THE SETTLEMENT

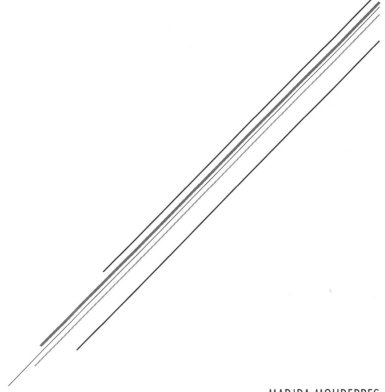

MADJDA MOUDERRES

DORRANCE
PUBLISHING CO
EST. 1920
PITTSBURGH, PENNSYLVANIA 15238

Dorrance Publishing Co
585 Alpha Drive
Suite 103
Pittsburgh, PA 15238
Visit our website at *www.dorrancebookstore.com*

ISBN: 978-1-6366-1539-4
eISBN: 979-8-88604-915-2

For my sisters, thank you for always supporting me, and for being my number one fans. I name you as the official heads of the fandom. You are the reason that this book exists.

For Mama and Papa, thank you for providing me with a life that allowed me to dream big. I could not have done this without you.

For my husband, thank you for pushing me to do the one thing that has always terrified me – sharing my work. Your love and support mean everything to me.

For my readers, welcome to The Settlement. The story has just begun…

Prologue

ENTRY #1:

Where do stories come from? Have you ever wondered when the first one was told? Throughout time, stories have been passed down from one generation to the next, changing as time progresses. I like to believe that the first stories to ever be passed down were real events that people experienced. There was no need to embellish the stories then; they had no other comparisons. But as time went by, new stories became a rare commodity. So one day, someone decided to make up a story and pass it on. Since this new innovation of making up stories was created, mankind got stories that would eventually end up shaping people's lives, and ultimately the world. Every story that has ever been told, real or made-up, is important. Now, what would happen if, one day, all of these stories were destroyed? And what if all of the people that still knew the stories were destroyed as well? How would humans function without this simple yet critical knowledge? After all, most stories do have a purpose. They teach us lessons: what or what not to do; the knowledge our ancestors had; all of the things we cherish as a race, as a species, as the world. Most people do not like to think of such awful things happening, but it already has. This leaves us with one story that has not yet been told...

The Great Wave swept over the lands, taking everything with it as it came. No tower was too tall, no city was too wide, and no person was too high for the wave. The Great Wave had no prejudice. It did not matter how rich or poor you were, because if you were anywhere near its path, it took you under. The Earth was undergoing an uprising. It was cleaning up all of the toxins and

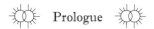

chemicals at their source. The cities, the hubs of the Earth's destruction, were hit the hardest of all. Some of the biggest cities in the world were situated near a coast or surrounded by large bodies of water, so they were the most vulnerable to the Great Wave. The Earth was sweeping away all of the unwanted waste and dust, leaving behind a smooth, clean, slate. But the thing that made the Great Wave so deadly was that it did not hit once. No, it hit over and over and over again. The few people that survived the first round did not have a chance to live for long. The wave soon claimed them as well.

After the damage was done, a proper cleanup was in order. The Earth took care of that too. Fires, volcanic eruptions, tornadoes, and earthquakes shook the earth. Anything that was left standing was torn down by the tornadoes. The fires burned every last scrap of metal, while the earth swallowed every last body left dead on top of it. The few people that survived up to this point lived in the scarcely remote areas of the world that were never conquered by technology in the first place. After about a decade, the Earth was no longer recognizable. Because of the changes happening on land, even bigger changes were happening underneath it. The constant earthquakes and the change in the Earth's mantle caused tectonic plates to shift, making all of the Earth's large landmasses meet up together where they were believed to have once started. The Great Wave had ultimately led to the reformation of Pangea.

The human race suffered greatly; we were almost extinct. But a few of us somehow fought through and managed to survive. It was truly the survival of the fittest, evolution at its finest. A lot of people thought that it was the end of the world; the Judgment Day. And honestly, maybe it should have been. We had failed as a species. We had destroyed the beautiful home we once had; we had let greed, arrogance, and jealousy claim our humanity. We tore through every last piece of beautiful sanctuary there once was. The skies turned gray, as did the lives of most. It was only a matter of time…yet, a few of us – the few that had not been corrupted – somehow pulled through. After about a century, the Earth had evolved, and the surviving humans had evolved with it. The earth was once again fertile. It grew lush plants and ran fresh streams of water. It was like the Earth was reborn. The skies were once again clear. But this was a new kind of sky, a sky that humans had long gotten rid of with the help of their factories and machines. The humans had also evolved. With their need to hunt and gather to survive, the humans changed.

Amongst other things, humans grew much bigger than they had once been. They grew larger hands to hunt and gather and longer legs to run fast after prey and away from other predators.

However, we never forgot where we came from. We never forgot the knowledge we had acquired 5,000 years prior to the present. We had answers. We had cures for cancer; we had the knowledge of the sciences, physics, even the technology of the world prior to this one. But we had to make a very important decision. Those that lived through the Great Wave understood, much more than we ever will. There was a reason the Earth punished mankind. It was the last and final warning that we needed to take care of it. There is a very thin line on which we have to balance if we want the human race to continue. We now have to use the technology and knowledge that we have to properly take care of the Earth, as we should have done centuries ago. The Elders of the new world got together and taught a few people – those who would become Elders later on – the knowledge that they needed to run the world and the humans on it. This all happened during a time we now call The Rebirth. For me, that was about 1,235 years ago. The world I was born into is called The Settlement. Humans have made a dramatic recovery, and I just so happen to be one of them.

Remember when I told you that there is still one story that has yet to be told? Hello, my name is Ivory Skye, and this is MY story.

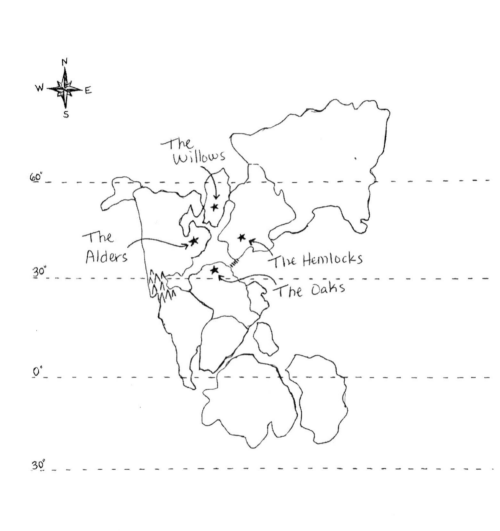

Chapter 1

ENTRY #2:

Hello. My name is Ivory Skye, I am twenty-two years old, and I am a part of the Western Assimilian Tribe.

Now, if you are reading this, only one of two things could have possibly happened. The first possibility is that a great catastrophe has struck the Earth yet again, and you have found my memory book to guide you with the information that you will need to survive. If this were the case, then I am most likely dead, so thank you for finding my book, and please remember to pass it on as a piece of human history.

The other reason you might be reading my book is the unlikely possibility that I have become an important person in human history, in which case I might either be dead or alive. I doubt that this will ever be the reason, but if it is, then I thank you for reading my book, in any case. This memory book will contain the history of my life. I hope that my life journey can help guide you to your destiny…

Now, before I get ahead of myself, and before I start talking about what life is like in the time period of The Settlement, let me start off by properly introducing my family and myself:

As I have already mentioned, my name is Ivory. I live in Western Assimilia, and my tribe is known as The Alder Tribe. I am the firstborn child of Nadi and Constantina Skye. My father, Nadi, is an Equestrian Professor, as well as the Head Keeper of the horses in the tribe. I will explain more about that at a later time; it is quite interesting! My mother, Constantina, is a Healer. She works with all of the other healers of the tribe at the Healing Clinic, but she also makes house calls when needed.

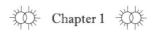

I was the firstborn of four girls for my parents. After my mother had me, she had two miscarriages, which explains the big gap in age between myself and my first sister, Hayden. After the miscarriages, my parents decided to take a break from trying to have another child. But before they knew it, my mother was pregnant again with my now fifteen-year-old sister. Three years after Hayden was born, Anya was born. And the following year, my last sister, Diana, was born.

Looks-wise, I am built like most of the females in our tribe. Height-wise, I am on the taller side of the spectrum. Average human height today is 250 centimeters, which is about eight feet, two inches. The last time I measured how tall I was, I was 267 centimeters, which is approximately eight feet, nine inches. I have long, brown, wavy hair that falls to my belly button. I also have dark brown eyes and fair skin. In terms of build, I have wide shoulders, long arms, long legs, a small chest, and larger hips. In a time period when childbirth is extremely important to carry on, to continue the growth of our species, having larger hips is an evolutionary norm. Overall, I am, for the most part, quite athletic – I mean, I have to be in order to hunt and survive.

As for my sisters, other than the fact that we're all girls, every time someone sees me with them and my mother, they tell us that we all look like exact copies of each other. This is true to some extent, but we all have our special little differences. Hayden, Anya, and Diana all have straight brown hair, unlike my unruly mess. My mother decided to give all three of my sisters bangs to keep their hair out of their faces. Hayden is the only one of the three with long hair, like myself. Mother always cuts Anya and Diana's hair chin-length because she says it is a hassle to take care of at their young age. Anya, who is eleven years old, came out with fair skin like myself. Hayden also has fair skin, but it is not as fair as Anya's. She has a hint of gold in her skin tone. Diana turned out to be the most different one out of all of us. She has a beautiful olive/golden skin tone that holds the most perfect tan you have ever seen. I do get jealous of her sometimes, because all I get is a burn when the sun is high in the sky. But I shall not complain over such trivial things.

One thing that all of my sisters and I have in common is our dark features. We all have dark, thick eyebrows, and really long, dark eyelashes. I believe our ancestors were originally from Southern Assimilia. Long, thick eyelashes were important for protecting the eyes from sandstorms, which are very common in the Southern tribe. Father also tells me that we have Willow blood running through us. He says that our great-grandparents had migrated from Northern Assimilia, thus explaining our fair skin. The Willows up North don't get as much sunlight as we do, which is why the majority of them have less melanin in their skin, hair, and eyes. Everything we are *today is because of evolution. Every human feature that evolved after the Great Wave was for one particular purpose – we were built for survival.*

At this point, you must be wondering what my parents look like. I mean, you might have an idea, based on how my sisters and I look...

Starting off with my father, he is very fair-skinned with hazel/green eyes and graying black hair. He is a couple of inches taller than me, so I am pretty sure I got my height from him.

My mother also has a lighter complexion. She wears her dark brown hair in a short bob that frames her small face perfectly, along with her long dark eyelashes, light brown eyes, and thin nose. She really is the epitome of beauty, in my opinion. And as she has gotten older, every little line she gets at the corner of her eyes or on her forehead just adds more character to her face. Can you tell that I want to look like her when I grow up? I love my family very much. I might not get along with them all of the time, but I really do love them. I have read books and heard stories of the people that lived before the Great Wave. One thing that I never understood about that time period is how families did not exist. I find it very hard to imagine. Today, we stand together and protect each other no matter what happens.

Like the tribes that lived before us, there are many written rules that the Collection of Tribes have to abide by today. But on top of those rules are some unspoken ones.

1. *The death of a human, any human, is a loss to be mourned by everyone.*
2. *The death of a family member, especially one that is not due to old age or natural selection, is one of the biggest tragedies that one could experience. This is especially true if the family member is of young age.*
3. *No matter where you are, or who you are with, protect each other against any other living species.*
4. *The human species must prevail over all. Our survival as a species is of utmost importance.*

So you see, the Great Wave has provided humans with a reason to live in peace and harmony. Every person is part of a family unit. Every family unit is part of a tribe. Each tribe is part of The Collection. Together, the four tribes form the human race. We are one; this is our way of life. We fight only to survive. We hide nothing from each other. We work together. And for this, the human race will continue to flourish.

Before I leave, however, I must make one thing very clear. Just as the human population has grown and evolved over time, so have the other populations, different species that also battle to survive in a world that is new to them as well. We live in a world where nightmares are greeted with open arms when compared to the true horrors that lie beyond the boundaries of the tribes. The world has changed in many ways. And although the continents have come together once again, the world is still a very big place. At this point in time, all that I know is what I have learned in the controlled environment of school. But I am hoping to soon change that.

This memory book will serve as my witness to the adventures that I know lie ahead of me. I do not know what to expect at this moment, but whatever it is, I know that it will be great.

And she was right…as Ivory signed her name at the bottom of the page, she did not know what the world was about to throw at her. She had no idea of the secrets she would soon uncover. She had made a prediction at the beginning of her second memory book entry, that the person reading her book would be doing it for one of two reasons. And she was dead-on, for she was about to embark on a journey that would leave her to be one of the most important people in the human history of The Settlement.

"Girls! Let's go; it's time to wake up! You're going to be late for school!" yells Constantina from the kitchen.

"I'm up and dressed; I just can't find my blue sandals," says Ivory as she walks into the kitchen.

"Did you check outside in the backyard?" asks Constantina.

"Why would they be out in the backyard? I always leave them next to the front door when I come inside," replies Ivory.

"There were a couple of shoes I washed the other day; they were filthy. You have to try and take a little more care of your shoes, Ivory; you know they're not easy to make."

"They weren't even dirty, Mama, it was just a little mud from when we went to the… Oh, never mind. I will go check."

"Hey, make sure your sisters are all awake and getting dressed. I do not want them to be late to school. There's less than two weeks left, so let us try to be punctual and finish off the year well."

"Ok, Mother, no problem!"

Heading down the hall on her way out to the backyard, Ivory passes by the room Anya and Diana share and peeks in.

"Are you guys almost done? You don't want Mother to get mad this early in the morning," she whispers to them.

"Don't worry, Ive, we're almost done," Anya whispers back.

Leaving her sisters to continue getting dressed, she passes by Hayden's room next, sticking her head in.

"You seriously must be kidding me. You're still sleeping?! Mother is going to kill you!"

"I'm getting up," grumbles Hayden from under her blanket. "Plus, unlike you, it only takes me two minutes to get dressed."

"Well, let's hope it does, because we're leaving in five minutes."

Ivory leaves her sister's room and closes the door. As she makes her way through the back door to the backyard, she wonders how different her life would have been if she'd had a brother. In a house full of girls, she'd always wanted a brother; an older brother, not a younger one, to be exact. A younger brother would just be annoying. But then again, how would she know…

Ducking underneath the hanging sheets and clothes outside, Ivory searches for the pile of shoes her mother had mentioned. As she turns, still searching, she spots a pile of shoes next to one of the poles holding up the laundry line. Peeking right through the pile of shoes is a pair of royal blue sandals, the ones she was looking for.

Holding her shoes in her hand, she heads back into the kitchen to grab an apple and get on her way to school.

"Wow, you're actually up and dressed," she says, surprised to see Hayden, who is sitting on the table, eating her fruit bowl and oats.

"I told you I only needed two minutes. I don't need to take forever to get dressed like you," Hayden laughs.

"Well, excuse me for having to deal with this crazy head of hair! You do not understand the struggle," Ivory says, shaking her head.

And she was right. She was kind of the unlucky duckling in the family. Her three sisters all had easy-to-deal-with hair. She, on the other hand, had a frizzy and completely unruly mess.

"Ivory, did you find the sandals you were looking for?" asks Constantina.

"Yes, thankfully, I found them! I was so worried; they're the most precious pair of shoes that I own."

"Honestly, they're so old and worn out; I don't see why you don't take better care of them if you don't want to recycle them."

"I love these shoes, Mother, they're just so comfortable. They've taken the form of my feet. And plus, they are the most beautiful shade of blue I have

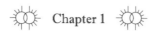

yet to see on any piece of clothing. Everyone always compliments me on them. And blue is my favorite color."

Ivory looks down at the shoes in her hand, admiring her treasured sandals.

"It is getting very late, Ivory. You have to leave now if you want to make it on time. Remember to tell Anya's teacher, Mrs. Osirnud, that I have the needles she's asked me about."

"Ok, I'll tell her. Where are the girls?" asks Ivory, looking around the small kitchen.

"They're sitting on the step outside, eating breakfast and waiting for you."

"Ok then, let's go, Hayden. I'll see you later, Mama; have a great day."

"Have a great day, Mother," says Hayden, giving her mother a hug before following her sister out.

Once outside, the two younger girls hold hands as they walk beside their older sisters to school.

On their way to school, the girls pass by the houses of Ivory's friends, who are waiting outside for them so they can all walk together. First on the way is one of Ivory's oldest friends, whom she considers more of a sister than a friend: Sparrow Avere.

"Hey, you're looking good this morning," says Sparrow as she walks up to Ivory, embracing her in a tight hug. "You know I love those sandals. I would give up three pairs of leather jackets to get me a pair like those."

Ivory laughs. "I know. If I ever see a pair like these again at the market, I will let you know. These were made by the Willows up in the North. I wonder when we'll get a new shipment of shoes and clothing again. Hopefully, they'll have a blue pair of sandals next time around."

As the girls continue heading toward their school, another friend joins them: Sevastyan Lanza. Sevastyan was also part of the original trio, along with Ivory and Sparrow. He was like the brother Ivory always wanted but never had. However, he was only a few months older than her. Nonetheless, they became best friends the moment they laid eyes on each other.

"Good morning, ladies, I hope your morning is going fine," says Sevastyan as he embraces each of the girls lightly on the shoulders.

"It's going great, thanks for asking," says Sparrow.

"Did you speak to Flora and Fauna yesterday, Sevastyan? Are they meeting up with us this morning?" asks Ivory. "I know that Flora said that they may have to help their parents carry some equipment early this morning."

"No, we're picking them up; their mother found a friend to help her out," replies Sevastyan.

"See, there they are."

And there they were, the newest members of the crew: Flora and Fauna Ilios, the twins.

Unlike Sparrow and Sevastyan, Ivory met Flora and Fauna only a few years back. The two had migrated from the Northern Assimilian Tribe to the Western Assimilian Tribe with their parents. The pair's parents were both healers. Because the Alders were known for their abilities to heal using the different parts of the Alder tree, along with other plants, most healers traveled to Western Assimilia to learn from them. Most healers that travel for the knowledge end up going back to their native tribes. However, when Flora and Fauna's parents saw how well the girls had adapted to the Alders, especially to their new friends Ivory, Sparrow, and Sevastyan, they decided to stay and live in Western Assimilia permanently.

Flora: "Good morning."

Fauna: "Thanks for picking us up."

Flora: "We appreciate it."

Ivory smiles. She loves it when the girls talk together and finish each other's sentences. They have a connection with each other that she had never seen before. They are an interesting couple; after all, they were originally Willows. But there is something about them – a gentleness, a kindness, and a fire at the same time that Ivory appreciates. She was drawn to them the moment she saw them for the first time. She could never really put her finger on it, but they made her instantly happy when she saw them.

"You guys look really pretty this morning," says Ivory. "Flora, I love the flowers in your braid. And Fauna, what kind of fur is that on your jacket?"

"It's snow leopard," says the wild-haired girl.

"Wow, how did you get that? They're huge. You didn't hunt it by yourself, did you?"

"Oh no, of course not. I actually didn't even have to kill it."

"This sounds like the beginning of a really interesting story," laughs Sevastyan.

"Well, I think it is," Fauna laughs back. "So I was in the woods one day, and I heard these little meow sounds. I followed the sounds, and they led me to a pack of baby snow leopards."

"Fauna, why would you go into the woods alone? It's dangerous! I don't know what kind of animals you had up north, but I'm going to guess they're just as dangerous as the ones we have here!" exclaims Ivory.

"Don't worry; it wasn't that far from our house. Anyway, I found the baby snow leopards alone. At the time, I have to admit, I was a little worried because I assumed the mother wouldn't be far off. And I knew that if I came across her, I could potentially have some big problems. Still, I looked around a little more, and I eventually found the mother. She was dead in the snow; something bigger had attacked and killed her. I felt bad for the babies because they were still really young, newborn, I believe, but it's also really rare to find snow leopard fur. So I went back home, grabbed my father, and we came back together to collect the fur."

"Wow, I would have been terrified if I were you. What about the leopard cubs; did you go back to get their fur? I'm sure they would have been easier to hunt, given that they were so young. And like you said, the fur is precious, so I bet you would have gotten a great trade for it. But I mean, I would feel bad about hunting cubs."

"Yes, I guess I could have. But I didn't have the heart to hurt them."

"Did you tell your father about them?"

"No, I only told him about the dead mother. I did tell Flora about them, though."

"Really? Flora, what did you think when Fauna told you what she found?" asks Ivory, turning to Flora.

"Well, there was nothing much I could do. Especially after she started feeding them and getting attached," says Flora, rolling her eyes.

"Wow, are you serious?" laughs Ivory incredulously. "You went back to them and fed them? How long did you do that for?" she asks.

"Well, the whole story happened months before we moved here, so they weren't full-size yet. But they were about the size of full-grown wolves before I had to leave them," Fauna replies with a shrug.

Ivory is stunned. She loves animals more than the normal Assimilian, and she's not fond of hunting the innocent ones, but she can't imagine being in the presence of a live wildcat and living to tell the story. In school, everyone was taught about the kinds of animals that lived out in the wild, outside the tribal boundaries. The animals Post-Great Wave (P.G.W.) had all evolved from their prior forms into new and improved species. Speed, agility, size – all of these traits had changed, mostly for the bigger, to allow the animals to survive in the new world.

"Well, you are a lot braver than me, Fauna, that's for sure," says Ivory, still stunned.

"No, that's not true. It's not about bravery; at least, I don't think so. I just have a connection with animals. I don't know how to explain it, but sometimes I feel like I can understand what they're feeling…"

"Okay now, let's not get carried away in our sappy, loving-wild-animals-that-will-most-likely-kill-us-on-sight imagination. Plus, we've finally made it to school," says Sparrow, cutting off Fauna, who is in a whole other world of her own.

"Can one of you please save me a seat? My mother asked me to talk to Anya's teacher," says Ivory.

"Sure, no problem, I will let Professor Ganlion know you'll be a little late," replies Sevastyan.

"Thanks. See you all in a bit."

During the time period of The Settlement, school is very important to the tribes. And within each tribe, there exists one big school. Seeking knowledge is one of the most important and most respected things a person could do. Learning about the world, how it works, and about the ancestors that survived when all odds were against them is required by all those under the age of twenty-three. At the age of twenty-three, the students will graduate from their studies and choose their place in society. Along with the regularly scheduled classes, the final year of study is also used to give students a chance to figure out what they want to do after they graduate. Students have the chance to hands-on explore the different careers they could get into after graduation. Most of the time, students already have some ideas about what they might be interested in, based on their hobbies during their spare time or their special talents. A lot of the really strong boys end up becoming warriors or hunters, while a lot of the girls end up becoming healers or medicine makers. Still, there are no rules that stop a specific gender from pursuing a specific place in society. The tribes have strong female warriors as well as soft-handed, skilled male healers.

In general, school systems are loosely based on the school systems of the past. Students study the usual courses, including mathematics, science, history, languages, and cultures. However, a lot of the courses are tailored to the time period as well, with new information that might not have been necessary before the evolution of the world. In addition, newer courses that are relevant to survival are also taught. These new courses include: horse-back riding, survival in the wild, hunting, archery, general weapon usage, and for older and more advanced students, flight simulation.

Flight simulation is a relatively new course for all four of the tribes. Although a lot of the technology from the past world was lost, some of it survived. The technological invention of wings that allowed humans to fly was a piece of technology that was not forgotten. And in a world where competition for space on land is brutal, to say the least, having a sky advantage is very much necessary for the human species. However, it is a very difficult course, with many having suffered grave injuries from it.

Ivory walks into her classroom, spotting her friends sitting toward the front. She walks to the seat Sevastyan had saved for her, putting her bag on the chair.

"You beat the professor," smiles Sevastyan.

"Yes, well, I ran," laughs the girl.

Ivory looks around the classroom at the buzzing students, all excited to graduate in less than two weeks. As she continues to make her way around the room, her gaze stops at one specific face – Cassius Zlato. As everyone sits on the edge of their seats socializing, Cassius sits leaned back in his chair, fiddling with a dagger, not paying attention to anyone else in the room. As people talk and laugh around him, he just looks straight ahead, his mind somewhere outside the classroom. *"Definitely bored,"* thinks Ivory. She turns back to socialize with her friends, but she can't help but look over at him every once in a while, checking to see if his face has changed. Nope, still the same. *How could someone think that they are so much better than everyone else?* Ivory thinks to herself. *The ego it takes to sit so quietly, yet still control everyone in the room, to have all eyes on you, it's insane – it's also kind of amazing.*

Ivory doesn't hate Cassius. But she doesn't particularly like him, either. At least, not the way she likes her friends. He is an interesting fellow, and they have an interesting relationship, to say the least. The two have practically known each other from the day they were born. Ivory's mother, Constantina, was a very good friend to Cassius's mother, Seraphina. The two women had grown up together in Western Assimilia, just as Ivory and Cassius had. One would think that the two's children would have a lot in common, therefore making them the greatest of friends. However, Cassius was also the son of Magnus Zlato, one of the most well-known warriors within The Collection. His bravery was legendary. Trying to live up to that would stress out anyone, so Ivory felt for Cassius. She especially felt for him after his mother had passed away when he was only ten years old. It was tragic, a hard time for the entire tribe. Ever since the death of his mother, Cassius closed everyone out, including Ivory. Everyone looked up to him because he was the son of the famous Magnus Zlato. But they were also afraid of him, so they stayed away. He, in return, took advantage of this – his father's reputation – and always got his way. Still, Ivory remembered his mother every time she looked at him, and that made it difficult for her to hold anything against him. With this in her head, Ivory gets up out of her desk and heads towards Cassius.

Ivory: "Hello."

Cassius: "Hello."

Ivory: "Haven't seen you around in a while. How've you been? How are Caius and your father doing?"

Cassius: "They're good. I was out on an expedition with my father about a few kilometers away from the border. We spent the weekend there."

Ivory: "Wow, that's amazing. Were you guys with a lot of other warriors? I mean, I guess you wouldn't really need THAT many people when you're with your father."

Cassius: "No, only two others. It's safer to look after a small group of people."

Ivory: "Oh, okay. Well, I just wanted to say hello and see how you were doing."

The corners of Cassius's mouth move up – a small smile betrays him.

"Thank you for stopping by. Oh, and please thank your mother for me. For the food, I mean. It's been a while since Caius has had a proper home-cooked meal. My father and I appreciate the kind gesture."

Caius is Cassius's younger brother. He was only two years old when his mother died, so he remembers her, but only vaguely. Caius is the only person that Cassius cares about more than himself. After Seraphina died, Cassius was the only person that Caius could look up to, as their father was always busy protecting the tribe. Cassius had taken it upon himself to help raise Caius so that he would never feel the empty space his mother had left when she died. In return, Caius almost worshipped his brother – more than his father, even.

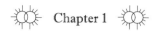

In Caius's mind, Cassius was the bravest, most loving person he'd ever seen. He was his ultimate role model. And the way that Cassius took care of Caius, it was not hard to tell why Caius felt that way. Caius was Cassius's only soft spot – and Ivory knew it.

"I will let her know," Ivory smiles back before turning around and walking back to her seat.

"Umm...excuse me, what was that?" smirks Sparrow, as Ivory sits back down.

"I was just being friendly," replies Ivory, rolling her eyes.

"Mhmm...being friendly. Sure, I totally believe that," says Sparrow sarcastically.

"Oh my God, you're so bad. Please don't try pushing your secret feelings for him onto me!" laughs Ivory, punching Sparrow on the arm, making her almost fall out of her chair.

"Oh paaaauuuuleeeaaaase...do not make me laugh! Also, don't try to deny that you were just talking to the best-looking guy our age in the entire tribe! Any one of the girls in here would die to get a single look their way, not to mention an actual smile!" laughs Sparrow, leaning in, trying to keep her voice down.

"He was just happy that my mother made his family food, that's all. You know I'm not into the self-absorbed, thinking-they're-better-than-everyone, too-cool-to-smile guys. Plus, I'm a little busy trying to figure out what I'm going to do after I graduate," says Ivory, frowning as she thinks about the future.

"Are you serious? I thought you were sure you wanted to be a horse keeper, like your father. You love horses, and you're the best rider of our generation. Everyone here knows it. You have Future Head Horse Keeper written all over you!" says Sparrow surely.

"I know, I still want to do that, but I don't know... I've been having this weird feeling these past couple of weeks...it's not that it's not enough for me, but I can't help but feel trapped, you know what I mean?" says Ivory.

"No, I get it. It's normal. It's going to be the thing you do for pretty much the rest of your life. The only different thing you'll end up doing is getting married and having children. Then, once the kids are the age of three, they start going to school, and you're back with the horses," replies Sparrow with a sigh.

"You know what I wish? I wish we could travel. To learn, to explore, to see new places...I don't care what reason it would be for. I just want to get out of here. We've literally never left this piece of land we call Western Assimilia. Sometimes I feel like everyone is so close to everyone else, I can't breathe," says Ivory, laying her head on her desk.

"Hey, it's good we're taking those flight simulation classes, then. I'm sure you can get a lot more oxygen up in the sky!" smiles Sparrow, giving Ivory a reassuring pat on the arm.

Ivory lifts her head to look at her friend. "That's true; I can't wait to fly – to feel the crisp, cold, breeze on my cheeks and through my hair. You know, sometimes when I ride I pretend like I'm flying. Flying somewhere unknown, somewhere beautiful," she says, closing her eyes, imagining the unknown beauty waiting for her out in the wild.

Just then, Professor Ganlion walks into the room. Sparrow gives Ivory one last reassuring smile before she turns forward in her chair to pay attention to their teacher. But Ivory can't shake the feeling that's been haunting her for weeks – freedom.

Chapter 2

"I don't care what anyone has told you about flying. Whether that it is the most dangerous thing you could ever try or that it is the best invention mankind has ever created. You see, it is quite simple – humans were not made to fly. Therefore, if you do not listen carefully and do everything that I am about to tell you, YOU. WILL. DIE."

ENTRY #3:
Professor Silven Drakonas: also known as Silver by his friends. The most badass son of a bitch there ever was. Okay, so I'm not exactly sure what that really means, but I overheard the warriors saying it once. I believe that's what people back in the day said when something, or someone, was really cool. We're not allowed to use that kind of language today, so I do apologize for the profanities, but in my defense, I really cannot find a better way to describe the professor. Seriously, though, along with Warrior Zlato, Silven Drakonas is one of the most well-known, feared people in our tribe. When I say feared, I mean it in a good way, of course. Along with my father Nadi and Headmistress Oriana Farinosa, Silven Drakonas is one of the three main Head Horse Keepers of our tribe. He also happens to be the Flight Simulation (flying) instructor.

So to start off, I'm sure you, the person reading my memory book right now, would like to know why he is known as "Silver." I must confess it is a bit random, but the story behind it is, in my opinion, interesting. Professor Drakonas is a very tall, very strong man. Along with his fair skin and shockingly contrasting jet-black hair, he has one random streak of silver hair growing right at the front of his head, above his left brow. I don't really know why or how it's only one small piece of hair that's silver; it just is. When he brushes his hair back out of his face, you can't miss seeing it. It's why his friends made up the nickname Silver for him. He is actually the same age as my father, but only that one streak of hair has dared to betray him thus far. I guess his hair is afraid of him, too. His long, pointed nose, sharp jaw, and piercing crystal blue eyes don't help make him any more approachable either, to be quiet honest. He's a scary guy overall – very serious all the time. A boy tried telling him a joke one time… he went home almost in tears.

But I respect him. A LOT. He was the only person in our tribe brave enough to learn how to fly alone and then teach everyone else how to do it. Yes, he broke a few bones in the process, and his pinky finger never fully healed, but that never bothered him. Actually, I think he's my ultimate role model. I wish I could be like him one day – unafraid of going on new adventures by myself. If I had the choice, I would love to do that now, but some things are easier said than done. I believe this is one of those things.

As the sun touches the earth and starts sinking into the horizon, the school day comes to an end. The students sitting on the tall, grassy hill looking over the school and the rest of the tribe start to pack up their belongings after their last class of the day with Silven (Silver) Drakonas.

"Please remember to pack your flight suits and an extra pair of dry clothes with you for tomorrow's trip. Horses will be provided for everyone, but I also know that some of you have your own horses. If you are riding on your own horse, please meet us at the front tribal entrance gate, ready to go, at dusk. The rest of you, please make your way into the stables to get yourselves set up with a horse. Also, please keep in mind that we *take off* at dusk. If you are not ready and waiting by then, you will be left behind. And if you're left behind, you cannot catch up on your own, unless you want to risk death out in the wilderness, alone. So to reiterate what I just said – because I know at least one of you will be late – you either make it, or you don't."

"Professor Drakonas, can we bring things like extra food or books with us?" asks one of the student.

"Yes, Aura, you may bring whatever you may need. Just keep in mind that the more you bring, the slower your horse will ride. Be efficient in what you bring along. You will not need any books for this trip. If you feel the need to bring your memory book, you may do so. Remember, this is only a three-day trip, people, most of which you will be in your flight suits."

"Thank you, professor," says the blue-eyed, long-haired, brunette girl.

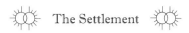

"I'll see you all tomorrow, sharp-eyed and ready to go. Get some sleep," says Silver, getting on his horse, riding off towards the tribe.

"So are you riding Thunder tomorrow, or what?" Sparrow asks Ivory.

"Of course, I wouldn't go anywhere without him," replies Ivory.

"Well, you have a few horses, so I wasn't sure if you'd take Thunder or another one."

"That's true…I was actually thinking about taking Onyx, he's one of the fastest horses we have, but Thunder is just overall more solid."

"And you pretty much grew up with him."

Ivory laughs. "That's true, he was my first horse. He's the reason I fell in love with horses. Well, that, and probably genetics."

"Yes, I have no doubt that genetics has played a role when it comes to your love for horses," says Sparrow, rolling her eyes jokingly at her friend. "Anyway, I have to head home and get everything packed and ready for tomorrow. I'll see you then!"

Ivory waves goodbye to her friend. As the rest of the students pick up their belongings and head home, she opens her memory book. The sun is just only caressing the horizon, and if she starts writing now, she should be able to get home by the time it sets completely.

ENTRY #4:

Tomorrow is the day we learn to fly. Now, don't get me wrong, I am extremely excited, but I am also really nervous. We are traveling to the coast for the first time in our lives. The students, I mean. Everyone that has learned to fly, including Professor Drakonas and the warriors coming with us on the journey, have visited the coast already.

Now, you might be asking yourself, why is it so weird to travel to the coast? Other than the fact that it is part of what we call "the wilderness," the ocean is there. Ever since the Great Wave hit, mankind has developed a fear of large bodies of water. It's why all of the tribes are located deep inland, as far away from the ocean as possible. I say as far away as possible, because when the tribes were made, they also needed to be somewhat close to each other. For some of the tribes, like the Southern Assimilian tribe, living far away from the water was very hard because most of the landmass in that area is dry desert. Therefore, the tribe is located only about thirty minutes away from the water when traveling by horse. The other three tribes are quite a bit farther away from the coast.

On our trip tomorrow, we will have to travel for five hours by horse through the woods to reach the coast. We will probably reach our destination sometime before noon, so we will have plenty of time to practice flight simulation before the day is over. We will then have a full day the next day to practice, and we travel back home at noon on the third day. This way, we can reach the tribe before sundown. The warriors all know that nighttime is the worst and most dangerous time to travel.

As she writes in her memory book, Ivory senses that she's not alone. She looks up from her book and sees none other than Cassius Zlato lower down on the hill, lying in the grass, eyes closed, taking in the last of the day's sunlight.

So, changing subjects, I have talked about some of the people in this tribe already, including my family and friends. One I have yet to write about is the famous Cassius Zlato. Hmmm... honestly, I am not sure where to start. I don't even know what to call him: Friend? Acquaintance? Enemy? Our relationship is a bit complicated, you see. Sometimes I like him, sometimes I hate him, sometimes I feel bad for him, and other times I just want to hit him over the head with a club. Anyway, I will start off with looks. Not including my friends, twins Flora and Fauna, most of the people in my tribe look about the same: light to medium skin tones and brunette hair. For this reason, Cassius, and the Zlato family as a whole, stick out like a sore thumb. Cassius has dirty blond hair that he wears brushed back all of the time. He puts some kind of invisible clay in it that holds it in place. Well, actually, a lot of the males in the tribe do that. They don't all like cutting their hair really short, but they can't tie it up unless it's really long, so the clay is the next best thing. Anyway, Cassius's hair, along with his eyebrows and eyelashes, are a golden dirty blond. His eyebrows are very structured; they're nice...I wish my eyebrows were perfect all the time...okay, not important, moving on to the most important part!

So the first thing I noticed when I first met Cassius when we were younger were his eyes. He has some of the most interesting, beautiful eyes I have ever seen. His eyes are a weird clear, gray/blue color with flecks of green. The outline of his iris is black, so the color inside the outline is very crisp. If you have ever looked at a stream of water that is super clean, with beautiful rocks shining from the inside, that's what Cassius's eyes look like. And because they don't really fall under a category of normal eye colors, I just like to call them clear. The girls and I kind of like to make fun of that, actually. We joke that because the eyes are the gateway to the soul, he must not have one, because souls have colors and his is invisible.

Ivory giggles out loud by accident as she writes.

Ok, so it's not that funny, but he is kind of cold to everyone. Actually, he's cold to the people he doesn't think are worthy of his presence. To the rest of us, he's just a bit, how do I say it...snobby. He does like to "hang out" with us sometimes, but the sarcasm and the "I'm better than you" vibe gets old, really quickly. These days, we just see him at tribal gatherings, and school, of course. Apparently, he's been spending his time with much more important people, like dumb girls who swoon every time he breathes. I swear, he could fart or burp in their faces, and they would think that it was the dream-iest thing that had ever happened to them. You would think that surviving a potential human extinction would straighten out people's priorities... But yes, I might as well stop trying to preach to the crowd, because the crowd is too busy swooning to listen.

All of a sudden, a shadow covers Ivory's book. She quickly closes it and looks up, a little startled.

"Hello, Ivory, how's it going?" says Cassius, amused at the fact that he managed to sneak up on her.

"Why hello, I am doing fine, thank you. And you, still going around the tribe breaking the hearts of some poor, unfortunate souls?" retorts Ivory, quickly recovering.

"You know it," laughs the boy, throwing Ivory a wink.

As he sits down next to her on the grass, Cassius looks over to what Ivory has in her lap.

"What is that you have there?" he asks.

"What, this?" Ivory asks, pointing to her little book. "This is my memory book. You know how Professor Ganlion told us in class to keep one, in case something like the Great Wave ever happens again?"

"Yes, I remember," he replies. "He said it was important that we never forget this time in history. If the human race does somehow get to a point near extinction once again, the memory books will be there for the humans to re-build the species. 'We must not forget our history, for within it lies all of the answers to our survival,'" says Cassius, pretending to be the professor.

"Exactly. Have you started yours yet? They're not going to check them, but you should do it anyway. After all, it is for a good cause."

"Yes, please do not remind me; I have not started mine yet."

"Ha, of course, typical Cassius," says Ivory, rolling her eyes as sarcastically as she could.

"Hey! Do not get all noble on me, Ivory Skye! I am eventually planning on starting it, and when I do I will write more in one day than you will write in a month!"

"Mhmmm, yes, of course you will," replies Ivory, rolling her eyes again, chuckling.

"You will see. I will do it. Anyway, I've just been busy lately, that's all."

"Busy? Busy with what?" Ivory asks, confused. "Case, school's almost done. We have not had any extra schoolwork for the past three months. Unless you're busy breaking hearts twenty-four seven – which is a horrible hobby, by the way – then you should have had time to at least get a book."

"No, I have not been breaking any hearts; that's just a rumor someone started for their own pleasure, and yes, I did get a book. I just… haven't written anything in it yet," says Cassius, looking down at his hands, a little flustered.

"Okay, well, what have you been busy with, then?" asks Ivory, looking directly at him.

Although it is slight, Ivory can see something uncomfortable about the way Cassius shifts – the way he now sits, and how he cut off their eye contact.

"I've just been busy with stuff," he mumbles, looking out into the distance.

Suddenly, he spins back to Ivory and looks at her straight in the eye. She swears to herself that he is probably going to have whiplash later from how fast he'd just spun back around.

"Why do you care anyway, Miss Ivory Skye?" says Cassius, in a sarcastic, snarky voice. "It's not like you actually genuinely care about me. I mean, why would you, when you have your three *best* friends, and your puppy dog-brother wannabe? Don't pretend like you're a saint in front of me, baby-face, because if you've forgotten, I know you. We grew up together, so I know how you manipulate people until you have them rolled around your little finger."

"Well, it doesn't seem to have worked on you, now, does it?" replies Ivory sharply, not breaking eye contact.

Cassius laughs out loud as he looks up at the lavender pink sky.

"No, it hasn't worked. However," he says, turning back to her, "as much as I despise you for knowing how to control people, I admire your ability to do so."

Ivory can see the fire burning inside Cassius's eyes – it could burn anyone who got too close. But there is something else there, too, something she can't quite put her finger on. It's chaotic, but it draws her in. She shakes her head, pushing whatever it is out.

"Ugh, Cassius, you really are crazy," she says, sitting back. "Actually, you're more delusional than crazy. But you know what? I'll just call you both. In fact, you're a delusional, crazy, privileged hater."

"Aren't we all?" he asks with a smirk.

"You know what? I don't have time for your weird, completely uncalled for, bipolar mood swings. Plus, I need to get back to my writing," says Ivory, looking back at the book in her lap.

"Alright, alright, I can see when I am not wanted around anymore. No need to get excited here," says Cassius with a half-smile crawling up his face. "I will leave you to your memories then, darling."

"Eww, please don't call me darling; it makes me feel like a dog with fleas," replies Ivory as she pretends to shake the fleas off.

"Ha ha, fine. Get back to your memories then, I-V-O-R-Y," says Cassius, stretching every vowel dramatically.

Ivory looks at him, giving him the obvious "you should leave now" look.

"Ah…thank you for a wonderful conversation. As much as I don't like you and your *posse*, I appreciate the intellectual stimulation I get from speaking to you. It's hard to come by around these parts," says Cassius. Ivory knows that this is as much of a compliment as she will ever get out of him. She sighs.

"As annoying as you are, thank you for stopping by, Cassius," says Ivory, softening up. "But seriously, get to writing. You want to get the memories down before you forget them," she says, pointing to her head.

"Thanks. I will," he says with a small smile.

Cassius gets up to leave, brushing the blades of grass off of his crisp, clean trousers.

"Alright then, Ivory, I will see you tomorrow at the gates. Until then," he says with a nod of his head.

"Until then," says Ivory with a nod back.

As Cassius heads down the hill, Ivory turns back to her book.

Anyway, as I was saying before the devil himself interrupted me, Cassius is one interesting guy. He must be interesting. Everyone seems to be interested in him, which means he has to be interesting… Right?

Ivory laughs to herself and shakes her head.

But you know what, as much as I hate Cassius, there's something about him that I really like. I know that there is good in his heart. He's annoying, that's for sure, but he can be really nice when he wants to be. And if I have to hang out with him, then I'll do it just so I can get a glimpse of that rare side of him.

That is all for now. More is sure to come soon, as I journey to the coast tomorrow on an adventure that is sure to be epic.

Chapter 3

Eyes wide open, hair flying with the crisp cold morning wind, Ivory gallops down a forest path with the rest of her classmates through green, lush trees. As she rides, she looks up into the treetops, discovering birds she has only heard about in books, red and blue birds with tail feathers as long as her arms and beaks as sharp as daggers. Through the trees, large elk flee at the sound of horseshoes pounding on the solid dirt path. In the bushes, large yellow eyes watch, waiting for an opportunity to attack, but no opportunities are given. Two warriors ride on either side of Silver Drakonas as he leads the pack of thirty students through the trees. Three warriors ride on either side of the group of students, while two more flank the backside of the group. It is the first time any of the students have gone outside the tribe into the unknown wilderness. That is, everyone except for Cassius. But even he had never gone out so far before. The ride to the ocean coast is long but beautiful. The path through the forest is lengthy, but it soon opens up to never-ending hills of lavender flowers on either side of a path that was created by generations of warriors and students who had traveled the same way before. The students marvel at the sight, at the colors, at the scent. The lavender hills eventually blend into open green fields as the group gets closer to the coast. The scent of lavender is replaced by a new scent the students have never experienced thus far in their lives. They taste salt on their tongues, and smell what they believe to be different kinds of fish in the air. As they get closer to the coast, they hear the water, crashing and curling. Birds – seagulls – can be heard from a distance, squawking and screaming. Soon enough, the group of travelers reach their destination: a large cliff top spanning as far as the eye can see.

As they all get off their horses and walk over to the cliff's edge, they see it. Blue. An expanse of blue, darker and deeper the farther away it gets. Down to their left, where the precipice they stand on ends, is what seems to be miles of white sand. The waves hit the shore, creating white, bubbly sea foam. The students marvel at the beauty that lies in front of them, overwhelmed by it all. Ivory closes her eyes as another sea breeze hits her face, making her hair dance around. This was what she'd been looking for all of this time. This is what she had been missing.

She can finally breathe – and she does. She breathes in the ocean. It fills her lungs and her spirit with its warmth, with hope. She opens her eyes and looks over at her friends, who seem to be experiencing the same euphoria. She reaches for Sparrow's hand, who opens her eyes at the touch. They squeeze each other's hands – there is no need for words. Professor Drakonas stands on the cliff edge with the rest of the silent group of students. He too had longed for the ocean – for the freedom it promised. Part of him knows that they have to get to work soon, set up camp, start practicing. But he lets the thought fly away with the wind, and gives the students a little more time to take everything in.

"So what do you all think? How do you like the ocean?" asks Professor Drakonas.

"It's beautiful," says Sparrow.

"It's breathtaking," says Ivory.

"It's so calm and peaceful," says Flora.

"Yet, you can feel a wilderness building inside, waiting to bubble up at any second," says Fauna.

The rest of the students nod their heads in agreement, unable to put their feelings into words.

"I am glad that you have all had the opportunity to enjoy this moment. However, the time has come to move on and start your training. Do not let the beauty of the ocean fool you into thinking that it will not hurt you. Although you will not find dangerous fish this close to shore, you are not safe just yet. The blue waters can pull you in and take hold of you very easily if you do not know how to maneuver through them," warns the professor.

"Now, let us set up camp and get ready with our flight suits. Girls, you can look toward warriors Jade and Raina to help you set up your tents. Boys, you have warriors Marceau and Emile to help you out. Once you are finished setting up, put on your suits."

"Professor, will we be flying today?" asks one of the boys.

"No, Lais, we will not be flying today," replies the professor. "We will, in fact, be swimming," he says with a mysterious smile as he looks at the shocked faces that some of the students have. "Do not worry; your flight suits double as wetsuits for the water. The material will keep you relatively warm in the cold."

"Staying warm is not what I am really worried about," whispers Sevastyan to Ivory.

"Yes, we have bigger things to worry about, like not drowning, for example," whispers back Ivory, a little nervous at the thought of drowning in the wild, cold, ocean waters.

"I can see by the looks on your faces that this, being your first swimming lesson, worries some of you. But fret not, swimming will come to you as naturally as walking once did," says the professor reassuringly to the group of pale-faced students. "Alright, let's go. Work fast, and get dressed; I will be waiting for you all down by the shore," he says, pointing to the white sand.

The students follow the warriors to set up camp and get dressed.

"I have to admit, this suit looks really cool," says Flora to her sister and Sevastyan as they wait for the other two girls to finish.

"Yes, the material is very breathable, yet it does not allow any water in," replies Sevastyan, pulling at his sleeve, watching it bounce back to the form of his arm.

"I like how smooth and sleek it is," says Fauna. "I wonder what kind of material they used to make it," she wonders out loud.

"I wonder where they got the material," remarks Flora. "I don't believe they got it from any animal."

"It is, in fact, synthetic. I would think you've seen this kind of material before, Flora. It is, after all, made up in Northern Assimilia," says Sparrow, walking towards the group.

"No, I have never seen it. All of our clothing is made from nature-made materials," replies Flora.

"It's just one of those things our ancestors remembered after the Great Wave," says Ivory, joining the conversation as she arrives to the group. "Making synthetic products like these suits is not the best for the environment, so we keep it to a minimum. Only flight suits are allowed to be made."

The group of friends continue their conversation as they carefully ride down the side of the big hill on their horses.

"Well, if I drown in my suit, make sure to save it before you bury me; I don't want to be the cause of the world coming to an end again," laughs Sparrow.

"Don't worry; you're not likely to drown, even if you fail at swimming. The suits are very buoyant. Even if you don't move at all in the water, you'll float to the top with these suits," Sevastyan reassures her.

The group reaches the shore, where Professor Drakonas stands facing the ocean. They leave their horses farther back on the shore and join the rest of their classmates next to the water.

"Is everyone here?" asks Professor Drakonas, turning back to the students.

Everyone looks around; it would seem so.

"Good. Now, I want everyone to walk into the water. Stop at the point where the water reaches your neck as you stand on the ocean floor."

"Here goes nothing," says Ivory with a nervous laugh to her friends.

The students walk into the ocean, the cold water shocking their senses as it covers their feet. The water does not directly touch the rest of their covered bodies, but they can feel the cold surrounding them. As their uncovered hands touch the water, it feels as though they may freeze to death. By the time they're in deep enough for the water to reach their necks, their feet and hands are numb enough that the water feels normal.

Professor Drakonas gets into the ocean as well, but only up to his waist.

"Okay, what I want you all to do now is lift your feet off the floor and pad-dle with your arms and legs, hard. This should keep your heads out of the water," he shouts over the waves crashing into the nearby boulders, underneath the cliff they had been standing on earlier.

The students do what they are instructed. Immediately, some heads dis-appear under the waves, but they soon come back out again. Staying afloat is difficult at first, but to everyone's surprise, the professor is right. Swimming, keeping their heads out of the water, is easier than they had expected.

"Good! Now, if you can, try swimming to your right, parallel to the shore, and back to where you started," shouts out the professor.

The students glide through the water, paddling with their arms, kicking with their feet.

"Great, now swim back to where you started, then back to shore!"

The students follow the professor's voice and do as they are told. And before they know it, they are all standing next to the professor, who seems to be very pleased at their accomplishment.

"Wow, that was exhilarating," breathes Fauna with excitement.

"I know, I want to swim a little more, that was so much fun," says Ivory, wiping the salty water from her eyes.

The professor overhears them. "I'm glad you said that, Ivory, because you are about to swim quite a bit in a few minutes," he says, with the same mysterious smile he had on his face earlier.

"Professor Drakonas, I understand that learning to swim is important, but what does it have to do with flying? I thought this was a flight simulation course," says Cassius, whom everyone had completely forgotten about.

Everyone looks from Cassius to their professor, interested in his response.

"No need to fret, Mr. Zlato, all will be answered soon enough," replies the professor, with a full smile now.

"Umm...is it just me, or is the professor scarier when he smiles than when he doesn't?" whispers Sparrow, wide-eyed, to her friends.

"YES," responds Sevastyan.

The rest of the friends nod along in agreement.

"Why do I have a feeling that Cassius just screwed us all over?" asks Flora.

"Um, because that wouldn't be the first time," replies Fauna, shaking her head in disapproval.

"I think the professor had this all planned out from the beginning," says Ivory.

"Here's to hoping we survive tomorrow," says Sparrow.

Everyone nods in agreement again, not having a clue as to what is about to go down in the very near future.

- - -

"We're going to what???" asks Cassius in disbelief.

"You are going to jump off this cliff, into the water. You are cliff diving, to be more exact." answers Professor Drakonas.

"Oh, you have got to be joking! What does jumping off a cliff into crushing waters have to do with flying, again?! I think I missed that part in the lesson book." Cassius rolls his eyes.

The nearby warriors snicker. They had obviously known what was going to happen the entire time. It would explain why they were all dressed in flight suits as well.

"You know, Cassius," begins Professor Drakonas, eyes hard now, "if you would shut your mouth and use your brain for once, you might have somewhat of a clue as to why you are about to jump."

"Ouch," whispers Ivory.

"Running his mouth like that, he had it coming," whispers back Sparrow.

Cassius doesn't say anything as his hardened face and ears turn slightly pink.

"So who wants to go first?" asks the professor, pacing back and forth on the cliff. The students look around at each other, not one of them stepping forward.

"Cassius? You seem to be the most interested person here. Would you like to go first?" asks the professor, amused.

Cassius continues to look forward, completely silent.

"Emile," the professor calls out to the tall, buff warrior. "How would you like to show these beginners how it's done?" he asks, not taking his eyes off of the students.

The warrior steps forward. "With pleasure," he smirks.

Then, he jumps.

The students rush to the edge of the cliff; just fast enough to catch him do a triple backflip before he lands in the water, executing a perfect dive. The warrior quickly reappears. He swims parallel to the cliff until the only thing to his left side is the white, sandy shore. He then turns to face the shore and lets the waves take him there. Some of the students cheer at this amazing feat. Ivory and her friends clap along with the rest of the students as they look at each other. This was not going to be easy.

"So now that you have seen how it is properly done, it is your turn," says the professor in a more serious tone.

"I have said it once, and I will say it again," he says, looking every single student dead in the eye. "You may have had fun learning to swim, but the games are over. Cliff diving is not for the faint of heart. Neither is flying, as a matter of fact. However, here we are, ready to learn. Before you can learn to fly, you have to trust yourself to fall. I can feel the fear burning inside you at this very moment. But I want you to take that fear and turn it into something greater. I want you to take that fear and let it drive you straight off this cliff, into the water. Take that fear, and make it drive your arms and legs to swim as they never have before. Take that fear, and make yourselves proud."

"Now," he says, looking around at the students, "who's first?"

Sevastyan steps forward. "Me."

The students all step back, leaving a path for Sevastyan to get a running start. He gives his friends one last glance, taking in a deep breath. He then makes eye contact with the professor; they exchange a nod, then he runs to the edge of the cliff and jumps. The professor looks over the edge, watching him as he falls. Sevastyan positions his body, arms and head first, in order to land the same way the warrior before him had landed in the water. He breaks the surface of the ocean hands first, pointed downward, followed by his head and the rest of his body.

Ivory and the girls all hold hands as they wait for him to reappear. *One, two, three, four...* Ivory counts in her head. It feels like an eternity passes as she continues to count the number of seconds. Suddenly, he bursts out through the waves. Sevastyan turns his body parallel to the cliff and paddles – hard. He lowers his head into the water and stretches his arms forward, seamlessly moving through the water, only pulling his head up to breathe every few seconds. In no time, he sees that there is only sand to his left side, so he turns toward the shore, letting the waves carry him. The students all burst into loud cheers and claps, his friends cheering the loudest of all. Warrior Emile walks to Sevastyan as he comes out of the ocean, giving him a tight shoulder grip, a sign of ultimate respect in the tribes. Sevastyan returns the grip and thanks the warrior.

Professor Drakonas, pleased, turns back to the students standing beside him. "Next?"

Silence, once again. Ivory steps forward this time, feeling the fire and adrenaline inside her, burning hot. She walks farther back on the cliff to give herself a running start as Sevastyan had. She looks over to the professor, who gives her the nod of approval, and she's off.

I can't wait to learn how to fly, to feel as light as a feather in midair, to feel free.

And there she was, airborne, her stomach floating inside her abdomen. The salt-laced sea breeze caresses her face as she falls. As she sees herself getting closer to the surface of the ocean, she positions her body as she had seen her friend do before her. She stretches her arms out in front of her, placing one hand above the other. Lowering her chin down to her chest and positioning her legs together, she breaks the surface. The icy water shocks her system again. Once in the water, Ivory brings her arms apart, placing them to her sides. She lifts her head toward the surface of the water that is now above her and moves her legs back and forth. As her head pops out of the water, she takes a deep breath, but a wave of water quickly sweeps over her. Water is inside her nose and lungs, the salt burning everywhere it enters. She opens her eyes underwater to see where she is in reference to the cliff, but there is not enough light shining through. Above her, Ivory can see the massive waves crashing together, making it impossible for her to get out. As she holds the little air still left in her lungs, she lets the adrenaline pulsing in her veins move her forward. She positions herself in a way where the sound of water crashing into boulders can be heard to her top left. She swims hard, using every muscle in her body. Just as she runs out of air, she senses beams of warm light above her – calm waters. She uses whatever she has left in her to burst through the ocean surface, desperately breathing in. She hears screaming from a distance, but is too blinded by the sun to see who it is or hear what they are saying. Closer to her left she hears her name being called out. She turns to see a tall, dark figure on the shore, running toward the water, toward her.

The shore, she thinks.

With one last push, Ivory swims. She catches a big wave that carries her all the way to the warrior standing on the wet sand. The warrior, Emile, runs to Ivory, helping her stand up.

"Ivory, are you alright?! It looked like the waves got you! As soon as you touched the water, the waves went wild!" Emile exclaims, frown lines accentuating the light wrinkles on his forehead.

Ivory stands up straight, coughing out the water and rubbing it from her eyes. Emile lets go of her arm as she turns to look at the now-calm water. She turns back to Emile.

"Um...yes. I am fine, I think," she says, not exactly sure what had just happened.

Emile looks at her, amused; she'd surprised him. He laughs out loud, then grabs her right shoulder in a tight grip.

"You are one incredible girl, Ivory. You have just proved it to me, to yourself, and to everyone else watching," he says, impressed.

Ivory smiles big and returns the shoulder grip. "Thank you, warrior."

She turns to the cliff to see everyone cheering for her.

"I will be keeping my eyes on you, sister. I have a feeling that this is only the first of many great things you will be doing. Just remember me when you become famous one day, alright?" says Emile, smiling, sweeping his wet brown hair back out of his face.

Ivory laughs, still not sure what had just happened. "Of course," she says as she makes her way to the horse waiting to take her back up the cliff.

At the top of the cliff, Ivory's friends, along with the rest of the class, all wait for her. As she gets off of her horse, Flora and Fauna run to her, embracing her in a giant hug. Sparrow and Sevastyan are right behind them.

"Oh my God, Ivory, are you alright?" asks Fauna.

"How are you feeling?" asks Flora.

"What happened?" asks Sparrow.

"Hey, let her breathe guys. She just almost drowned," says Sevastyan to the girls.

The twins let go of Ivory, giving Sparrow a chance to hug Ivory next.

"Ive, I swear, for a second there I thought you were gone. The waves just went wild…" says Sparrow, face pink and eyes watering.

"Ivory," says a booming voice.

"Yes, professor," Ivory replies, turning to face her professor.

Everyone makes a path for the professor to walk forward toward the girl. Sparrow lets her go and stands to her side with the rest of their friends.

"What you did out there, it showed great thought and courage. You could have panicked and let the waves take you, but you used your brain and allowed your body follow. You have made me proud," says Professor Drakonas, a smile dancing on his lips and wonder in his eyes. He turns to the rest of the students, looking at each and every single one of them.

"We were made to survive!" he yells out, for everyone to hear. "Even in the toughest situations, we can survive! But in order to survive, you have to listen. Listen to what your body is telling you, and then use your brain and instinct to move forward," he continues, moving to the edge of the cliff.

"You are the future! You are the warriors, the hunters, the caretakers of the next generation!" he yells from the cliff's edge. "I am here to give you the tools to thrive! All it takes is one strong push, one jump! Students, follow your senior into the depths of the unknown, and you shall emerge stronger than you could have ever imagined!"

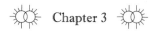

And with a wicked smile, Silver closes his eyes, and lets himself fall backwards off the cliff. The students all look at each other, his words burning in their heads and in their hearts.

"Follow…"

"Follow…"

One by one, students join in.

"Follow!"

A boy runs toward the cliff's edge and jumps. Two more girls follow behind him. One after the other, the students all jump off the cliff. Sparrow looks over at Ivory. "See you at the bottom?" she asks.

"See you there," Ivory replies, giving her friend a squeeze on the arm.

Flora, Fauna, and Sparrow jump, while Sevastyan and Ivory are left standing alone on the cliff. Sevastyan looks at Ivory, determination on his face. "You coming, Skye?" he asks, with a challenge playing over his smile.

"I'll be right behind you, Lanza," replies Ivory, accepting the challenge.

Sevastyan jumps. Ivory takes a moment alone on the quiet cliff overlooking the vast blue, taking it all in. She closes her eyes one last time, breathing in deep, filling her burning lungs with air. She opens her eyes and runs to her destiny. Professor Drakonas had told them to follow him into the unknown. Ivory does not know what the waves will hold for her this time, but she is willing to risk it all to find out. After all, there is no better way to embrace your destiny than to splash right into it.

Chapter 4

ENTRY #5:

First day of flight training complete.

It is currently an hour past sunset. Tonight, the moon shines bright, brighter than I think I have ever seen. I once thought that no sky could be as clear or as beautiful as the one I see from my room's window every night. I was wrong. The stars here shine brighter than I could have imagined possible. Looking out over the cliff at this time of night, I do not know where the ocean ends and where the sky begins. It is all a canvas of deep, dark blues. The only hint I have is the bright lights, the balls of fire, burning high above my head.

Today has been an eventful day, to say the least. The journey to the coast was beautiful, beyond anything I have ever experienced. But swimming in the ocean, I cannot even begin to fathom, to explain, the feeling. And then there was the falling. I must admit that I had trouble with my first jump – trouble that I surprisingly overcame. Do you know that feeling that you get when you, or someone else, is in trouble? You feel it somewhere between your chest and your stomach. It makes your arms and legs move on their own, before your brain can even begin to comprehend what exactly is happening. That's what it felt like today. I was scared; I couldn't hold my breath for much longer under the water. But part of me just knew what to do to survive. I have never felt this feeling in my life before. I guess it's probably because I have never been in real danger before. That's the thing with adventure, it is exhilarating, it makes you feel alive in ways you did not know were possible. But there is no guarantee that you will survive through it. That's when your survival instinct emerges. That's what

33

happened to me today. I am happy that I was able to overcome my troubles. However, this leaves me worried for what is to come in the next two days. What if I cannot overcome the new troubles I run into? What if my instinct alone is not enough...?

As I sit around the fire with my friends, all writing in our memory books, I think about life back home at the tribe. Although it has only been a day, I long for my family greatly. I wish they could be here to see me as I jump into the water, as I swim through the ocean, as I conquer my fears one at a time. I know my sisters would cheer me on, louder than anyone else. My father would stand tall, arms crossed, impressed at my feats, my mother by his side, eyes shining with pride. Anya and Diana would run up to me as I walk out of the water, embracing me hard as they tell me how brave I am, how they want to be like me when they grow up. Hayden would be right behind them, greeting me with a tight shoulder grip and a nod of approval. She would walk me back to the group of warriors and students, head high, making sure everyone knew that I was HER sister. I can see it all now. In the end, that is what matters to me the most – making my family proud. I really just want to make them proud.

"Good morning, students. I hope you all got a good night's sleep after our exciting day yesterday. I am well aware that you all must still be exhausted. However, I would be lying if I told you that the hardest lesson is behind you. We have a lot of work to get done today, so eat up, put on your flight suits, and meet me at the cliff. You have one hour," says Silver Drakonas before he heads off toward the warriors.

"How did you girls sleep last night?" asks Sevastyan as he joins Ivory, Sparrow, and the twins.

"Like a baby," replies Sparrow, taking a big bite out of her apple.

"My lungs and nostrils are still a little sore from the saltwater, but I do not think that I have ever slept so soundly in my life," says Ivory, as she refills her water canteen.

"Yes, you slept like a rock," laughs Fauna. "Flora woke me up in the middle of the night to check if you were still alive."

Everyone laughs. "It is true; I woke up for some water, and you were really still when I looked over at you. You had not moved from the position you had fallen asleep in. I was genuinely worried for a moment," says Flora, with worry lines on her forehead as she remembers the sight.

"Well, do not worry, I was fine," laughs Ivory, putting down her canteen, giving Flora a hug.

The friends continue to talk about their experiences from the previous day as they eat their breakfast and get ready for the day. Once they finish eating, the girls go to their tents to get dressed, while Sevastyan joins the boys. As she is the first to finish getting dressed, Ivory heads to the cliff to wait for the lesson to start. As she gets closer, she sees one person already standing, looking out at the horizon.

"Hey," she says to the standing figure.

"Hey," replies Cassius, turning back to look at Ivory.

"So, are you ready to jump again?" asks Ivory.

"I think so," replies Cassius, looking back out at the ocean.

The two stand in silence for a while, listening to the waves, watching the seagulls circle over a school of fish.

"Good job yesterday," says Cassius, keeping his gaze on the horizon. "You surprised everyone, Skye. Even me. I'm not sure I know you as well as I thought I did," he says, voice steady.

"Thanks," replies Ivory, a bit surprised at the genuine compliment. "Honestly, I don't think I knew myself in that moment either," she says, thinking back to the moment she came out of the water.

"Look, I know that you don't like me. I know that most people don't like me. I can be conceited, egotistical, even mean. I haven't been the nicest person to you, Skye. But what you did yesterday, it deserves recognition. We might not get along, we might fight, but I just want you to know that you have my respect. You deserve it," says Cassius, turning to face Ivory.

Ivory is speechless. He was right, she didn't really like him. Actually, she just felt bad for him, for the most part. And those feelings are what drove her to be nice to him. Respect is a big word, Ivory knew. For Cassius to say this to her, she was sure he meant it. And no, this did not mean that they were friends, by any means. But it did mean that they could have a cordial relationship, at the very least.

"Thank you," replies Ivory, holding eye contact with Cassius.

There is no need for any more words; the two turn back to the ocean, watching silently.

- - -

The students gather up at the cliff once again, standing in a half moon around Silver Drakonas and four of the ten warriors.

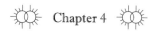
"So yesterday, you played in the water. Today, you play in the clouds," proclaims the professor, anticipation in his voice.

The students all look back and forth at each other, feeling the excitement in the air.

"This is a new day, so let us not dwell on any problems we may have encountered yesterday. However, let us also not forget the lessons we have all learned. I have scared you in the past, saying that if you do not follow my directions, you will die. If I am honest now, it was somewhat of a lie, at least, at this point in time. Those that have tried to fly on their own in the past have been injured quite seriously. However, now that you have all learned to trust yourselves to fall and swim, you are ready for the last step."

Silver takes one of the large bags warrior Raina holds, pulling out a pair of very large gray wings. The large wings are mainly composed of two different materials. The first, which is what the majority of the wing is made of, is a very supple material. Ivory did not know the exact name of it, but the professor had earlier explained that it was similar to synthetic sailcloth that was used long ago in other flying contraptions, such as hang gliders. This material moves with the wearer as he glides through the air. The second material Ivory sees as she looks at the wings seems to be harder, in contrast to the thin, supple, synthetic material. According to the professor, it allows the wings to keep their shape and hold well under heavy winds. As she looks closer at the wings, Ivory knows that the second material could not possibly be normal metal, for that would make the wings much too heavy to fly. She recalls Professor Drakonas saying that it was a very rare, lightweight metal that works the same way steel metal would. Since it can only be found in Eastern Assimilia, the Hemlock tribe is the main producer of flight simulation wings. The rare metal allows the wings to work the same way a bird's wings would while supporting the much larger weight of a human.

Attached to the wings is a harness consisting of many belts, all attached together, made of black leather. The professor takes hold of the harness, slipping it over his shoulders. He ties the belts onto his chest and stomach and tightens those around his shoulders. The wings, larger than his body, hang off of the harness on his back.

"As you can see, each wing is composed of three pieces that work together to give you stability and equilibrium as you weather different winds. Each piece has a separate harness that corresponds to a different part on your arm. The first piece," he says, pointing to the top harness on the inside of a wing, "is for your upper arm."

Warrior Marceau steps next to the professor to help him as he puts the first harness on his left upper arm.

"The second harness is for your forearm. You can see here, the first two pieces of the wing move with your elbow joint, allowing for comfort and flexibility," he says, pointing to the different parts of the wing as he puts on the second harness.

"The final harness is a little different and slightly more complicated than the first two," he continues, pointing to the final piece of the wing. "This harness is made of several small pieces. The first is a piece that goes around your wrist. This is where the third piece of the wing begins. Attached to this wrist strap are four smaller straps, one to be placed between every finger. The four smaller straps all attach together at a metal ball that you hold in your palm, which attaches to the underside of the wrist. Now, this ball," he says, pointing to the ball in his hand, "is the most important piece of equipment on these wings. This is the controller that will help you maneuver the full lower half of each wing, for starters. This ball is attached to the skeleton of the wing, so it also essentially helps hold the wings together."

The professor finishes putting on his left wing, then moves on to the right one.

"As you can see, the top side of the wings is layered with long, thin feathers. These feathers, along with your suit, will help you glide smoothly through the air. The feathers are also very important while flying because they can help speed you up or slow you down. This will become imperative when you want to come in for a landing. They naturally lay flat on the wings. However, you can regulate their positioning with the controller you hold in your palms," he says, showing the students how the feathers move with the movements and rotation of the ball in his hands.

"You also have to keep in mind that each wing works on its own. Each wing can be controlled by its corresponding arm. This will allow you to rotate in flight, as well as flip, change directions, or fly diagonally."

The students all listen to their professor, taking in every little piece of information, more excited by the second.

"Now, before I start the demonstration, does anyone have any questions?" says Professor Drakonas, looking around.

A hand goes up.

"Yes, Sevastyan, what is your question?"

"Professor, I was just wondering, how is it possible that we have this kind of technology today? After the Great Wave, everything was destroyed. How is it possible that we can build such an advanced machine today?"

"You are correct, Sevastyan; everything was destroyed by the Great Wave. That is, every physical piece of technology. You see, Sevastyan, there is nothing more technologically advanced than the brain," says the professor, pointing to his head. "As long as smart humans survive, knowledge will never die. But the problems that we ran into as a species over and over again throughout history was that a lot of us did not store the important knowledge. A lot of us were simply not smart. Our brains have great storage capacities, but we never took advantage of them. We were not smart enough to be smart, if that makes sense. Tell me something, have you ever asked yourself why you attend school from the tender age of three until you reach the age of twenty-three, Sevastyan? Any of you?" the professor asks, looking around.

"Yes, sir," Sevastyan nods, along with the rest of the group.

"We do not want to waste your bright young minds," answers the professor. "We learned this from our past experiences; our past failures. So to answer your question, Sevastyan, no, the physical technology did not survive. But the people who knew of it did. Those people who survived, they were the smartest of any of those that lived before them. That is, after all, why they survived in the first place. They. Wrote. EVERYTHING. That way, the people who would come after them could carry on the knowledge. It's why we ask each of you to keep memory books. To write what you know, what you have been taught, new ideas…whatever it may be that may help you or anyone else in the future."

"I understand now; thank you, professor," says Sevastyan.

"Good. Now, if there are no more questions, we will get started."

The professor looks around, not spotting any hands in the air.

"Alright, here we go."

Turning around and placing his arms to his side, the professor steps to the cliff's edge and jumps.

As he had shown his students the day before, Silver Drakonas falls head first toward the water, holding himself steady in his downward position. As he gets closer to the water, he opens his arms, pointing his wings out. He rotates the metal controllers in his hands, slightly turning up the feathers. Just as he is about to hit the water, his wings catch the wind, swooping him up into the air. He tilts side to side with his wings, bringing himself higher up into the sky before leveling off. He flies about a mile out over the ocean, disappearing into the thick gray clouds, before making a large U-turn back toward the cliff he started out at. When he reaches the cliff, he circles around, over his students.

"He is amazing," breathes Ivory to her nearby friends.

"He is the original flyer," Sevastyan replies to Ivory. "There is not one person in any one of the four tribes that can do it as well as he can. He was born to fly."

The professor looks down, spotting the perfect landing area farther back on the small mountain. He flies towards the open grounds, slowly rotating the metal controllers in his palms. Turning the feathers against the wind, he slows himself down before landing perfectly on his feet. As he lands, he turns to face his students.

Stunned, the students all clap for their professor.

"That was so cool!"

"When can we do that?!"

"How does someone get so good at flying?"

"No one will ever be as good as him!"

The students buzz over the demonstration.

"That did not look very complicated, did it?" asks Silver, making his way back to his students.

Everyone laughs at the joke. It was obviously a lot harder than he made it look.

"Do not worry, I promise you that if you pay attention and do as you are told, you will be flying like this by the end of the day," he says, chuckling, as he walks back to his students.

"I bet you my blue sandals that he just showed us the most basic flight plan he could make up," whispers Ivory in Sparrow's ear.

Sparrow tries to hold in her laugh, snorting in the process, making Ivory laugh along with her.

"Yes, I don't think anyone would disagree with you on that," Sparrow whispers back.

For the next half hour, Silver and the warriors help the students put on their wings, each slightly different in color, showing them how to hold and

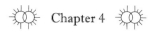

rotate the controllers in their palms. Silver then gives his students the directions they need to lift themselves up as they fall into the ocean, turn in the sky, and how to navigate their landing.

"For the present time, I want all of you to land in the water. Landing is the trickiest lesson to learn in flight simulation; this is where most people get hurt. Once you get the feel of landing, of slowing yourselves down, we can try it on dry land. That will probably happen the next time we make the trip to the coast. As you know, there will be a follow-up flight simulation trip after you graduate and get placed in your future tribal position. But for the moment, the ocean will provide a softer landing. As a warning, what you DO NOT want to do is dive into a landing. EVER. It may feel like the right thing to do when you are in the sky, but it can get you killed if you do not slow yourselves down at the perfect moment, even in the shallow waters. It is possible to do, not impossible, but very difficult and much too dangerous for beginners. Again, it does not matter so much now as you land in the deeper parts of the ocean, but it would be to your displeasure to get yourself used to this idea. Have I made myself clear?"

The students all nod their heads in understanding as they get ready to line up to take flight.

Chapter 5

The sun hides behind the low-hanging clouds as the students prepare to take flight. A cool ocean breeze rips through the high tidal waves, lightly ruffling the feathers on the students' wings. *Perfect flight weather*, the professor had said.

"Sparrow! Sparrow, we're doing it! We're flying!" shouts Ivory to her nearby friend, both mid-flight.

"Woooooh…this is so amazing!" shouts back Sparrow.

The two girls fly together, hovering low over the water. Professor Silver Drakonas flies higher up above the duo, yelling out directions as they go.

"There is a high wave coming up! I want the both of you to slightly lift the feathers on your wings to pick up more wind and move up!" he shouts at the girls.

Ivory looks at the big wave forming out far in front of her and back at Sparrow. The two make eye contact and together start rotating their controllers slowly – but not slowly enough. As another big breeze hits their wings, the girls suddenly soar up into the sky, past their professor. Ivory quickly rotates her wing feathers back down, shakily stabilizing herself. Sparrow, however, continues to climb.

"Sparrow!" calls out Ivory, looking up at her friend.

"Ivory, hold steady, I'm going after Sparrow!" barks Professor Drakonas as he quickly flies up past Ivory, after Sparrow.

The two quickly disappear into the clouds.

Ivory looks up at the clouds, trying to spot her friend and professor as she holds herself steady.

No sign of the two.

Higher up in the sky, past the thick, gray clouds, the sun shines bright. Silver Drakonas calls out to Sparrow, who climbs higher and higher still.

"Sparrow, rotate the feathers back down!" he orders.

Still holding her arms and wings out, Sparrow looks down at her professor.

"I am trying!" she yells back, "It's not working; the controllers are stuck!"

Sparrow desperately tries to move the pieces of equipment in her hands once again, with no luck. Then, she has an idea. As she continues to climb, she lays her right wing down the front side of her body, and her left wing down the back side. Silver Drakonas watches, taken by surprise at the girl's quick thinking as she spins in the air before snapping her wings open again, finally regaining control of them. Sparrow brings her wings back to her sides, still close to her body, and slowly descends to her professor.

"I am so sorry, professor; I lost control of the wings. But I believe I have regained it once again," she says apologetically as they both descend back into the clouds.

Ivory watches the sky, worried sick for her friend, not realizing how far out into the ocean she has flown. Remembering what the professor had said about making a U-turn, Ivory lowers her left wing, very gently. She slowly starts to turn back toward the direction of the beach. Just as she stabilizes herself once again, Sparrow and Silver break through the clouds in front of Ivory.

"Oh my God, Sparrow, you're alright!" yells Ivory to her friend flying far ahead of her.

Sparrow looks back at Ivory, relieved to see her as well.

"Ivory, are you holding up alright?" the professor yells back at Ivory.

"Yes, professor, I am stable!" she yells back.

"Make your way to the beach; we will meet you there when you land!"

Sparrow and Silver fly back to the shore, landing in the water. Ivory follows in right behind them. As soon as she lands, Ivory stands up and runs to her friend, embracing her – or at least she tries. The two's wings get in the way, cutting their attempted hug short.

"Are you alright? What happened?"

"The feathers on my wings got stuck. No matter what I did, I couldn't move them back down!"

"So how did you end up coming back?"

"She used her brain and her instinct," replies Professor Drakonas for Sparrow, obviously impressed.

"Great job, Sparrow, that's exactly what I want to see from my students," he says, giving her shoulder a squeeze.

"Thank you, professor," replies Sparrow, beaming.

The trio walks out of the water and ride back up to the cliff.

Sevastyan meets the girls at the top, unsuccessfully trying to hide an eager smile.

"Do I want to know what happened?" he asks, laughing.

The two girls look at each other and laugh.

"We'll tell you later."

"Yes, if you can make it back in one piece, we'll let you know what happened."

"You girls really are quite the pair," Sevastyan laughs as he makes his way back into the line.

Ivory and Sparrow look at each other again – this time laughing and high-fiving.

"We are, aren't we?"

"Of course, always."

"Forever."

Tonight is the last night we spend on the coast. Tomorrow, we travel back to the tribe.

I don't even know where to start with today's entry…

I feel like I have so much to say, but at the same time, nothing to say at all.

You know what; looking back at my first entry, I realize now that I never had the chance to talk about my friends. So I will take this moment to introduce each.

Starting with one of my oldest friends is my best friend, my sister, Sparrow Avere. Sparrow and I had an interesting relationship from the start. We hated each other. Yes, you read that right, we HATED each other. I thought she was a mean girl and she thought I was a spoiled know-it-all. I think the thing that made us feel that way was the fact that we were both exactly the same, in a way. It took our male best friend, Sevastyan Lanza, to help us see it. And although we had that not-so-great moment in the beginning, Sparrow and I soon became inseparable. We have walked to school together every day since we were eleven years old.

Sparrow is a free spirit. She is the type of person who will say it exactly the way she means it. I admire that about her. She also happens to be very beautiful. Her chin-length,

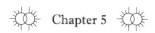

pin-straight raven hair beautifully complements her dark olive skin tone and her light, chocolaty brown eyes. She is shorter than me by quite a bit – the top of her head reaches slightly above my shoulder – but she is to never be underestimated. She is a firecracker, just waiting for the perfect moment to pop! I am so blessed to have someone with such a beautiful heart and soul as my friend.

Moving on to my second oldest best friend; Sevastyan is the brother I never had. I met Sevastyan around the same time that I met Sparrow. He was friends with both Sparrow and I before she and I were friends. If Sparrow is a free spirit, Sevastyan is a gentle spirit. He is a very calm, level-headed boy. He is known and loved by everyone in our tribe. He puts on little shows for the children of the tribe, sometimes dragging me up to help him. It is quite the sight, Sevastyan in all his height, pretending to be one of the children. If my mother could have it her way, I would be the next Mrs. Lanza. I must admit, Sevastyan is a very good-looking fellow. He is one of the taller young men around; I have to look up to look him in the eye. His build is a little more slender than the majority of the males here. He has dark brown hair that he keeps cropped short, with longer bangs that he either wears up or to the side, and dark green eyes that pop against his light/medium skin. Even his rather large nose seems to fit perfectly on his face. I cannot deny his good looks, but I also cannot make our relationship something more than it already is. I have never thought of him as more than my best friend or my brother. It is just too weird. I talked about it with Sparrow one time, and she said the same thing. We just know each other too well to ever have the kind of relationship my mother hopes for.

Now, when it comes to the twins, Flora and Fauna, I cannot say the same. The two migrated with their parents to our tribe exactly three years ago. I was drawn to the two the moment we met, and once I introduced them to Sparrow and Sevastyan, our trio quickly grew into the group it is today. Growing up in Northern Assimilia, where sunlight is scant, Flora and Fauna look like the majority of the Willow population: very fair, almost transparent skin, baby-blue eyes, and strawberry blonde hair. The two girls are slimmer than the rest of the girls of our tribe. Our tribe is known for having some of the strongest warriors within the Collection. The girls in general are built wider, more muscular. The twins, in comparison, have very small muscles and are built taller than most. As I am taller than most girls here, I am the same height as the twins.

Flora and Fauna are identical, for the most part. The only way most of us can tell them apart is by hair. Flora has long, straight hair that she usually wears in a braid or a ponytail. Fauna, on the other hand, has chest-length, wild hair. She looks like a lion most of the time with her hair down. Once in a while, she lets Flora fix her hair in a braid, but she draws the line at putting flowers in it. Flora, like her name, loves flowers. She always has some kind of flower in her hair. And when she braids it, she puts lots of little ones in it. Fauna, on the other hand, doesn't want anything to do with plants. She has a tendency to do more dangerous things, like take care of wild snow leopards, for example. She and Sparrow have quite a bit in common, now that I think about it. They drive Flora and me crazy at times. Flora falls more on the calm side of the personality spectrum, more like Sevastyan. Secretly, Sparrow and I think Flora and Sevastyan would make the perfect couple. I'm not sure they know it yet, but I can't wait for the day they do.

Anyway, that is pretty much the end of my friends' list. Well, my best friends' list, anyway. All of us have other friends, of course, but we like to spend most of our time with each other when we can.

I shall stop here for now. Today has been a long day; we flew out to the ocean and back many times, only taking a small lunch break, and continuing on till sunset. It is now only an hour to midnight, so I shall head to sleep and prepare for our last day tomorrow. Because we have done so well with our flying lessons, Professor Drakonas is allowing us the whole morning before we leave tomorrow for time to explore. We will most likely be traveling in small groups, each with a warrior, but it is exciting, nonetheless.

Goodbye for now.

- - -

"Ivory! Ivory, run!"

Thud, thud, thud, thud.

"Why is my heart beating so hard? Why am I running so fast? What am I running away from?"

A girl screams in the distance.

"No! Stop!" Ivory holds her hands tightly over her ears, trying to block the screaming out.

"It's so dark; I can't see where I'm going."

"Someone, please, help me!" Ivory yells out into the vast darkness as she continues to run, feet pounding hard over the dead leaves.

Suddenly, the ground disappears from underneath her feet, and she falls, rolling down a steep hill, only stopping when she gets to the bottom at a forest clearing. Looking up, Ivory sees the first sign of light, a full moon.

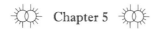

Thud, thud, thud, thud, THUD, THUD, THUD THUDTHUDTHUD-THUD...

The sound gets closer, louder.

Ivory holds her hands to her ears and puts her head between her knees as she sits, rocking back and forth. She screams.

- - -

"Ah!" Ivory shoots up from her sleeping bag, breathing hard.

She brings her shaking hands to her forehead, wiping off the warm sweat. She then puts her index and middle fingers together and brings them to her throat, feeling her fast-beating pulse.

She knows that it was just a dream, a nightmare, but she can't shake away the fear. And, as if someone tapped her on the shoulder, she looks around the large tent. On the far end to her right is a girl, also sitting up, quietly crying. Ivory gets up and quietly crawls over to the girl before sitting opposite her on her sleeping bag.

"Hey, are you okay?" she asks the crying girl, putting a hand on her shoulder.

The crying girl nods her head as she attempts to wipe away all of her tears.

"I'm... I'm alright. It was just a bad dream," mumbles the girl, still a bit shaken.

"Trixie. That's your name, right? Don't worry; you're not alone," says Ivory, caressing the girl's shoulder.

"Yes, I'm Trixie. Thank you, Ivory," she replies.

Trixie was a very shy, quiet girl. Ivory had seen her around, but she had only heard her name once or twice in the past. She seemed like a very nice girl, making Ivory wonder why she hadn't taken the time to get to know her before.

Keeping to her gentle nature, Trixie moves her shoulder-length brown hair all to one side, wipes her face with both hands, and takes in a deep breath.

"Thank you, Ivory, I really am alright now. I have no idea where that all came from," she whispers.

"No problem, it happens. Sleep well," whispers back Ivory, exchanging a quick hug with Trixie before crawling back to her own bed.

Snuggling back up in her sleeping bag, Ivory watches the quiet girl she'd officially just met do the same. Ivory turns to lay on her left side as she tries to remember her dream. Why was she running? She couldn't remember a thing.

"Tomorrow is going to be a long day; I better head back to sleep," she thinks to herself.

And she does, as sleep slowly takes hold of her again. Still, as she falls to sleep, there is a small piece of her brain that keeps turning, wondering…

"Morning! Time to wake up, sleepy!" whispers Flora excitedly to a drowsy Ivory.

"Ugh, really?" she grumbles, eyes still closed. "Do I have to?"

"Yes! We don't have any time to waste, time to get up!" says Flora, a little louder, as she gets up to leave.

Ivory turns to lie on her back as she opens her eyes, looking up at the tent above her. She sighs.

"It's now or never, I guess," she says to herself.

Sitting up and looking around, Ivory finds herself the last person in the tent. Everyone had already gotten up and gone out to eat breakfast. Against her will, she drags herself up off her bed and out the tent. The sunlight hits her eyes in the most unpleasant way possible. Squinting, Ivory walks over to the group of girls sitting together, eating.

"Well, well, look who's decided to finally wake up! What were you doing last night while we all slept, running a marathon or something?" Sparrow jokes.

"You have no idea," Ivory says, rolling her eyes at her friend.

She plops down next to Flora, reaching for a piece of bread. Taking a big bite, filling her entire mouth, Ivory looks around the camp. A little over to her right, she spots Trixie sitting with another group of girls, eating. Trixie and Ivory make eye contact with each other, and wave to one another. Ivory smiles at the girl before turning back to her friends.

"Who's that?" asks Fauna, who had caught the short, silent dialogue between the two girls.

Sparrow looks over at the second group of girls, following Fauna's gaze.

"Do you know her?" she asks Ivory, surprised. Flora turns to look at the girl, interested in who everyone was talking about.

"Umm…kind of, I guess. I met her yesterday," replies Ivory, a little unsure, taking another bite out of her bread. "Her name is Trixie," she says with her mouth full.

"That's a pretty name," says Flora, still looking at the girl. "I think it suits her, she's so cute."

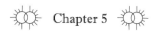

"Hmm…weird," says Fauna.

"What's weird?" asks Sparrow.

"I feel like this is the first time I've ever seen her," replies Fauna.

"Her face is a little familiar, but I've never personally met her either," says Sparrow.

"She's a really nice girl," says Ivory, reaching for some berries. "She's a little shy, though, which is probably why we don't know her."

"Hmm…anyway, are we exploring together today? Where do you guys want to go?" asks Sparrow, changing the subject.

"The beach!" the twins say at the same time.

"Oh yeah, I want to explore the beach too," agrees Ivory.

"The beach it is!" says Sparrow, satisfied with the choice.

After they finish eating, the girls start heading back to their tent.

"Hey, Ivory!"

Ivory turns around, spotting Sevastyan jogging towards her.

"Hey, what's up?" she greets him.

"Nothing, I was just wondering if you guys decided where you wanted to go. I want to dress accordingly," he says.

"Of course you do," replies Ivory, shaking her head at her always-prepared-for-anything friend.

"We all want to explore the beach. The professor said that we might spot some tide pools further down."

"Alright, sounds good! I'll meet you guys at the horses, and we can all leave together."

"Alrighty, see you then!"

"Don't leave without me!" shouts Sevastyan as he walks away.

Ivory laughs. "Do not worry, you know I would never leave you behind, brother!" she shouts back. "Don't you leave without us, either!"

"You know I would never!"

Sevastyan reaches his tent, going inside to change into his clothes for the day. As Ivory reaches her tent, an idea hits her.

As she goes inside, she looks around, and then heads straight for Trixie.

"Hey, good morning."

"Good morning, Ivory!" replies Trixie, a little surprised but pleased with the interaction.

"I just wanted to say hello and make sure you're feeling better," says Ivory.

"Oh yes, thank you. I apologize for the erratic behavior; I have no idea what got into me last night," replies Trixie, cheeks flushing pink.

"Oh no, please, no need to apologize! I had a nightmare too, I know exactly how you were feeling!" Ivory reassures her.

"Thank you," says Trixie, looking back up at Ivory.

"So do you know who you're exploring with today?" asks Ivory, out of curiosity.

"Umm…yes, I guess. The girls I was sitting with wanted to explore the grasslands, back near the path we came through."

As Trixie talks, Ivory can see that she is unsure about the entire situation.

"Do you want to explore that area?" she asks.

"Well…it's ok," says Trixie, stammering. "I mean, I did kind of want to stay more on the beach, but it's alright," she says with a shrug.

Ivory looks back toward her friends, who are looking her way as they dress.

"You know what; my friends and I are exploring the beach. Would you like to join us?"

"Wow, are you sure?" asks the quiet girl, unable to hide the excitement from her elevated voice.

"Yes, of course! My friends and I would be very happy to have you along with us." Ivory smiles reassuringly at Trixie.

"Well, if you say so! I will let the other girls know that I won't be going with them," says Trixie, excitedly looking around for the other girls.

"Meet us at the horses when you're done getting dressed," yells Ivory at the girl, who's already disappeared.

Ivory walks back to her friends and starts to change her clothes.

The girls look at her silently, waiting for her to say something.

"That was really nice of you to do," Flora finally speaks up.

Ivory looks over at her, smiling back.

"I just…she's a very nice girl, and she didn't have anyone to explore the beach with," she says, shrugging.

Sparrow walks over to her, putting her hand on her shoulder.

"We're happy you did that, Ive. We wanted to meet her at some point, anyway. This is the perfect time." She winks, putting Ivory's heart at ease.

Ivory looks over at Fauna, who gives her a reassuring smile as well.

Ivory continues to get dressed as her friends start heading out.

"See you out there, Ive."

"See ya, Sparrow."

Chapter 6

Ivory walks out of her tent and heads toward the group of students and warriors standing near the horses. She and Sevastyan reach the three other girls at the same time. Warrior Emile walks to the group as they excitedly prepare for their quick excursion.

"So it seems like I can't stay away from you five this trip," he says jokingly as he approaches them.

"Hey, warrior Emile, you're going to be our guide today?" asks Ivory, ecstatic.

"Yes. Have you all agreed upon a place you want to explore?"

"The beach," the five say in unison.

"Perfect. If you have everything you need, we can head out," says Emile.

"Actually, we're waiting for one more person," says Ivory, looking around, spotting the quiet girl as she makes her way to the group.

"Hey," she says to Trixie as she takes her hand and leads her to her friends.

"So, everyone, this is Trixie. Sevastyan, you didn't know about this, but she is going on the excursion with us today," says Ivory, turning to Sevastyan, who had not known about the girl before this moment.

Sevastyan walks up to Trixie with a big smile on his face, extending his hand. "It's a pleasure to meet you, Trixie; I'm Sevastyan."

"Thank you, it's a pleasure to meet you as well," replies Trixie, accepting Sevastyan's handshake.

The rest of the girls all introduce themselves to Trixie, giving her hugs and making her feel like she is part of the group.

"Okay, it seems that we have everyone here. Let us all get saddled up and head down to the beach. I have a really cool place I want to take you," says Emile to the group.

Ivory fixes the saddle on her horse Thunder, feeding him a sugar cube in the process as a treat for being the best horse she could ever have. Once she finishes getting him ready, she hops on and heads down the cliff with her friends and their warrior. As the group rides down the small mountain, Ivory looks at her friends in front of her, how they interact with Trixie. Fauna and Trixie seems to have more in common than Fauna had thought. This makes Ivory happy. Seeing her friends all get along with her new friend proves to her that she had chosen the right people to surround herself with.

Sevastyan lags a little behind everyone so he can ride with Ivory.

"That was really nice of you. Flora told me what you did," he says to Ivory.

Ivory smiles. "She really is a nice girl. I'm actually surprised she doesn't have more friends. But hey, the girls seem to really like her, so I think I made the right decision," she replies, looking at the girls all laughing at something Trixie had said.

"I think so too."

Ivory and her friends reach the white sandy shore and stop behind warrior Emile, waiting for further instruction. Emile takes a moment, looking to his left at the miles of white sand and to his right at the cliff they had just come down from. He turns his gray horse around to look at the six students behind him, waiting.

"Do you guys want to explore the beach, or do you want to go on a *real* adventure?" he asks with a mysterious smile.

Ivory and her friends all look back and forth at each other, a little confused.

"Do you guys trust me?" asks Emile.

"Umm…yes," everyone answers, a little hesitantly.

Emile thinks a little bit longer, then makes up his mind.

"Alright then, it's decided. I want all of you to take off your shoes and put them away in your saddle pouches. We're going in the water," he commands, excitement filling his voice.

"Warrior Emile, I hope you're not going to get us in any trouble," laughs Ivory.

"Oh, I probably will. But don't worry, it'll be fun!" Emile winks back at Ivory.

Emile and the students all take off their shoes and head into the water on their horses. As they go further out into the water, the horses lift off of the sandy ocean bottom and start to paddle.

"How much farther out are we going to go?" asks Sevastyan.

"Just a little more, so we can be far away from the rocky cliff bottom when we swim past it," replies Emile.

The group swims for a while longer before they turn to their right side and swim parallel to the cliff.

"It's so cool that the horses naturally know how to swim," says Trixie out loud.

"Most land animals have had the ability to swim in the water for ages, even before the Great Wave and the evolutionary event that followed. It really is very cool," replies Fauna.

Waves pass by, hitting the horses and the people on top of them, completely soaking them, but the horses never falter. Out in the distance, Ivory spots a small splotch of white, which she believes to be sand.

"Is that where we're going?" she asks Emile.

"Yup, you've spotted it," laughs Emile. "But you have yet to see anything. Trust me, you're going to love this."

The group swims with their horses for about ten more minutes before they make it to the shore on the other side of the cliff.

"Not a lot of people come to this side of the cliff because you can't come down on your horses," says Emile. "Look there, do you see that?" he asks, pointing to the cliff. "It's a sharp drop. The only way you can make it here is if you swim. However, it is a little risky, which is why not a lot of people know about this spot."

"Um… hold on, wait a minute. If it's risky to come here, why are *we* risking it?" asks Sparrow, eyes narrowed.

"Because you guys are special. I know you guys are *sooo*… much braver then the rest of the students," Emile says, exaggerating his words.

Everyone laughs as they jump off their horses and bring them higher up on the shore, where they tie them up together.

"Put everything you might need in your backpacks, including your shoes, and bring them with you. We have a bit of a walk ahead of us, and we can't take the horses down any further," instructs Emile.

The students do what they are told and start heading down the beach. The sunlight makes a full reappearance, hitting the water and the sand, making them lighter and even more beautiful than they had seemed before. As they continue to walk, Ivory spots a little pool of water surrounded by rocks. She runs up to it, everyone following behind her. As she reaches the small tidal pool, she climbs on top of the rocks and looks over into the water. She can't believe her eyes. The little pool of water is filled to the brim with small fish, corals, urchins, and starfish of all shapes, sizes, and colors. The rest of the group joins Ivory, all finding a spot to stand and look over into the pool.

"Wow, look at that black slinky one; it looks so slimy," says Sparrow, both captivated and repulsed at the same time.

"I love the corals; they're so pretty," says Flora, mesmerized.

Everyone nods in agreement. The corals are beautiful. They are all different shades of orange and pink and red.

"I like that one. I never knew they came in blue," says Trixie, pointing to a small starfish sticking to the inside rock wall of the pool.

"Wow, that is interesting," agrees Ivory. "Is it safe to pick up and touch?" she turns, asking Emile.

"Yes, I believe so. I don't believe they are harmful. They're not sessile, like barnacles, but they are, for the most part, harmless. Just watch your hands when you handle them; you can cut yourselves if you're not careful."

"Who wants to reach in and grab it?" asks Sevastyan.

"I can do it," replies Fauna, putting her hand in the water, taking hold of the starfish and gently pulling it off the rock. The sunlight hits the starfish as it's taken out of the water, making the water droplets on top of it sparkle. Fauna examines the starfish before passing it to her left to Trixie.

Trixie's eyes open wide as she holds the organism in her hands. She looks down at it in wonder. She had never seen anything like it before; she'd only read about it in books. She turns it around in her hands, lightly going over the little ridges with her fingers.

As the starfish gets passed around the circle, Fauna reaches her hand into the pool once again, this time touching the little sea anemones dancing in the water.

"They look like little flowers," says Flora to her sister, who sits to her left.

As Fauna touches the anemones, they close at her touch, only to open again moments later.

"Be careful which anemones you touch, Fauna, some produce toxins that can sting you," warns Emile gently.

Trixie turns to Ivory. "This is the most amazing experience I have ever had; thank you so much for inviting me with you, Ivory," she says, obviously overwhelmed by everything.

"Hey, we're friends now. There's no need to thank me. That's what friends are for," says Ivory, winking back as Trixie.

About ten more minutes pass before Emile speaks up again to the group.

"I think you have explored this little pool enough. The time has come for me to take you to the main attraction," he says excitedly.

He climbs off the rocky tidal pool wall and starts heading further down the beach. Fauna takes hold of the blue starfish, gives it one last look, then puts it back in its spot on the rocky wall. She climbs down back to the sand, puts on her shoes, and follows the rest of her friends. Up ahead, the sandy shore slowly becomes more and more rocky, hence the need for shoes. And as the rocks accumulate, they lead to a wall; a high, flat, rock wall.

"This way," says Emile, getting into the water once again, going around the wall, and disappearing behind it.

Ivory walks right behind Emile. She can't believe her eyes as she makes her way into the water and around the wall. The wall is only one side of a cave, a cave that holds a very big, shallow pool of water. On the other side of the cave is also a wall, but right in the center of it is a large hole, like a window. The entire cave top is also a big hole, allowing the sunlight to shine through. All along the perimeter of the pool is a strip of white sand. Inside the shallow pool are shells of different sizes and colors.

As Sparrow, Fauna, Trixie, Flora, and Sevastyan make their way into the cave behind Ivory, they all stop dead in their path, taking in a collective gasp. Emile walks through the pool to the back of the cave, where he sets his backpack and shoes on the sand and sits, putting his feet in the crystal-clear water.

"Enjoy," he says, satisfied with everyone's reaction.

Ivory looks around the cave, dipping her feet in the warm, shallow water. She puts her belongings down next to the cave wall on the sand and then walks over to the center of the pool, looking up at the large hole in the ceiling. It had been chilly the past few days as a result of the ocean breeze. But standing in the warm waters and looking up at the clear blue sky above her head, Ivory doesn't feel cold anymore. There is something about this cave; it feels *magical*. Ivory looks over to her friends; Sparrow, Fauna, and Trixie running around in the water, Sevastyan and Flora exploring the cave walls, and Warrior Emile sitting on the sand, eyes closed, enjoying the sunlight. She smiles, then sits down where she stands, right in the middle of the pool. The water comes right up to the bottom of her chest. She puts her hands in the water, wading them back and forth, watching the light hit the ripples she makes in the calm waters. Then, reaching out in front of her, she pulls out a pink and coral-colored shell from the sand inside the pool. Running her right hand through the sand she pulls out another, and another, and another. Before she knows it, she has a handful of different, beautiful, shells; souvenirs for herself and her family, she thinks. Flora and Sevastyan make their way to Ivory, sitting on either side of her.

"What do you have there?" asks Sevastyan, peeking into her lap.

"They are lovely," exclaims Flora, eyes wide.

"Reach into the water," says Ivory. "They're buried in the sand."

Flora and Sevastyan do as they are told, soon filling their hands with brightly colored shells as well. The other three girls soon get interested and join the others in the water, also searching for seashells to take home with them. Ivory gets up out of the water, walking over to her backpack to store her shells. She walks over to Emile and sits next to him on the sand, leaving her feet in the water like him. They sit quietly together for a while.

"How on earth did you find this place?" she finally asks, looking around the cave in wonder.

"Well, once upon a time, when I was your age, I was a curious fellow. Risk, danger – these words did not exist in my vocabulary. Of course, I was also very lucky – the risks I took never ended in tragedy. I remember when I came here for the first time with Silver. He was younger then, but still the most skilled flyer our tribe had ever seen. We did not have the same big age gap between us as you guys have with him, but we still referred to him as professor. It was only until after we graduated from our studies that he pushed us all to call him by his first name – as he will to you one day."

"I don't think I could ever do that. I feel like he will always be Professor Drakonas."

"Oh, he will, there is no doubt about it. But in time, when you acclimate into the tribe as an official contributing member, you will find that some things change. You become one of us. We are all the same. You will still respect your elders, but you will be a respected member of the tribe as well."

"Wow. That all seems so far away, but it's so close."

"Yes, you will soon start to wonder how fast time goes by. It feels like just yesterday when I left my excursion group and discovered this place for myself. Silver was furious, to say the least, but I know that he liked my drive."

"Has he seen this place?"

"Yes, of course. He had to see the discovery I risked my life for."

"And? What did he say?"

"Hmmm… not much, actually. I know he was stunned, that's for sure. I think he kept silent so as to not compliment my idiotic choices. But yes, I am sure he was as impressed as you all are today."

"Well, warrior, you are a lot braver than I think I could ever be. I would be too scared to disobey the professor, even if I knew I could be discovering something as amazing as this."

"Actually, I think you're a lot braver than you realize, Ivory. And I think, well, I know, that the professor, Silver, he thinks so too. He overheard you and your friends talking about the beach. He was the one who suggested I bring you here. I was the one who was hesitant about it at first. But I think I can see what he sees in you – your friends as well. I wouldn't trust any one of the other students to make it here with me as I did with you."

Ivory is stunned.

"Thanks."

"There is no need to thank me, Ivory; I am simply stating what I see. I think you know that I am not the sugarcoating type," laughs Emile.

Ivory smiles at the thought, then laughs. "Actually, yes, I do know that."

"Good. Now, don't let this conversation get to your head. You have a lot of work ahead of you, and if you don't work hard, you will not reap the rewards. Greatness, Ivory, does not come with lineage, as some people might think. It is not passed down. It also doesn't just happen overnight. It is worked for – hard. You have come a long way, and it is starting to show. Don't stop now. I – we – see great things coming your way. If there is one piece of advice that I would give you, it's to embrace your destiny. Take life as it comes at you – no shortcuts. Then come tell me all about it," Emile finishes, looking Ivory directly in the eye.

"I will, I promise."

"Good."

Emile stands up, brushing the sand off of himself. He picks up his backpack, then yells out to the rest of the students.

57

"I know you must all be enjoying yourselves, maybe a little too much, but it is time we head back to the cliff and get on our way home," he says as he makes his way to the edge of the cave.

Ivory takes the last few moments she has to look around the big cave, thinking about everything Emile had said. She had always thought about life as something that she had to make for herself. She never really thought about destiny before. *Embrace your destiny,* he had said. But what if her destiny wasn't what she wanted, she thinks to herself.

"Ive, let's go," calls out Sparrow.

As Ivory gets up to leave she thinks, *"Well, my destiny, so far, has brought me here. And this was an unexpected but amazing journey. I guess I'll just have to wait and see what happens next. I just pray that it's as amazing as this was."*

"Are you all ready?" asks Emile, standing in the water.

"Yes," replies everyone.

One by one, the students turn the corner of the cave wall, heading toward the rocky shore they had passed in order to make it into the cave. As the last one out of the cave, Ivory gives it one last, long look.

"One day," she whispers. "One day I'll be back. And I will do it on my own," she promises herself.

The group heads back to the cliff, where they meet up with the rest of their class, then head back home.

"This was the most amazing trip we've ever had," says Sparrow to Ivory as they ride back home.

"I know. I can't wait to come back after we graduate. It'll be a whole new experience," replies Ivory.

"You know what I can't wait for? To sleep on my bed! My back is killing me!" yells Fauna, laughing.

"Oh, Fauna," laughs Ivory with the rest of her friends.

And just like that, the group travels back home, excited to share the stories of their adventures with their loved ones waiting for their arrival.

Chapter 7

"I'm home!" yells Ivory as she walks through the front door.

She drops her backpack down on the floor next to the door and starts taking off her jacket. The house seems really quiet. Then all of a sudden, she hears little feet running on the hardwood floors. She gets greeted with big hugs and kisses from her sisters as they tackle her where she stands.

"Ivory, you're home! We missed you so much!"

"Tell us all about your trip; you were gone for so long!"

"She wasn't gone that long; it was just for a few days."

"Still, we missed you so much!"

"Did you bring us back any souvenirs?"

"Guys, one by one, I have no idea what you're all saying," Ivory laughs out loud.

"Girls, get off your sister and let her breathe. I'm sure she's exhausted. She's had a very long trip," says Constantina, waiting patiently to also greet her daughter with a big hug.

"Hey Mama, I missed you so much," says Ivory, burying her face in her mother's shoulder as she embraces her.

"I missed you too, baby. How was your trip? Were you all safe? Did anything bad happen?" asks Constantina, holding her daughter's face in her hands, examining it.

"No, of course not, Mother. It was really nice," Ivory reassures her.

"Okay, good. Well, go set your things down in your room and get changed. Then come over for dinner."

"Okay. Where's Papa?"

"He should be home soon. Rain had her foal, so they're a little busy at the stables."

"Ohhh, that's so cute. I can't wait to see it!"

"Well, you'll have to wait until tomorrow morning. Go now, get yourself settled."

"Alright, I'll be right back."

Ivory picks up her heavy backpack once more, dragging it on the floor all the way to her room before she sets it down in a corner.

"I'm not opening you any time soon," she says sternly to her backpack, as if it could respond back to her.

She undresses, throwing her dirty travel clothes in the same corner as her backpack. She thinks about taking a shower before putting on her house clothes, but the thought of sitting next to the stove as she heats up a big pot of water to shower with sounds too tiring. And showering in icy cold water at night can get her sick. *Tomorrow*, she thinks.

Once she is dressed, Ivory lays on her bed and closes her eyes.

"Oh bed, oh soft, comfortable bed, how I've missed you so," she whispers lovingly into her pillow. "Yes, I know you missed me too. And don't worry, pillow, I've missed you as well," she smiles, eyes still closed.

"Hey, don't fall asleep without having dinner first. Mother worked hard to make your favorites," says Hayden as she walks into the room and sits at Ivory's feet.

"Hayden, my lovely sister…"

Hayden laughs. "Let me stop you there, sister. I know what you're about to say."

"Pleeeeaaase and thank you!"

"Oh, alright. Because I know you're dead."

"Yay!!"

Ivory snuggles up in bed while Hayden massages her tired feet. Ivory had gotten massages from all three of her sisters, but Hayden's touch could not be replicated by any other. And although Hayden likes to make a fuss about giving Ivory massages, it was a bonding time for her and her sister. And when it came down to it, Hayden never let anyone else take the job.

"So, anything exciting happen at the coast?"

"It would be hard for me to choose a moment that wasn't exciting, I think."

"Ugh, you're so lucky."

"Why, did anything cool happen here?"

"Umm…really? What do you think?"

"I think I'll take that as a no, then."

"Obviously. That's literally all I pray for, every day, for something exciting to happen. It doesn't even have to be exciting, just something different. At one point, I literally lied outside on the grass and just watched it grow for an hour or two."

"Why don't you study? Don't you have exams at school or something?"

"I already studied. I've pretty much memorized the entire lesson book. I'm so sick of school! You're so lucky you're graduating in a little over a week!"

"Well, yeah, I am excited about finally finishing school too, but it's not going to be any easier trying to find my place in the tribe, you know. Finding a career, a position, where I can actually make a difference and still be happy with what I do, that's not easy to do. This is it for me; I'm going to officially be an adult."

"I'd rather be an adult," mumbles Hayden.

"Guys, Papa's here! And Mama says come to the table; it's time to eat," says Anya, popping her head into the room.

"Okay, we're coming," replies Ivory, sitting up in her bed. "Thanks for the massage, Hayden; I needed it."

"No problem, I know you can't get it better anywhere else!" winks Hayden.

The two leave the room and walk together to the kitchen. Ivory's father, Nadi, is drying his hands off after washing them.

"Hey, look who's decided to join us for dinner today!"

"Hey, Papa," says Ivory, walking up to her dad, embracing him in a hug.

"Hey, Ive," he says, kissing her on her cheeks. "Did you have fun?"

"Yeah, it was awesome! You should have been there!"

"Oh, don't worry, I've been there, and I've done everything that you did. It's beautiful out at the coast. How was the ride there and back; bumpy?" he asks, as they all sit at the table.

"Um…no, not really," Ivory tries to recall the travel portion of her trip. "I mean, getting out of the woods was a little interesting. That was probably the bumpiest part. Same thing when we came back. But once we hit the open hills and the lavender fields, it was all smooth riding."

"Nice. And how was Thunder? I passed by him on my way out of the stables; he looked happy eating his hay."

"He was solid, didn't falter one bit. And I bet he looked happy; I gave him a mini mountain of apples along with his hay before I walked home," laughs Ivory.

Everyone laughs. "Yes, I'm sure he was ecstatic about that," replies Nadi.

"Okay, so," starts Constantina, "tonight I made waraq ainab, merguez, and a cucumber and tomato salad. Ivory, what would you like first?"

"Everything!" laughs Ivory.

Her mother had made some of her favorites. Waraq ainab – pickled grape leaves stuffed with rice, with the tiniest bit of ground beef – cooked in a lemony sauce. Merguez – long, thin sausages, filled with ground beef and aromatic spices; a bit spicy on the tongue. And, of course, cucumbers and tomatoes with a light, lemony vinaigrette. There was a small ingredient that ran through most of the foods Ivory liked to eat: lemon. She could literally put lemon on anything.

Constantina, knowing what Ivory loves, puts the lemon wedges right next to Ivory.

"Mama, I think this is the best meal you've ever made. Seriously. It's amazing!" raves Ivory.

Everyone at the table agrees, complimenting Constantina on her always-marvelous cooking skills.

"Oh, here," says Constantina, pulling out a kitchen towel enclosing fresh, warm bread on the inside.

Ivory laughs, almost choking on her food. "You know me so well, mother."

"Don't choke!" Constantina laughs back.

Ivory takes the fresh bread, opens it up, and puts the merguez inside, making a small sandwich.

"Mmmm…so good!"

Ivory finishes up her plate and leans back in her chair, stuffed.

"That was so delicious; thanks, Mama."

"I'm glad you liked it," smiles Constantina.

"I hope you have some space left for dessert," says Hayden.

"Dessert? There's more?"

"I would hope so!" says Nadi. "Dessert is the best part!" he laughs.

"Hayden, help me pick up these dishes so I can set out the pie," says Constantina.

"Pie? Ohhh…what kind of pie are we talking about?" asks Ivory, eyes wide with excitement.

"Ive, I thought you said you were full!" says Anya.

"Yeah!" agrees Diana.

"I always have space for dessert!" replies Ivory, pretending to be flabbergasted at the insinuation that dessert was not important.

Constantina comes back to the table, placing the pie in the middle.

"Cherry pie," she says, pleased with the outcome of her hard work.

"YEEEEEEEEEES!" exclaims Ivory, fist in the air.

Constantina cuts slices of pie for all to enjoy. Ivory tells stories of her time at the coast over cherry pie, then heads to bed soon after. She had missed these special moments with her family while away. They were all very close, as were most families during the time period of The Settlement. This was a time when all you really had was your loved ones. They were one's reason to survive and live on. After all, what's the point of living when you're all alone?

- - -

"Ivory!"

"Ivory, help us! Please!"

"Help!"

Ivory turns, searching for the voices, all yelling for her help. But as she looks out into the pitch-black darkness surrounding her, she cannot find the source of the screams.

None of the voices sound familiar, but they all sound desperate.

The screams become more desperate, bloodcurdling, by the second.

They soon become too much for Ivory handle. She covers her ears in an attempt to muffle the heartbreaking sounds.

But through her hands, she hears another voice. One that is clearer than any of the others. But it doesn't scream for her help like the others do. The authoritative voice yells at Ivory one time:

"Ivory, wake up! WAKE UP!"

And she shoots up in her bed.

- - -

The cold water feels amazing on Ivory's warm, clammy forehead. She had made a good decision to take a cold shower early this morning, as opposed to the hot one she had planned the night before. As she lathers her hair and body in soap, Ivory thinks about her dream. She can't quite remember all of it, but what she does remember is the last voice she'd heard. *It was a woman*, she thinks to herself. It wasn't a voice she was familiar with, either. It was a little raspy, *probably that of an older woman*, she thinks. But the authority it held drove Ivory right out of her dream.

Ivory had never had nightmares before. Vivid dreams, yes, but never nightmares. *It was probably all of the excitement of the past couple of days*, she thinks to herself before rinsing and wrapping herself up in a large towel.

As she heads to her room to change, she hears her father wishing her mother a good day before he leaves to the stables. Everyone else is soundly asleep this early in the morning.

Ivory goes into her room, closes the door as quietly as she can, and starts changing into her clothes for the day: a short-sleeved, loose-fitting, light green blouse that she loosely tucks into her favorite pair of tan jodhpurs. She also puts on socks to wear with her riding boots. When she finishes getting dressed, she sits on her bed and starts towel-drying her hair.

The door to her room slowly creaks open.

"Good morning, you're up early today."

"Good morning, Mama. Yeah, I couldn't stay asleep any longer."

"What's wrong, excited to be back?" smiles Constantina as she sits next to her daughter on the bed.

"No, not really," says Ivory, looking down at her hair.

"Hey, what is it? What's wrong?" asks Constantina, a little concerned.

"I don't know. I've been having nightmares. It's happened the past two nights in a row," replies Ivory, now looking up at her mother.

"Oh, that's not a good sign."

"Really? Why?"

"Well, if it was just one random nightmare, I would say that it's ok, it happens sometimes. But nightmares in general are never a good sign, I guess… You know what, don't think about it. The more you think about your nightmares, the more likely they are to affect you. So forget about them, and move on with your life," Constantina finishes, pleased with her advice.

"Okay, I'll try," replies Ivory with a small smile.

"Alright. Well, I have to go and start waking up the girls for school," says Constantina, getting up off the bed.

"Mama, wait, can you please braid my hair? I don't want it to be in my face all day. Plus, I have riding lessons today."

Constantina sits back down on the bed and makes Ivory sit on the floor in front of her so she can braid her hair.

"There, perfect," she says as she gets up to leave once again.

Ivory takes a look in the mirror. Pleased with her mother's work, she heads out to look for her riding boots.

"Ugh, are you kidding me?!" she says out loud, staring at her now filthy riding boots.

"You have time; wipe them down with a damp cloth. Don't go into your riding lesson with dirty boots; you know how your father feels about that."

Ivory thinks back to the lesson her father had given the students about always being clean and tidy when riding. He had said something about that being half of the riding experience.

"Yes, I think I will do that," replies Ivory, going back into the house to fetch a damp cloth.

By the time Ivory is finished cleaning her boots and eating breakfast, the girls are all ready to head out as well.

"I want you all to have a wonderful, productive day. Stay safe. Anya, take care of your younger sister. Hayden, keep Anya and Diana in your sight when you can. And Ivory, well, you already know."

Ivory laughs. "Yes mother, I will keep it in mind."

The girls all give their mother a kiss before they head out the front door.

Ivory, Hayden, Anya, and Diana follow their usual path to school, picking up Ivory's friends along the way. When they get to their school, Ivory wishes her younger sisters a good day before making her way to the stables with her friends.

"So, did you guys hear the news?" asks Sparrow.

"What news?" asks everyone at the same time.

"We are hosting the most famous man in The Collection during the Full Moon Festival, which also just so happens to fall on the same day as graduation this year!" replies Sparrow, unable to contain her excitement.

"Wait a minute. You're not talking about Nazar Yilan II, are you?" asks Sevastyan, stopping dead in his tracks.

"Who is Nazar Yilan II?" asks Fauna.

"And why is he the second? Who came before him?" continues Flora.

"Nazar, my friends, is the middle man that helps keep connections between the four tribes running smoothly, making them The Collection that we know them to be today," says Ivory.

"How have you never heard of him? He is the first man to brave the oceans since the Great Wave," says Sparrow, bewildered.

The group starts walking again, making their way into the stables as Ivory continues to tell the twins about Nazar.

"Nazar is the only child of the famous Southern Assimilian Elder Nazar Yilan. His mother died giving birth to him, and his father refused to take another bride. For this reason, Nazar Yilan I decided to name his only child after himself, so that he may one day be his successor. That is why Nazar is known as Nazar Yilan II," explains Ivory.

"Okay, that makes sense. But hold on, I thought that Elders can't have successors because that could lead to greed and one family trying to dominate an entire tribe," says Flora, confused.

"Yes, you're absolutely right, Flora. If Nazar had become an Elder just because his father was one, it would have not been fair, and the Oaks would never allow that to happen. However, Nazar did what no one else could. He built a ship, all by himself, and sailed through the ocean to all three tribes. His bravery was spoken of throughout The Collection. And for this, his tribe chose him to be their Elder so they could learn from him and hopefully follow in his footsteps."

"Wow, I'm speechless. I can't wait to see this man. When is he coming?" asks Fauna.

"I'm not sure when exactly; I just overheard some kids talking about it. But it will likely be very soon, as we are only a few days away from the festival and graduation," replies Sparrow.

"Hey, look out!" yells a voice from behind.

Ivory turns, then quickly ducks, taking Flora and Fauna down with her.

"Oh! That was close!" exclaims Fauna.

"Hey! What do you think you're doing?! You know that balls aren't allowed in the stables!" yells Ivory furiously as she walks toward the trio of boys responsible for almost knocking her head off.

Sevastyan and Sparrow look at each other with a smug grin. Ivory is a generally calm, gentle person; very few things really tick her off. But when she does get angry, she goes from zero to a hundred, real quick. To Sevastyan and Sparrow's enjoyment, this was one of those moments.

"Hey, I'm talking to you, knuckleheads!" yells Ivory as she walks right up to the three boys, who slow down to a halt.

"Skye, calm down; it's just a ball," says the tall, lanky boy on the right.

"Yeah, it's not like anyone got hurt," says the muscular boy in the middle, who seems to be about Ivory's height. The two boys on the outside push around the boy in the middle, all laughing at his rather unfunny joke.

"Oh, really? The last time someone walked in here with a football, I do believe a girl got bucked off her horse and broke her arm," replies Ivory in a matter-of-fact manner, arms crossed.

"Well, maybe you should teach your horses not to be so scared," says the dark-skinned boy on the left, making his friends laugh all over again at a joke that Ivory still can't seem to find funny.

"Are you three mentally retarded, or are you just, I don't know, mentally retarded?"

"Umm…is there a third choice?" asks the boy in the middle, trying to compose himself.

Ivory shuts her eyes tight and tries to hold her fists to herself before she makes the mistake of punching all three of the boys in the gut.

"Kai, Yuri, Acyl!" yells Nadi Skye from behind Sevastyan and the girls, making everyone jump.

"I know that this ball is not yours," he says holding it up for everyone to see. "Because if it were, we would have a problem," he says, walking up to the three boys. Ivory moves to the side, giving her father space to look the three boys in the eye.

The boys stumble over their words, terrified of the head horse keeper.

"N-n-n…no, no sir. No, we would never bring a ball into the stables on purpose," chokes out Kai, looking ridiculously childlike, even in all his height.

Yuri, the blue-eyed middle boy, looks down, not able to say a word. Nadi puts his arm forward, ball in hand. The three boys all look at each other, trying to decide what to do at this point.

Finally, the dark-skinned, green-eyed boy reaches forward to take the ball.

"We apologize, sir. It will not happen again," he says solemnly, eyes down.

"Correction; it will NEVER happen again. If I ever see this ball around here again, I will come for you three. Have I made myself clear?" says Nadi sternly.

"Yes, sir," reply the three boys, bowing their heads in shame.

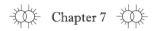

"Good. Now, make your way to your horses. We have no time to waste."

"Yes, sir."

Nadi turns, making his way to the arena to continue warming up his horse before the students make their way in. As he passes by Ivory, he gives her a wink and a quick smile. Ivory tries holding her laugh in. She gets her calm personality from her father, who is as serene as they come. That is, until someone pisses him off. That's when he becomes the scariest person there ever was. Ivory calls it "scary eyes." Thankfully, she'd never had to experience their full force.

"Come on, Sevastyan, girls, you all need to get started as well," he says more kindly to the familiar faces of his daughter's friends as he walks past them.

"Yes, Mr. Skye," they all reply.

Ivory follows her father and friends down the stables, turning to give the three boys one last glare and a triumphant grin. The three follow quietly behind, defeated.

"Hey, boy, how are you?" Ivory coos at her beloved horse while she strokes his face and gives him tiny kisses on his nose. "Did you enjoy your apples yesterday? Did you have a good night's sleep?"

Thunder neighs back at Ivory, nudging her softly on the shoulder. Ivory takes a brush to Thunder's mane and back, making sure he's completely clean before she rides him. She finishes cleaning the little dirt she finds inside his shoes, then saddles him up. She walks Thunder into the large outdoor arena, where her father is already mounted on his horse before she mounts him. She makes a few rounds around the arena, passing by Yuri and his friends; the three trying to be as efficient as possible in order to redeem themselves in front of the head horse keeper, who also happens to be their riding instructor. Soon enough, the rest of the students make their way into the arena for their lesson. And once the lesson is done, the students all give their horses a good brushing, feed them, pick up any mess they may have made in the process, and head off to lunch. Today, Ivory and her friends are invited to have lunch at Flora and Fauna's house.

"I am so hungry; I can already smell the food!" shouts Sparrow in excitement as the five make their way through the tribal center, heading in the direction of the houses.

"Me too! I hope you guys made a lot of food, because riding turns me into a hungry beast. And that lesson we had today…whew, I haven't sweat that much in a while!" says Sevastyan, making everyone laugh.

"Don't worry, I made sure Papa made extra sandwiches," laughs Flora.

"Yes. And Mama made you guys a special little treat to go along with that," winks Fauna.

"Sounds good to me! Can't wait!" laughs Ivory.

The five continue on their way, enjoying the beautiful end-of-summer weather they are having, laughing and making jokes.

"No, I know! I was trying so hard not to laugh at his face when... AHHH!!!"

THUD.

Ivory falls to the ground, hard. Flora screams.

"HEY!" yells Sevastyan, taking a defensive stance in front of the girls.

Sparrow rushes to Ivory's aid, picking her off the ground. Fauna stands right next to Sevastyan, ready to attack.

What is happening? thinks Ivory to herself as she hangs on to Sparrow, trying to balance her spinning head. Flora comes to help her up as well, but Ivory takes her hand to get to Sevastyan. She grabs his shoulder for support to peek past him, to see what he was shielding them from.

She regrets her decision immediately.

Eyes black, surrounded by dark, sunken-in circles. Skin, tanned and weathered from too much sun exposure and hard labor. Lips curled up, teeth snarling in warning. Three men, looking more like animals, fiercely crouched down, ready to attack.

Ivory takes in a sharp breath. But the scream she fears might escape her lips comes from somewhere else – a little girl, a bystander. As Ivory holds on to Sevastyan, with her two friends holding her from behind, she witnesses the quick reaction of the people around them.

The warriors are the first ones on the scene. Five of them quickly step in between Sevastyan and the three men, taking a defensive stance. About seven more surround the three men on the sides and from behind. At this point Sevastyan turns to look at Ivory, his eyes widening as he catches a glimpse of her face.

That's when it all gets blurry. The last thing Ivory remembers before her eyes roll up into her head as she passes out is the taste of salt and iron between her lips.

Chapter 8

Ivory opens her eyes slowly, afraid of what might be on the other side of her eyelids. A voice in the distance calls her name, followed by another.

"Ivory…" the voices start softly. "It's time to wake up."

"Let's go, Ivory, we don't have all day," another teases.

Small, sharp giggles ring through the background. "Ivory…Ivory… IVORY…"

The voices get more impatient by the second. Ivory opens her eyes now and looks at the unfamiliar faces of the people calling out to her; bright, young faces. Silence rings through the air as Ivory looks back at the staring eyes. Then, all of a sudden, the earth opens and they start to sink. Ivory's feet move before her brain has time to process the picture.

One by one, the boys and girls sink into the ground. Ivory runs to try and save them, to take their hands and pull them out, but her feet become heavier. With every step she takes, her feet sink further into the ground as if she's running on quicksand. Before she knows it, she's struggling to keep herself out of the ground. The more she struggles, the faster she sinks. The screams of the sinking boys and girls decrease one by one as they're completely sucked in. Soon enough, Ivory is left with her own scream; one she is unfamiliar with. As she takes her last breath before she gets completely sucked in, she feels a sharp, shooting pain on her forehead. That's when it all goes black.

"Ivory…" the voice starts softly. "It's time to wake up."

Ivory's heart pounds fast. *No please, not again*…she thinks to herself.

"Ivory, I know you can hear me," the voice says. "Come on, baby, you're alright, you can open your eyes now."

Wait. I know this voice. Where do I know this voice from?

She feels a hand run through her hair and the side of her face.

"Don't worry; she's fine," says the voice. "She'll be waking up in a few minutes. I gave her a muscle relaxant, so she's going to be a little out of it."

"Her friends, along with a few other people, have been waiting for her outside for a while now. Should I let them know she's waking up?" asks another voice, a male voice, Ivory decides.

"No. I want to wait until she's completely awake first. Don't worry, I will call them in before I leave," replies the first voice, a female.

"Alright, Healer Skye, I will leave you, then."

"Thank you, Vail."

Did he say Healer Skye? MOTHER?

Ivory's eyes fly open. "MAMA?"

Constantina quickly turns back to her daughter on the Healing Clinic bed.

"Oh, there she is! Ivory, how are you feeling?" she asks, kissing Ivory on the forehead.

That's when Ivory feels it again; the sharp pain. "OW! That hurts!" she says, trying to reach for it and touch it.

"No! Don't touch it until it heals, I've bandaged it. Or at least, don't touch it until the blood clots and stops flowing out. You have one annoying little cut there," she says, looking a little tired.

"I'm so sorry, Mama."

"You don't need to be sorry, Ivory; you did nothing wrong. Just...pay attention to where you are walking next time, okay?" laughs Constantina.

"Okay, I will."

"Good. Now, your friends have been driving me and the other healers a little crazy for the past hour or so. I think it is high time I call them in to see you."

"Yes, of course! Are they all doing well? Did anyone else get hurt?" asks Ivory, concerned.

"No, do not worry; all of them are perfectly fine. I'll go call them in and return in a little bit. Is that okay? If you need me, just yell; I will be two rooms down."

"Yes, of course, go ahead. Thanks, Mama."

Constantina kisses her daughter's forehead one more time before she leaves. And although it's not obvious, Ivory can see the worry lines on her

mother's forehead as she walks out. She also overhears some of the conversation she has with her friends.

"She's still not completely there, so be gentle and slow when you talk to her, please."

"Is she going to be alright, Mrs. Skye?"

"Her forehead will heal, will it not?"

"Yes, it will heal; that's the least of my worries at this point."

"Then what is it?" asks a male voice.

"She took a pretty bad hit to the head. It knocked her out for a while. The next couple of days will be crucial in figuring out if she suffered any real brain damage."

*Wow, brain damage. I didn't think it was that bad…*thinks Ivory, looking around the white, sterile clinic room.

Slowly, the door creaks open, and one by one, Ivory's friends walk in. Ivory has never been happier to see her friends; she can't tell if they feel the same way.

Sparrow and Flora take in a collective shocked gasp, followed by a river of silent tears. Fauna nudges them both, trying to calm them down for the sake of Ivory. Sevastyan is a little taken aback at the sight of his best friend, his sister, in such a bad condition. But he quickly regains control of himself and walks to Ivory's bedside, kneeling down to her eye level.

"Hey, Sis, you gave us quite the scare there, you know," he says softly, taking her hand gently in his.

This makes Ivory smile. "Sorry," she manages out.

Sparrow walks to Ivory's other side, followed by Flora. Unsuccessfully wiping the tears from her eyes and face, Sparrow sits on the bed next to Ivory, taking her other hand.

"I'm so happy you are fine," she says, looking down, laughing and crying at the same time. "I don't think I've ever been so scared in my life."

"Me, too. I still can't believe everything that went down," says Flora, sitting at Ivory's feet across from her sister.

Sparrow turns away from Ivory to wipe away her tears.

"Hey, stop crying; why are you crying? I'm fine, I'm right here," says Ivory to her best friend, trying to sooth her.

"Yes, thankfully you are. But have you seen yourself in the mirror, Ive? You look a little…beat," says Fauna, concerned.

"A little? She looks like she was hit with a metal club on the forehead," Flora whispers to her sister. The two exchange a quick, silent conversation, just through their eyes, soon after turning back to look at Ivory.

"I thought it was a small cut," says Ivory, a little confused, turning to look at Sevastyan, who quickly turns on a smile for her.

"Well, yes, it is somewhat of a small cut. But it was deep; there was blood everywhere. And the whole area on your forehead and down the right side of your face is bruised," he says.

"Is it really dark?"

"It's as dark as the souls of those crazy Oaks," spits Fauna disgustedly.

"Oaks? Wait...can someone please explain to me what happened, exactly? Because all I remember is talking to you one second, then you guys helping me up, then the three animal-looking men, people...whatever they were. I want the full story, like, right now. Please."

Ivory's friends all look at each other. "Sevastyan, why don't you say it; you were in the front; you witnessed it all," says Sparrow, emotionally exhausted.

"Well. It went something like this, I think," he starts. "So remember how we were all walking to Flora and Fauna's?"

"Yes," replies Ivory.

"Sparrow was talking to Fauna, while Flora, you, and I were in the middle of a story. You were walking backwards so you didn't see them coming. Honestly, I wasn't paying attention either; it was all so quick. But anyway, I think you bumped into one of them as you were turning around, or maybe you hit him with your backpack. I'm still not 100% sure."

Ivory tries to think back to that moment, but it just hurts her head, so she stops and listens to the story.

"He could have said something. He could have even made you apologize if he was so UPSET," says Sevastyan, shaking his head, infuriated. "I mean, to shove anyone for that reason, especially a non-suspecting girl... He was literally TWICE your size! I don't know how they raise them down South, but I'll tell you now, you'll never catch me going that direction, EVER. Anyway, that was pretty much it. He shoved you to the ground, where you hit your head on a sharp rock. Fauna and I got in front of you; I was afraid he would continue to attack you or anyone else. And Sparrow and Flora helped you up."

"The men, the three men...you said they were Oaks?"

"Yes. Sparrow was right about Nazar coming. But apparently he sent some of his people before him. I find it very irresponsible if you ask me, sending your uncontrollable wild folk."

"So, what happened then? I just remember seeing them and then waking up here."

"Well, the warriors were very close by, and they saw the whole incident, so they were quick on the scene. All of the other people that were around came to help you. Professor Drakonas was riding by when the whole thing happened, so he gave me his horse to come here and tell them to get everything ready for you while he carried you all the way here."

"Professor Drakonas…he carried me the whole way?"

"Yes, and he was furious!" jumps in Fauna.

"From the quick conversation we caught, he apparently isn't that fond of Nazar to begin with," says Sparrow. "So the fact that his 'people' came and did that, to not only one of us, but a student…thankfully, your father was there to calm him down," she says, shuddering at the thought.

"My father was there too?"

"Yes, and he came in here to spend some time with your mother while you were still out," replies Sparrow. "Don't worry, I know that look on your face. I am sure your mother reassured him," she smiles.

"Well, all that matters now is that you are doing better, Ivory," says Flora with a small smile.

"Oh, I almost forgot," she says suddenly, turning to the small pouch hanging on her pants belt. "Here, I brought this for you."

Ivory puts her palm out for the small leather pouch. "What is it?"

"Remember when we went to the coast and passed by the lavender fields? I filled up a bag with lavender when we had that quick stop on our way back. Lavender is very soothing, and it has a lot of healing properties. I want you to keep it on your pillow for the next few days at least, and make at least one cup of tea with the flowers every day as well. It will help with the healing."

"Thank you so much, Flora; I will definitely do that," says Ivory, touched by the thoughtful gesture of her friend.

"It's time we get going, girls. I will walk you home," says Sevastyan, standing up.

"Thanks for waiting to make sure I was alright, my friends. You have no idea how much it means to me," says Ivory, almost teary.

"Hey, hold up, you're not getting rid of me that easily!" laughs Sparrow, also getting up off the bed. "Your mother said that you're spending the night here, just in case. I've already talked to my parents and they said I can stay here with you tonight. So I will be back later in the evening."

"Awesome, can't wait! All of you have a safe walk home, and I will see you later, Sparrow!"

The girls and Sevastyan all give Ivory a kiss on the forehead before they leave.

"Take a nap; you must be exhausted. Before you know it, I'll be back," whispers Sparrow on her way out, blowing Ivory one last kiss before closing the door.

Ivory looks around her small room for a bit, trying to familiarize herself with the place. She wishes desperately that the room had a window, but its location in the building would not allow for that. The small movement of looking around exhausts her very quickly, making her eyes close again. But right as she is about to fall asleep, she hears a gentle knock on the room door.

"Yes, come in," she says, voice hoarse.

The door opens slowly, and Kai, Yuri, and Acyl walk in. Ivory is surprised; they were the last people she had expected to see.

Were they the "other" people healer Vail had mentioned to Mother earlier? I wonder if they have been waiting outside the whole time... she thinks to herself.

"Hello, Ivory," says Yuri, standing three feet away from Ivory's bed with his friends.

"We are so sorry that you got hurt today," says Kai.

"Yes, we hope you feel better," says Acyl, walking forward to place down a bouquet of flowers at Ivory's bedside.

"Umm...thanks," she says, still a little unsure.

Yuri looks at his friends, then walks forward, kneeling down closer to Ivory.

"We, umm...we wanted to apologize, about earlier today," he says solemnly. "We were real big jerks. Knuckleheads, like you said. It's just..." he sighs, "It's so easy to forget what this whole thing is about, our existence, essentially. It's so easy to get all caught up in the silly things; tribal gossip, social hierarchy... It's so easy to forget about what's really important, like protecting and loving one another in order to ensure our survival. I – we – know that the rules are there for that sole purpose. And we lost sight of that. The whole incident today, it really put things into perspective for all of us. Those other people, they obviously are not lucky enough to live in a *community* like we do. They are brutal; they have to be, in order to survive in the wilderness that they live in, so much so that they have almost become a part of it," he says, looking at his hands.

"We were right there too, when it happened. We were actually so close; we could have probably stepped in to help before the warriors got there. But we didn't. We just froze. And for that, we also apologize," says Yuri, taking Ivory's hand and looking her straight in the eye.

"Hey, it's ok," says Ivory, finally finding her voice. "I think that anyone would freeze in a situation like this one. We were never trained to fight other humans. We've been taught how to hunt animals for food and how to protect ourselves when attacked. But all of that pretty much just consists of running."

"We didn't even run," chuckles Acyl. Kai seconds his statement with a disappointed shake of his head.

Ivory smiles, turning back to Yuri.

"I forgive you, and I thank you for stepping forward with an apology. There are no hard feelings between friends."

Yuri smiles with relief, then stands up.

"Thank you, Ivory. And I promise, we will make it up to you," he says.

"Yes, and the next time we run into those three imbeciles again, we'll get them for you," winks Acyl.

"Yeah, we'll get them!" seconds Kai, high-fiving Acyl.

Ivory can't hold back her laugh. "You guys are crazy! Just make sure don't end up in here too," she winks back at Acyl. The three boys laugh along with her.

Yuri takes Ivory's hand once again, giving it a small kiss. Acyl and Kai follow right behind, doing the same.

"Rest well, Ivory. And thanks for everything," says Yuri to Ivory, walking out with his friends, closing the door behind them.

"You're welcome," she says as the door closes.

Ivory tosses and turns in her bed as she sleeps, eventually kicking off her blanket. She groggily opens her eyes, searching for a fan in the small room. She had fallen asleep after the three boys had left, and Sparrow, who sleeps to her right, hadn't the heart to wake her up when she came to stay with her. But Ivory couldn't sleep any longer; it was just too hot. The nights had weirdly been hot ever since Ivory had left on her trip to the Coast; an oddity for the time of year they were in. At this time, at the end of summer, the nights would usually be very cool, while the days would still be warm.

Ivory sits up in her bed, quickly feeling the effect in her head. She closes her eyes for a minute to settle the spinning room a bit. She opens her eyes again and finally spots the small fan peeking behind the open door. Although the moon is not yet full, its light reaches through the window in the outside hallway, through the doorway, and into the room. Trying to be as quiet as she could as to not wake up Sparrow, Ivory gets out of her bed, hesitating for only a second to make sure that she is stable enough to walk across the room. Slowly, she starts making her way to the fan, but stops when she gets to the door. Instead of grabbing the fan, she stands at the doorway, clinging on to it for a little support, and then makes her way out of the room to the large window across the hallway.

She looks out into the night at the now foreign-looking tribe. Standing at a higher-up floor, she can see as far as the houses and Weaponry, as well as the Tribal Center, which includes the Elder Council Building. The window she stands at is only slightly cracked open, so she pulls one side open, leaning over the edge as she does. She can hear the stream of water that runs into a small lake right behind the Elder Council Building. The Alders, long ago, had built many small bridges over the stream, as it runs right through the tribe, dividing about one-third of it from the rest. Ivory takes the bridges every time she needs to get to the stables. That side of the tribe also holds the Animal Training facility along with the Hunters' Headquarters. Ivory had only been there a few times when it was relating to her school studies; it was more of a common place for Fauna to visit, as it actually related more to what she wanted to do after graduation. On the other side of the stream are the Gardens and the Medicine Center, a place that was more familiar with Flora than any of the others.

As Ivory looks out into the quiet darkness, she is startled by a new sound: wolves. One by one, the wolves start howling. The sound makes its way around the Southeastern corner of the tribal boundary, near the Weaponry. The wolf howls die down but are soon replaced by a large exploding sound and light, lots of light.

"Sparrow! Sparrow!!"

Sparrow runs out of the room, disoriented, getting to the window just in time to see the smoke rise up into the sky. She looks at the now wide-eyed

Ivory in total confusion. Before she can even begin to ask Ivory what had happened, healers run out of the adjacent rooms, quickly instructing any patients that might have been woken to stay in their rooms.

"Hey! Get away from that window!"

Ivory looks at the burning flames, desperately trying to understand what is happening. And just as the healer reaches the two girls to escort them back into their room, another sound cuts through the air. A scream, as desperate as one can be. Ivory and Sparrow run back to the window, sticking their heads out, looking for the source. The scream did not sound far, but it had come from the other side of the building. Still, the two look out, trying to find any clue they can. The startled healer quickly regains his composure and grabs the two by their arms, dragging them into the room, locking the door behind him on his way out. Sparrow quickly lights a lamp as Ivory makes her way, blind, to the bed. Sparrow soon follows, holding the shocked Ivory in her lap.

"Whaa...what...? What is happening? Why?"

"I don't know Ivory...I don't know."

Chapter 9

The explosion, the fire, the smoke; it's all anyone can talk about early this morning. The thing is, I was one of the very few people who actually witnessed it as it happened, even if it was from afar. But for the sake of avoiding an interrogation by literally everyone in the tribe, I think I'll keep that little detail to myself. The only other person that knows at the moment is Sparrow, and she knows that there is no way I could know how it all happened from where I was standing. I do not have a lot of time to make this entry much longer; I shall write in the details of last night sometime later. However, if there is one thing that I know I need to take account of right now, it's that something weird is happening around here. I don't know what it is, but my stomach is in knots and I have not slept since the incident hours ago. They are finally going to let us leave this room, so I need to leave now and finish getting dressed before Sparrow comes back from the lavatory.

More to come later. I promise.

Ivory closes her memory book and puts it back in her backpack. There are so many things she needs to write about, so many new revelations. But the sunlight calls out to her much more than her book ever will, especially after being locked in the small clinic room for hours, anxious at what was happening in the outside world. The healer had apologized for locking the two girls in. It was a "security protocol," as he called it – to keep the patients and their loved ones safe. But it was more like a mental game, *a mental breakdown,* Ivory thought.

Just as she finishes putting her shoes on – a job much harder with a spinning head – Sparrow walks back in.

"Come on, you ready to go?"

"Yes, please. I can't stay in here for a second longer."

Sparrow helps Ivory up, giving her an arm for extra support. The two walk out of the room, down the hallway and a flight of stairs, and out into the open. Ivory takes a few deep breaths, in and out.

"Do you want to go sit on one of the benches?" asks Sparrow.

"Yes, but let's choose one closer to the front door. I am almost certain we will be seeing Sevastyan and the twins very soon."

Sparrow leads Ivory to the small garden of flowers outside the Healing Clinic, helping her sit on one of the beautifully carved wooden benches. Ivory runs her hand over the different flower carvings on the back of the bench.

"Beautiful…" she whispers.

"Hey, look over there," says Sparrow, poking Ivory's knee.

Ivory looks in the direction Sparrow points, spotting her three other friends hastily making their way to the Healing Clinic door.

"Sevastyan!" she yells so he can hear her. "Over here!"

Sevastyan and the twins pause at the voice, looking around, quickly spotting the girls in the garden to their left.

"Come on, they're over there," says Sevastyan to the sisters.

The three make their way through the garden, hugging the two girls when they reach them.

"Hey, how did they let you out?" asks Sevastyan, a little out of breath. "I was scared they wouldn't even let us through to see you."

"Please, don't remind us of the lockdown we had. We were stuck in that tiny room up until thirty minutes ago!"

"Yeah, it was a bit stuffy in there. Not the best place to be stuck," agrees Sparrow. "How about you guys? Is it alright for you to be out? What's happening in the rest of the tribe?"

"We were on lockdown too, down at the houses. Warriors were everywhere; no one was allowed to leave their house," replies Sevastyan, shaking his head.

"Did you guys see it? When it happened?" asks Ivory, leaning in to her friends.

The three friends get ready to answer, but Sevastyan stops them for a second, looks around, then pulls up another bench right across from the two girls. He, Flora, and Fauna all sit down and lean in to Ivory and Sparrow, making a small, intimate circle.

"So, we didn't see it when it happened, but from out of our bedroom windows, we could see the smoke rising," whispers Flora.

"So it woke you up, then," says Ivory, curious.

"Try jolted us out of bed," replies Fauna. "The whole tribe heard it."

"How about you, Sevastyan?" asks Sparrow. "Did you see anything that might help us get an idea of what might have happened?"

"No, I was farther away from it, so I only heard the loud boom. By the time I got out the front door and started making my way toward the sound, warriors were already there, making people go back inside."

Sparrow looks at Ivory knowingly. Ivory had told her about the things she had witnessed, and they both agreed that they should keep it to themselves but also include their friends.

"Ivory saw it," says Sparrow, whispering real low.

The three others all look at Ivory, shocked.

"Wait, wait, wait, what do you mean you *saw* it? What exactly did you see?" asks Sevastyan.

Ivory tells her three friends everything she had heard, everything she had seen, including the final scream that shook her to her core.

Sevastyan doesn't say anything as the rest of the girls discuss the events, trying to make something out of the clues they had. Ivory notices this.

"Hey, what is it? What are you thinking?" she asks him.

"I don't know," he says, looking down, still in deep thought. "I overheard something, but I didn't get it all."

"What is it? What did you hear?" the girls all look at him expectantly.

"Honestly, I don't know. I couldn't understand what they were trying to say, exactly, the two warriors. But we won't have to wait long before we find out. We're having a tribal meeting, an assembly, in an hour. It's one of the reasons they lifted the lockdown. Everyone is expected to be there."

"Then what are we waiting for, let's go!" exclaims Sparrow, standing up.

- - -

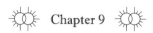

"Throughout history, we have learned over and over again that in times of darkness, we must stick together to ensure our survival," starts Warrior Zlato, standing on the stage in front of the Elder Council Building.

"The events that took place late into the night, and early this morning, were not only tragic but still somewhat of a mystery. At 2.0 hours, an explosion blew up a chunk of the southeastern fence surrounding the Weaponry. We have yet to figure out how this explosion happened, whether it was an accident or somehow executed by an outside force. Sadly, there were two warriors on duty close by who got hit with the flaming debris. However, they are said to heal in a few days' time with no permanent damage, so please feel free to pay them a visit and praise them for their hard work protecting us as we all slept. The zone of the Weaponry that holds the weapon-making materials was damaged quite a bit, so any further Weaponry courses will take place outside the weaponry on the adjacent grassy fields as repairs are being made. Starting today, we will be holding mandatory tribal meetings at this same time, every day, in order to keep you all updated on this sad situation. On that same note, the Elders have been in discussion with the head warriors, and it has been decided that starting tonight there will be a curfew as to what time everyone needs to be home. We are very sad to announce that our security was breached yesterday and a student has gone missing, that student is Yuri Lyasin."

Gasps of shock run through the audience, hitting Ivory the hardest. She can't believe what she is hearing.

"Please, I know the concerns you must all have at this moment in time, but please, the last thing we need is widespread panic in the tribe. We have currently sent out warriors into the surrounding woods to search for the boy while others still search in here. At this time, I would like to ask you all to keep the boy's family in your thoughts and prayers. This is a big blow for the entire tribe. If one of us is hurt, we all hurt. If one of us is harmed, we all bleed. Stay strong, my brothers and sisters. And keep an eye out for any suspicious activity or signs of Yuri. And most importantly, follow the new rules we are setting down for your safety, and take care of yourselves. Remember, always pay attention to your surroundings. And do not, under any circumstances, stray near the tribal boundaries, or worse, go out," he finishes with a warning.

"As for Yuri, we will give you all an update as soon as we get one, so please stay tuned in for that."

"Now, on to a brighter note. As of early this morning, we are officially joined with our brothers and sisters from the South: the Oaks!" he yells in excitement as a dark figure emerges from the side of the building.

Ivory squints her eyes to try to see who it is.

"For the next few days, we will be joined by the famous explorer, warrior, and now Elder, the one that helps connect us all; Nazar," announces Warrior Zlato, introducing the cloaked figure making his way around the stage.

Nazar walks onto the stage, slipping off his hood, exposing his face.

"Wow, he looks a lot younger than I thought he would," whispers Ivory to Sparrow, whose gaze does not falter away from the stage.

Ivory looks back at Nazar, who has a full head of jet-black, wavy hair. He also has a small beard and mustache, as black as the hair on his head. He doesn't look like what Ivory believed explorers to look like. Unlike the three men she had seen from Nazar's tribe, he was not worn out. He was perfectly coifed, his skin holding only the slightest tan; his eyes, a light chocolate brown, popping out in contrast to the black kohl on the inside of his eyes. Although it was not unseen for people of the desert to wear kohl for medicinal purposes, it was still striking to see.

Underneath his cloak, Nazar wears a black and burgundy suit, also something Ivory was not expecting. And then there is the jewelry. His beautiful golden rings and necklaces glimmer bright in the sunlight. So do his teeth when he smiles.

Where did this man come from? Ivory asks herself incredulously.

Nazar smiles big as the crowd cheers. He shakes Warrior Zlato's hand and then takes his place on the stage.

"Brothers, sisters," he starts off. "Words cannot describe the happiness I feel as I look down on your beautiful faces. I would like to extend to you my greatest sympathy for the recent events and offer my warriors to help you with your quest in finding the boy and rebuilding your Weaponry. I have traveled far. I have seen much. But I have yet to find a people as kind or as gracious as you. You have stolen my heart, dear Alders. And for that, I am at your service," he finishes with a bow.

The crowd goes wild. Everyone starts cheering his name.

"Nazar, Nazar, Nazar, Nazar…"

Ivory slowly claps along, turning to look at Sevastyan, who also doesn't seem to be as into it as everyone else. The two exchange quick eye contact.

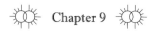

They both know that there is a conversation that has to be had, but now is neither the time nor place.

"Thank you! Thank you, all! May you all have a beautiful day, and I so look forward to celebrating this year's Full Moon Festival with you all!" he shouts excitedly at the roaring crowd, giving them a wave, returning the stage to Warrior Zlato.

"Thank you, Warrior Nazar, your help is greatly appreciated at this time. As for you all, this assembly has now come to an official close. Please return to your regular daily routines, and to all a good day.

"To you a good day," returns the crown in unison.

Warrior Zlato turns back to Nazar, who is making his way to the Elders sitting in the background on the stage. When he reaches them, he bends down on a knee and kisses each Elder on the hand and forehead. The Elders, flattered, try to urge him back up, but he insists on showing each Elder the respect they deserve. Once he is finished, Nazar stands up and receives the hugs the Elders have waiting for him. Although he himself is an Elder of the Southern Assimilian tribe, Nazar is much younger than any other Elder in the time period of The Settlement. For this reason, he shows much more respect to the Elders of the tribe than another Elder might.

Ivory looks back at Sevastyan, who nods for her to follow him out of the crowd. Before she follows him out, she catches a glimpse of Cassius making his way onto the stage, to where his father and Nazar stand talking to the Elders. The last thing she sees is Nazar's excited face as he embraces Cassius in his arms.

"I think I lost the girls on my way out," says Ivory, trying to spot Flora, Fauna, and Sparrow.

"Just as well, I need to talk to you; alone," replies Sevastyan, looking around, making sure no one else can hear him.

"So what did you think about all of that?" he asks Ivory curiously, leaning on the tree next to her. "I want to hear your opinion first."

"I don't know. I felt really uncomfortable. I mean, we just found out that someone is missing; Yuri, out of all people! I didn't tell anyone this, but he visited me yesterday when you guys left. He, Acyl, and Kai came in to apologize to me about everything. We laughed, we made amends, they even brought me flowers!"

"Wow," says Sevastyan, almost speechless.

"All of a sudden, this man we do not even really know comes up, and everyone is cheering like nothing ever happened. It just, it feels so wrong," she says, shaking her head.

"Exactly! Thank you! I couldn't believe it when they started cheering. It was like, did everyone just forget what happened all of a sudden? It was like a mob mentality. That's why I can't hold it against the girls, because they were just cheering with everyone else. But I just couldn't get myself there. It was wrong," says Sevastyan, disgusted at the thought.

Ivory nods in agreement with Sevastyan. He had summed up exactly what she had been feeling at that moment.

"We need to talk to them!" she says suddenly, startling Sevastyan. "I bet you anything that they were together later on; yesterday evening as well," she says, pacing back and forth.

"What?" Sevastyan asks, a little confused.

"Sevastyan, we need to find them. I can't wait for the girls to come; we have to go now. If anyone has any clues about this whole situation, it's Acyl and Kai," she says, eyes wide, impatient.

Sevastyan quickly catches on to Ivory's thought process, then starts thinking himself.

"Morning classes were canceled today in light of what happened, and the tribal assembly…"

"So that means that they're probably not going to be at school," finishes Ivory. "If it were any one of you, I think I would probably try to find answers from the closest source; your family." The answer hits Ivory.

"Let's go," says Sevastyan, taking Ivory's hand.

Chapter 10

Ivory had known that the Lyasin family house would be full of people offering their help to Yuri's parents, but that just made it difficult for her to accomplish what she had in mind.

"How are we going to find them through all of this?" asks Sevastyan, looking around.

"I don't know. I just hope they're here."

"I have no doubt that they're here. With all these people, they have to be. Let's go to the back; it doesn't look as crowded."

"Okay," agrees Ivory, following Sevastyan to the back of the house.

As they make their way through the hanging linen, the two don't see anyone. But as they get closer to the back door of the house, they hear faint voices, voices Ivory recognizes.

"Acyl! Kai!" she calls out as she spots them sitting on the small doorstep.

The two boys look up at Ivory and Sevastyan, standing up as Ivory rushes to them, embracing them both. Sevastyan gives both a grip of support on the shoulder.

"I'm so sorry, I don't know what to say," she says to the boys.

The two look at each other, not sure how to respond either.

"Look, I know that everyone has probably asked you about everything you know, but if there's anything you know that might help us find him, we will do whatever it takes," says Ivory.

"Some people think that he might have ran off, that he did something stupid," replies Acyl, looking up.

"Whaa…what?!?" exclaims Ivory, baffled at the crazy accusation.

"One of the warriors asked us if this was some kind of trick," says Kai, shaking his head in disbelief.

"I KNOW for a fact that something bad happened to Yuri," replies Ivory sternly.

Acyl and Kai now look at each other and back at Ivory.

"How?" asks Kai.

"Because she heard it," replies Sevastyan, looking back at Ivory to make sure it was alright to say to the two boys.

"What do you mean?" asks Acyl, eyes wide, fire relit.

"I heard him. Yuri. I heard him scream when he was taken," replies Ivory, now sure of what she had heard. After the announcement that the boy was missing, the pieces had all fallen into place for her. But hearing that the warriors had other thoughts made her reconsider telling them about what she had heard.

"Don't tell anyone," says Acyl after hearing the details from Ivory.

"Why not?" asks Sevastyan. "It might help them find him."

"No, Acyl is right," says Kai, finally speaking up. "All that will get you is a 24-hour interrogation. Plus, they won't believe you."

"Why wouldn't they believe me?" asks Ivory, confused. "I have no reason to lie, especially about something like this."

"They'll say that you were out of it. That you imagined this whole thing."

"But Sparrow was with me, and she heard it too. Actually, now that I think about it, so did the healer that was standing near us. That's three people; we couldn't have all been imagining things."

"No, no…you don't understand. This whole thing is a lot bigger than they're making us believe it is. They have it in their minds that this must be Yuri's fault, that he did something, and this was the outcome," insists Acyl.

"How do you know that?" asks Sevastyan.

"Because we told them what happened before we left him," replies Kai. "We told them about the Oaks we ran into on our way home. We told them how Yuri told us to be careful as we went our separate ways. What they're not telling everyone is that we think they did it. And…" Kai's words drift.

"And what? What else?" asks Ivory.

"And that they found some blood," finishes Acyl.

Ivory gasps, holding her wide open mouth with her hands.

"Shit," replies Sevastyan.

Yuri is gone. Missing. We – my friends and Yuri's friends – think that this was no accident. I can't even get myself to write what our theory is because it's a dangerous one. Whether it's true or not, our theory could end up severing the ties between the Western and Southern Assimilian tribes. To assume that the Oaks could have had something to do with Yuri's disappearance, whether it's true or not, is an insult to the trust our tribes have with one another. For this reason, we have all decided to keep our knowledge of what might have happened to ourselves.

Although it has yet to be announced, a few drops of Yuri's blood were found on the pathway down in front of his house. The warriors believe that he made his way outside after the explosion, as everyone did, and either hurt himself by accident or was attacked by an animal. Putting the Oaks anywhere near the equation is definitely out of the question at this point. Acyl and Kai seem to be positive that unfair play was somehow involved in this. I'm scared for them. We warned them over and over again not to go looking for him, and they eventually agreed, but I cannot be certain. If it were one of my friends, I know that I would not be as calm as these two have managed.

It is currently one hour past sunset, and the curfew officially started an hour ago. As I write this entry, I keep checking outside my closed window, hoping for a sign, anything, that Yuri is alright, that he is alive. I cannot even begin to imagine that he is somewhere not breathing, cold to the touch…dead. No, I shall not dwell on such horrible thoughts, for the fear that they may come true. I am hopeful. Tomorrow will be a brand new day. School will continue, along with the other regular tribal activities. Graduation is only a few days away. And I still have no idea what I want to do with my life when it's over…

Ivory sighs at the thought. She wishes someone could just tell her what to do and how her life will go. But then again, what if she doesn't like what she hears? She can't decide what's worse, someone deciding her fate for her or her having the choice but then choosing the wrong thing.

She quickly signs her name at the bottom of the page, then closes her book and slides it under her bed. She lays her head down on her pillow and turns to her left to look out her window. The day's events have left her on the edge, but sleep somehow finds its way in and engulfs her in its embrace. As the minutes pass, her muscles relax. Her body slowly starts shutting down for the night. But one part of her brain starts preparing for what's to come. After all, what's a good night's sleep without the regularly scheduled nightmare?

- - -

"Ivory, wake up. Wake up, child."

The voice. It's the same voice.

Ivory's eyes open, and she finds herself surrounded by the darkness again.

"Hello?" she calls out, looking around, trying to get somewhere. But she gets nowhere. It all looks the same.

"Hello?" she calls out again. "Is anyone here? Hello!"

"Ivory," whispers the voice, right in her ear.

This startles Ivory, making her spin around to find the source. Nothing.

"Ivory," it whispers again.

Ivory stops moving and concentrates on the voice.

"Ivory," it whispers a third time. "There is still time."

"What do you mean?" she asks back. "There is still time for what?"

"There is still time, child. Wake up."

"I, I don't understand…there's still time for what? You haven't answered my question!" she yells out at the voice.

"Open your eyes…Wake up… WAKE UP!"

- - -

Ivory jumps up in her bed, heart racing. It was the same woman. She had jolted her right out of her dream, just like the last time.

"What do you mean?" she whispers to herself. Looking out the window to her left, she sees the light starting to make its way up from the horizon. Dawn.

She lays back down on her pillow. Her parents will be waking up soon, so there is no reason for her to go back to sleep now.

Ivory thinks about her nightmare. Although it was a nightmare, it made her a little hopeful, for some strange reason. Maybe it was what the woman had said.

There is still time…

But it also brought up so many questions. If only she could figure out what there was still time for.

"So do you have permission to fight today?"

"No," sighs Ivory. "I begged mother this morning, but she said she'd hit me on the head herself if she heard I participated. Apparently, I need a few more days to make sure I am completely well," she says, rolling her eyes at Sparrow.

"Well, you can help us out with our form then!" winks Sevastyan.

The girls all laugh.

"Of course Sevastyan is the one who finds a way to make the most out of the situation," laughs Fauna, punching him in the arm.

"Honestly, I could use a little advice about balancing the sword with the rest of my body, Ive. You're so good at it, I would really appreciate it," says Flora.

Ivory laughs. "Of course I'll help *you* out, Flora," she says, giving her a side hug as they all make their way through the Weaponry doors. "But you can forget about Sevastyan!" she laughs out loud.

"What?! Wait, wait, wait…why are you going to help her but not me?!" he laughs incredulously.

"Umm…because she asked nicely! And she's not in competition with me to see who can win the most sword matches! I'm ahead of you by two wins, and not participating today is not going to help my numbers. So why would I help you?!"

Everyone laughs at the two quarrelling back and forth.

"Oh fine, don't help me. I don't need it anyway," winks Sevastyan, sticking his tongue out like a child.

Ivory laughs again as they make their way to the grassy arena.

"Ivory," calls out Professor Spyridon as he sees her making her way towards him. "I am surprised to see you here, child. Are you fighting today?" he asks, surprised.

"Unfortunately, no. My mother will not allow it just yet. She says I need to give it at least two more days," she says with a huff.

"Ah, yes, that is what I expected," chuckles the professor. "It's alright, you can watch for the day. Actually, you would be surprised to find out how much you can actually learn just by watching. I think you will enjoy it," he says matter-of-factly.

Ivory nods at her professor before he turns to walk away. Ivory and her friends stand around for a few more minutes as the rest of their classmates make their way into the arena.

"Everyone, gather!" calls out Professor Spyridon. As everyone gathers, he starts splitting everyone up into two groups.

"Sevastyan, Flora, you will do the sword matches first. Fauna, Sparrow, you two will start with archery," he orders. "In about an hour, the two teams will switch activity. The sword fighting team will practice archery, while the archery team has a chance to practice sword fighting. Is everything clear?" he asks.

"Yes, sir!" the students reply in understanding as they start splitting up into their groups.

"Ivory," calls out the professor. "You can choose which group you want to watch. However, if you would like to take my advice, watch the archery practice right now. You are already a skilled sword fighter. Plus, Sparrow is practicing archery right now, and as she is the most skilled archer of your generation, I would think watching her closely will give you some great insight."

"Hmm…that is very true. I still have trouble holding my arrow steady. Thank you, professor!"

Ivory makes her way to the archery group as they set up. As usual, Sparrow is the first to shoot. Everyone stands far behind her, giving her space to move around and set up her arrow. Ivory moves a little forward, closer to her friend. The short-haired girl takes a few deep breathes before pulling her bow up to her lips. *Her form is nothing but flawless*, thinks Ivory as she looks at her friend preparing her shot.

As Sparrow holds her bow in place, ready to shoot, she takes a few quick breaths in and steadies them just as she finds her sweet spot on the target board. It's almost too quick to see as Sparrow releases her bow and her arrow flies straight into the small red X.

"I never aim for the target; I always aim past it," Sparrow had told Ivory once.

Ivory believes her, as her arrow not only *always* hits the target right in the center, but also digs in deep and comes out of the other side.

Ivory watches the arrow as it hits the X right in the middle, as always, with a muted thud.

The crowd of students goes wild. It never gets old, watching Sparrow shoot. It is an art form more than anything else. It's like a graceful dance that she does, with her bow and arrow as her partner.

Ivory claps along with the rest of her classmates as Sparrow makes her way toward her, leaving her spot open for the next shooter.

"Showoff," jokes Ivory as Sparrow gets close enough to hear her.

Sparrow winks at her friend, making them both laugh at the same time.

"Was it good?" asks Sparrow as the two make their way to the back of the shooting line.

"Really? Are you actually asking if it was good?" replies Ivory sarcastically.

"Hey! I have a reputation to uphold here!" laughs Sparrow.

"OF COURSE, it was amazing, as per usual," replies Ivory, reassuring her friend. "And as per usual, I am very jealous of your incredible talent."

"Well, thanks!"

When the girls get to the end of the line, they turn to see their friends in the other group sword fighting.

"Hey, is that who I think it is?" asks Sparrow, narrowing her eyes to see if she was right.

"Umm…yeah, I think that is Trixie," replies Ivory.

"And she's about to go up against Sevastyan? Well, you can kiss your record goodbye, girl!"

"Hey! Haha…you never know, she could surprise everyone and win!" replies Ivory with a small shrug, not really believing what she is saying.

"Really?! Ive, you know that's just wishful thinking. She lost when she went up against the weakest students here. And that one time she won, Lena was still healing from a sprained ankle. Do you REALLY think she's going to beat Sevastyan?!?"

Ivory gives Sparrow a dirty look. "I hate you."

Sparrow laughs out loud, unable to contain herself until she starts crying. Ivory shoves her away, turning her back to her crazy friend.

Just as Sparrow gets ahold of herself, Flora moves into the fighting circle across from Vain. Vain is a pretty tall guy, but Flora is tall too, so they are almost at the same eye level. However, Vain has much more muscle tone than Flora, making her look small in comparison. Ivory shushes Sparrow as the two begin their scrimmage. Vain lets Flora get a few digs at him, easily ducking away from her sword. Slowly, he starts returning hits. The two hold each other off for quite a while. Ivory and Sparrow watch proudly from the sidelines as their friend actually holds her end of the match evenly. Some of the students even start cheering her on, but she is too into the match to pay attention to anything happening on the outside.

"You have one more minute to disarm your opponent, or else this match will be a draw!" calls out the professor.

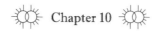

That's when Vain's friends start yelling at him from the sidelines.

"Come on Vain, finish it!"

"You're going to lose; what are you doing?!?"

"Finish her off, let's go!"

The sweating boy quickly looks from his friends back to his opponent. Flora catches him in that moment, hitting his sword hard, making it fly into the air. But the boy quickly runs for it and catches it before it touches the ground, flipping on the grass in the process. In a desperate attempt to get back in position, the dark-haired boy jabs his sword forward, actually hitting Flora on her side.

Flora screams and falls to the ground, clutching herself, just as Vain realizes what he has done. He throws his sword to the ground and runs toward her, alongside the professor and Sevastyan.

"Oh my God, I am so sorry, Flora! Are you okay? I'm so sorry, I didn't mean to hurt you!" he says desperately at the girl as she lays on the ground in a fetal position. The professor picks the girl off the ground and starts making his way to the sidelines.

"Andraes, get me the first aid kit, now!" he calls out to the warrior standing nearby.

The warrior runs to get the first aid kit.

Sevastyan holds Flora's hand gently as the professor sets her down again. "Flora, it's going to be alright, don't worry," he reassures her.

"I'm so sorry, Flora, it was a complete accident…" says Vain right behind Sevastyan.

Sevastyan stands up and turns around, getting up in the other boy's face.

"Oh yeah, how about I show you a real accident, asshole," he spits, shoving the boy hard.

Vain stumbles but catches himself quickly, getting back up in Sevastyan's face.

"Hey, why don't you stay out of this, Lanza; it doesn't concern you!"

As quickly as the fight between the two starts, others come up to the two, quickly taking sides. Vain's friends start arguing with Sevastyan's friends. The professor, tending to Flora's wound, doesn't have a chance to turn around and stop the fight that's about to break out, but Ivory has a quick thought.

She screams. She screams at the top of her lungs. Sparrow, who is standing right next to her, is beyond startled. Everyone in the fight circle, including Sevastyan and Vain, turn to her direction in shock. She knows that she has everyone's attention, but Ivory continues to scream, the pitch getting higher by the second. The students all stop and stare, wide-eyed and confused. Some pull their hands to their ears, unable to withstand the loud screech. When Ivory finally stops screaming, it is dead silent. If a needle had been dropped on the grass in this moment, the sound would be deafening. Even Flora stops crying and looks at Ivory, confused.

Cheeks now pink, Ivory takes a deep breath before she starts talking.

"Sevastyan and Vain, you two better take a step back from each other right now before I come and do it for you," she orders, looking the two straight in the eye. But the two are still in too much shock to grasp what she's really saying.

So she closes her eyes and starts screaming again, making all of the students wince and hold their ears shut.

After a few seconds, she stops screaming and shouts at the two boys again. "I said, take a step back from each other, RIGHT NOW!"

Startled, the two boys look at each other and back at her. This drives her half-mad. "Are you two seriously deaf?!?" she says as she stomps her feet all the way to the two with no trouble as the students all move out of her way. She shoves both Sevastyan and Vain away from each other.

"Go! Now!" she barks. "I want both of you to walk away right now, or so help me…!"

The boys and their friends quickly move away from Ivory, opening up the space for her to see her friend and professor on the ground. Flora just stares at her, completely unaware of her wound now. The professor gives Ivory a look of surprise and approval. He is definitely happy she broke up the fight, even if it was very unconventional.

Fauna finally has space to make her way to her sister. The two whisper to each other and the rest of the students start talking in hushed voices as well. Ivory takes a big breath and sigh, and makes her way to Flora on the ground.

"That was kind of terrifying," says Flora with a small smile.

"Honestly, I almost shat myself. Like, I legitimately almost shat myself, Ive," says Fauna in a serious tone that makes Ivory bust out laughing. Sparrow joins the group, laughing nervously with Flora.

"Umm…Ive, I love you, you know I do, but WHAT IN THE HELL was that? Like, could you not have given me just the slightest warning?" asks Sparrow, making Ivory feel the slightest bit guilty.

"Look, it wasn't planned, okay! It was all very sudden. I kind of scared myself too…" replies Ivory, looking to the side, a little embarrassed.

The girls all laugh at her confession.

"Hey, at least Flora is fine," says Ivory, trying to change the subject. "You are fine, aren't you, Flora?"

Flora gets her sister to help her stand up. "I'll be fine. It really hurts, but it's not too deep."

"You still need to get stiches," says Fauna to her sister, concerned.

"Flora, do you think you can walk to the Healing Clinic from here? You can go with your sister," says Professor Spyridon.

"Yes, professor, that shouldn't be a problem," replies Flora with a nod.

"Good. Ivory, can you help Fauna take Flora to the Healing Clinic? You will not miss much around here, and I would feel better knowing that Flora has the both of you with her."

"Yes, professor, I'll go," replies Ivory.

The professor waves the three girls goodbye and turns back to his students. "The rest of you, get back to practice! Let's go!"

Ivory, Fauna, and Flora make their way through the tribe to the Healing Clinic, where Ivory's mother greets the three with a disappointed head shake and a warm hug.

Chapter 11

"You girls need to start being a little more careful with yourselves. As much as we would all like to believe that girls and boys can do everything the same way, we are definitely not built the same. You need to take care of your bodies because, at the end of the day, you have to remember that our biggest goal in life is to help carry on our species. And a damaged body will do no good in that department," lectures Constantina.

"She's right, you know. You girls need to listen to Constantina and take better care of yourselves. We are old; we have done our part in helping carry on our species. You girls are next in line to do that," winks Fleur Ilios, the twins' mother, as she walks in the room.

"Hey, Mama," stands Fauna, giving her mother a hug.

"Hello, Healer Ilios," says Ivory, also standing up to give the woman a hug.

Fleur hugs Ivory and walks to Flora and Constantina as the healer closes up the stitches.

"So how are we looking? What's the damage?" Fleur asks Constantina.

"Well, as I was telling the girls, we were very lucky this time. It wasn't too deep, and it fell right between the bottom two ribs on her left side. Definitely make sure she doesn't put excess pressure on that side in case the incision opens again. Other than that, her vitals are looking great and she is ready to get out of here now," Constantina reassures Fleur with a smile.

"Well, you heard her, girls. That means no rough playing," says Fleur with a wink, helping her daughter off the clinic bed.

The twins look at each other with sheepish smiles.

"Okay, Mother," they reply in unison.

"Alright, you girls start making your way to the tribal center for the assembly. Constantina and I will follow in a bit," says Fleur to the three girls.

"Okay Healer Ilios, we will see you then," replies Ivory. She turns to her mother to give her a quick hug before she heads out with the twins.

"Stay safe and watch your step, okay, baby?" whispers Constantina to her daughter.

"Yes, Mama," whispers back Ivory, giving her mother a kiss on the cheek.

The three girls leave the Healing Clinic, leaving behind the two healers.

"I wonder what they're going to talk about at today's assembly," wonders Flora out loud.

"Yeah, I wonder if they found anything new about Yuri. Or if they found him…" continues Fauna.

"I think I might have an idea of what they are going to announce, but I am not sure. They may have found out more," replies Ivory, suddenly reminded of the horror that she'd almost forgotten. "It's so crazy, isn't it?" she asks her friends.

"What's crazy?" asks Flora.

"It's crazy how fast we forget," she replies, shaking her head. "Let me ask you something. When you woke up this morning, when we were around our other friends, laughing and happy, did you remember Yuri?"

Flora and Fauna look at each other with a frown and then back at Ivory.

"No, we didn't. I don't want to say we forgot about him, we just…I don't know, we got busy with what was happening in our own lives, I guess," replies Fauna, still frowning at the thought.

"Exactly. Don't get me wrong, I totally forgot about him at some point, too. But out of everyone, I shouldn't have. Knowing for a fact that he is hurt and that he is still out there…it's crazy how the human mind has a way of playing tricks on us, making us believe that everything is going to be okay when in reality, it isn't," says Ivory, looking down at her feet as she walks.

"Wait, what do you mean, you know for a fact that he is hurt? Do you know something that we don't?" asks Flora, a little confused.

Ivory gives the twins a quick recap of the conversation she had with Acyl and Kai the earlier day. Flora and Fauna stop dead in their tracks when Ivory mentions the blood, looking at each other, sharing some kind of silent conversation.

"Do you think they are going to share that piece of information with the rest of the tribe today?" asks Fauna.

"Honestly, I have no idea. I don't know what they're thinking at all at this point. If they don't share it, we are the only ones that know," replies Ivory with a sigh.

The three start walking again, in silence.

"Well, we don't have to wait much longer to find out what they have to say. We're here," says Fauna, breaking the silence as she makes her way into the Tribal Center clearing.

"Greetings! Greetings to all of my fellow Alders as well as our visiting Oaks!" shouts Warrior Zlato over the buzzing crowd, quieting them down.

"I would like to start off by thanking each and every one of you for not only putting down whatever you had been doing to be here with us today, but also for making the first night of our implemented curfew an overall success. The warriors appreciate the cooperation of each and every one of you. If it were not for your continued support, we would not have the updated information that we have for you today. So, thank you!"

The crowd starts buzzing again the moment Warrior Zlato mentions the update. The twins and Ivory look at each other.

"It means they're going to tell everyone," whispers Flora.

"Do you think they found something else?" whispers Fauna.

"I don't know, but that's what I understood from the way he said it," whispers back Ivory.

The three look back up at the stage in unison as Warrior Zlato makes sure he has all of his papers and information in order. The three girls stand close to one another, nervous at what the warrior might reveal. In fact, the entire tribe seems to be on edge, waiting for a positive update. But a positive update is not in the cards.

"As of right now, the boy has not been discovered yet. We do, however, believe that he is most likely in a compromising situation. Warriors have found traces of the boy's blood in front of his house, as well as near the tribal boundary."

A sharp gasp takes over the crowd.

"Along with the blood of the boy, the warriors have also discovered blood that they believe belongs to some kind of animal. The animal's blood was found mixed with the boy's at the boundary, along with animal prints we are unfamiliar with."

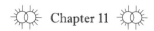

"What?" gasps Ivory out loud.

"Wow…this is new…did you know this?" asks Fauna, flabbergasted.

"N…no. This is the first time I've heard about this…" whispers Ivory back.

"Shhh…he's not done," says Flora, trying to hear the warrior speak.

"We've tested the blood samples that we found and we are definite that some of it belonged to the boy. The other DNA we found is something we have never seen before. And if we take the prints into consideration, we are dealing with an animal that is quite large, one that we are completely unfamiliar with. This means that there is a definite danger still out there, and we are not sure if our security can hold if the animal decides to attack again. So in order to protect you, the curfew will stay in place until further notice," finishes Warrior Zlato.

Everyone in the tribe is shocked. A lot of people are also very frightened by what they have just heard. Ivory wonders to herself if Yuri's parents made it to the assembly or if the warriors had told them the news before telling the rest of the tribe. She wishes the latter is true.

Before Warrior Zlato walks off stage, he takes a brief moment to give one last word.

"Look, I know that you are all worried right now, both for the boy and for yourselves. And I also know that the uncertainty of this whole situation does not help one bit. But if I can give any one of you a little peace of mind, it would be that the boy, Yuri, still has a very real chance of being alive. The quantity of blood we found was very small. In fact, we couldn't be sure it was his until we tested it. So do not give up hope just yet. But whatever you do, please, do not, under any circumstance, try to go out and look for Yuri yourselves. We have trained warriors out right now as we speak, sweeping the forest floors and tree-tops, looking for him or any sign he might have left behind. Please, keep him in your prayers, because if he ever needed it, it would be right now."

As Warrior Zlato walks off the stage and joins the rest of the warriors, Ivory knows that the assembly has come to an abrupt, bone-chilling end. It has left her with more questions than answers.

"Let's go, I think we're done here," says Fauna to the two other girls.

"Yes, let's," replies Ivory, head spinning with this new information.

As the girls try making their way out of the crowd, they hear their names being called. It's Professor Spyridon.

Flora stops the two other girls and points to the waving professor. When Ivory and Fauna catch the professor waving them over, they change direction and start heading toward the stage.

"There you are; I was afraid I wouldn't catch you in this crowd," says the professor to the three girls.

"We were just heading back to the Weaponry to rejoin the class," says Fauna.

"I know. I made an announcement at the end of class, but you were not there to hear it. I have a special treat for all of you today. I told the rest of the students to meet up with us here after the tribal meeting."

"What's the surprise, professor?" asks Flora.

"You will see; I cannot tell you just yet," he says with a wink before walking away.

"Hmmm…Oh, hey! Sparrow! Over here!" yells out Ivory as she spots her friend amongst the dying crowd.

Sparrow turns around, looking for the voice calling out her name, spotting Ivory standing next to the stage with the twins. She waves to the three girls and starts making her way to them. At the same time, Sevastyan spots the girls and starts making his way to them as well.

"Hey, you're all here!" exclaims Sparrow, hugging each one of the girls.

"Flora, how are you doing?" asks Sevastyan as he joins the group.

"I'm fine, thank you," replies Flora with a smile.

"Umm…how are YOU feeling, after that little incident, sir?" Ivory asks Sevastyan with a smirk.

Sevastyan sighs. "I'm fine. And I apologize for my behavior. I honestly have no idea where that came from; that was the first time I really snapped at someone like that," he replies, looking out into the distance, trying to recall the moment.

"Yeah, that was a little too much, brother. Like, just a little," says Fauna, laughing. "Ivory was about to whip your behinds if you hadn't gotten it together."

The girls all laugh at the thought of Ivory kicking Sevastyan and Vain on the butt repeatedly.

"Alright everyone, gather around!" shouts Professor Spyridon to his students.

Ivory and her friends finish laughing and join the rest of their classmates.

"So, you are all probably wondering why I have brought you all here. Like I said, I have a very special surprise for you all. I brought you here today to meet the man himself, Nazar Yilan II," says the professor with an ecstatic smile.

The students all break out in cheers, excited at this amazing opportunity. That is, everyone except Ivory and Sevastyan. The two look over at each other immediately, not sure how to take this news. From the first moment that they had seen him, they didn't like him. He made them almost uncomfortable.

Ivory and Sevastyan break eye contact just in time to see Nazar walk out from behind the stage. They clap along with the rest of their classmates at his arrival. As he makes his way to the students, Nazar takes down his hood, revealing his dark curly hair and piercing brown eyes. His black cloak flows to the ground but never touches it. Ivory marvels at how beautiful his cloak is, with its inside trimmed with blood red velvet. Again, she wonders how someone living in the desert can be so regal. It's not that she doesn't think desert people cannot be regal, it's that he was a little too regal, like he had never picked up a sword once in his life. As Ivory's mind wanders, one by one, Nazar meets the students, listening to their praise and kindly shaking their hands in response. When he reaches Ivory, he stops and silently looks her over. This takes Ivory by surprise. She feels Sevastyan's stance hardening at her side.

Nazar leans in to Ivory, his nose almost touching hers. His kohl-lined, smoldering eyes look into her wide-open eyes. He holds her gaze for a second, then smiles.

"You are Ivory Skye," he says, finally leaning back into a normal stance.

Ivory tries steadying her breath.

"Yes," she manages out.

"I could tell by the bruise on your forehead and face. It still looks fresh. Your eyes too…you have the eyes of a warrior," he says with a mysterious smile.

Ivory is speechless. How does one answer such a comment?

"Um…thank you, sir."

"Oh, please, you can call me Nazar. I feel so old when your generation calls me sir. I mean, I understand that you do it for the respect, but there is no need for such formalities between friends."

"Yes, sir. I mean, Nazar."

Nazar chuckles and then suddenly grabs Ivory's hand, startling her.

"I really must apologize, dear, for the stupidity of my Oaks. To hurt such a beautiful, talented girl…" he coos, reaching for her bruised forehead, running his fingers down her face.

Ivory holds her breath, not sure what is happening and wondering if her friends were seeing it all.

"I really wish that you can find it in your heart to forgive us all," he says, reaching down with his face, kissing Ivory on the hand.

Ivory's face flushes red.

"Of course, sir, Nazar. There is nothing to forgive, it was honestly my mistake, I wasn't watching where I was walking…"

Nazar, lips still on Ivory's hand, looks up. A smile dances from his lips to his eyes. Ivory tries to put on a smile for him, barely managing to do so.

"I don't know what it is, Ivory, but when I look at you, I see the same thing that I see in myself," says Nazar, standing upright, still holding Ivory's hand. "I have a feeling that this is the first of many meetings between us. So, until next time…" he finishes with a wink, finally letting go of Ivory's hand.

Nazar walks away, leaving Ivory in somewhat of a brain mess. She can't begin to think of everything that has just gone down.

"Oh…"

"My…"

"God…"

Flora, Fauna, and Sparrow stare as they walk up to Ivory, who is still frozen in her spot.

"What the hell was that?" asks Sevastyan, looking over at Nazar, who laughs at something a student had said.

"Ivory. Ive. Are you okay, babe? You're looking a little shocked right now," says Sparrow, holding her friend by the shoulder.

Ivory shakes her head, trying to snap herself out of it.

"I…umm…I don't know. What…ahhh…" Ivory picks her hands up from her sides, turning them over, examining them as they shake. "Did anyone else see that?" she asks in a hushed voice, still examining her hands.

"Umm…everyone saw that," says Fauna.

Ivory looks up at her, eyes wide. Fauna shrugs apologetically.

Three girls walk up to Ivory and her friends, squealing in excitement.

"Oh, my, God!! Ivory, you are so lucky!!" says the first girl.

"I know; I would literally do ANYTHING to have been in your spot!" says the second girl.

"What did it feel like?" asks the third girl.

"What? What do you mean?" asks Ivory, still a little lost.

"What did it feel like when he touched your face and kissed you, of course!? What do you think we're talking about!?" replies the girl, a little too excited.

"I mean, seriously, for a second I thought he was going to kiss you on the lips, his face was so close to yours!" squeals the second girl.

"Okay, you girls need to calm down," says Fauna, annoyed. "He is a grown man, not a teenage boy. He kissed her hand platonically as an apology, not because he is in love with her. And he is way too old for her, or any of you, for that matter!"

"It was fine," replies Ivory quickly, finding her voice again. "He just felt bad that his warriors hurt me, that's all."

The three girls look at each other, disappointed that they're not going to get anything juicy or dramatic out of Ivory.

"Okay, well, we have to go. We'll see you guys later!" says the first girl, pulling her friends away, heading toward the group of students around Nazar.

"Those bubbleheads seriously need to get it together," huffs Fauna.

"Seriously, he's old. I don't know what they see in him," says Sevastyan in agreement with Fauna.

"Well, he's not that old…" says Sparrow. "And he looks amazing for his age."

"Oh, come on! Are you serious right now?" asks Sevastyan, mind blown.

"Flora thinks so too," says Sparrow, looking over at the girl.

Sevastyan looks at Flora, bewildered at the idea that she would think Nazar is good-looking too.

"Hey, I never said anything! Do I think he's terrible-looking? No, he looks pretty great for an older gentleman. But I definitely think that he is way too old for any of us," replies Flora, defending herself.

Ivory sighs to herself as her friends argue over Nazar's looks. All she wants to do is go home and write about the whole situation in her memory book so she can reflect on it. Not paying attention to her friends, she looks around at the other students unconsciously. Her gaze travels past the different faces, then stops and moves back to a specific one. She quickly realizes that Cassius is looking, no, staring at her. His eyes narrowed, focused on her; he holds her gaze. Startled, Ivory looks around to see if anyone else sees Cassius staring her down, but she is alone. She turns her gaze back to Cassius, narrowing her own eyes in question. Cassius smirks, then shakes his head and looks away.

What the hell was that? What is happening? thinks Ivory to herself as her friends try pulling her back into their conversation. The only thing she knows for sure is that she has never felt so uncomfortable in her life, and she has been through some weird situations.

Chapter 12

"So I heard you guys met Nazar today. Sounds exciting! How was it?" asks Constantina over the dinner table.

"It was alright, I guess," replies Ivory, pushing the food on her plate around with her fork.

"Mama, we learned that a long time ago, there used to be these things called cars that people used to travel in. But did you know that they lead to the earth being polluted, which lead to the Great Wave?" says Anya excitedly.

"Oh, that's an interesting subject to learn about! And yes, they were very bad for the environment. That's why we don't use them anymore," replies Constantina.

"Yes, that's why we use horses. They're good for the environment, and they make great friends!" laughs Nadi. The girls all laugh, except for Ivory. But thankfully, no one notices.

"Mother, is it alright if I leave for my room? My head hurts a lot," says Ivory.

"Yes, of course, baby. Would you like me to make you some more of that lavender tea that Flora gave you? You said it helped," replies her mother.

"No, thank you, I think I'm just really tired. I need to sleep. I will see you all tomorrow," says Ivory as she gets up to leave. "Goodnight." She waves to everyone before heading off to her room.

Ivory had written in her memory book as soon as she had gotten home, so she just lies on her bed, waiting for sleep to embrace her in its arms. But every time she closes her eyes, she sees his eyes – smoldering – burning right through her and leaving a hole behind. She hugs her pillow, trying to find some kind of comfort in it, just enough to doze off. She lays awake for another half hour before sleep finally catches up with her.

- - -

"Hello, Ivory. Welcome."

Ivory opens her eyes, but she is not where she expected to be. She expected darkness. But instead, she is met with a beautiful room, decorated in red velvet drapes and big statues with colorful gems. She turns around, trying to take everything in. Then, suddenly, it occurs to her to look down at herself. She is dressed in an emerald green off-the-shoulder silk dress that flows to the floor, with a train following behind her as she walks. On top of her dress, covering her shoulders, is the cloak, the beautiful black cloak with the smooth, velvety, red inner lining. Underneath the cloak, Ivory's arms are covered in gold and jade bracelets. She walks forward and sits on a little chair in front of an intricately-made vanity and mirror to get a better look at herself. Her hair, flowing down to her waist in waves, holds a delicate little crown encrusted in rubies and diamonds.

Eyes lined in black kohl, skin as smooth as porcelain, and lips as red as cherries, Ivory looks at herself in awe. She has never seen herself so beautiful before.

"This can be you, every day, for the rest of your life. If you'd like," whispers a voice to Ivory's side.

When she looks over at the talking stranger, she finds Nazar, dressed in a beautiful suit and matching cloak. He walks over to Ivory and stands right behind her. Ivory looks at him through the mirror as he takes something out of his pocket. He then reaches out in front of her and places the necklace around her neck. The necklace is beautiful and long with an interesting pendant hanging off of it, two intersecting suns.

"Pledge yourself to me, and I promise to make you the happiest you will ever be," whispers Nazar in Ivory's ear before walking away.

Ivory looks back at herself in the mirror and touches the necklace. It's cold to the touch.

"Gold is cold," she hears a familiar voice whisper in her ear. "Do not let its beauty pull you in. Because although it may feel good now, it will burn you later…"

Ivory looks around, searching for the woman. This was not the setting she was used to hearing her in. But her search for the woman is cut short as the necklace on her chest starts to get hot. Ivory screams and struggles to break it off as it burns her skin anywhere it makes contact. When she finally breaks it off, she turns back to the mirror to see her bleeding chest and hands. Tears running down her face, Ivory looks back at the necklace on the ground as it melts down into a puddle of gold.

Gasp.

Ivory's eyes open to her bedroom ceiling. Carefully, she pulls up one hand at a time, examining each where it had been burnt in the dream – nothing. She then reaches for her neck and chest, afraid of what she might find. But again, she finds nothing. As real as it felt, it was just a dream. At least, that's what she tries to convince herself.

- - -

"Today, we review all of the positions available to you after graduation. All of these positions allow for growth and advancement. Please open your books to page thirteen, where you will find an outline containing every position."

Ivory flips through her book until she reaches the page her professor had told the class to turn to. The title of the page reads: *Different Job Positions Available to New Graduates and Seasoned Professionals.*

Ivory reads through the choices and their quick descriptions as the book has them arranged:

- ***Hunters***:
    - *Job description: Go out into the wild to hunt game (bears, elk, antelope, bison, etc.)*
    - *Hunting Rule:*
        - *Animals can only be hunted for food, not for sport.*
        - *Exception: An animal can be killed in self-defense.*
    - *The position of gamekeeper is available to those of older age. These are former hunters who are no longer young enough to keep up with the harsh wilderness. They keep goats and cattle for milk.*
- ***Wolf/Animal Trainers***

- ○ *Job description: Train wolves and other canines to obey and help humans in their hunting activity. These animals are also used to guard the borders of the tribes when wild animals are nearby. They scare the smaller animals away and howl when something big is coming toward the tribe.*
- ○ *This position allows you to work alongside the hunters.*
- **Horse keepers/Trainers/Riders**
  - ○ *Job descriptions for each position follows:*
    - *Horse keepers: Take care of the horses by cleaning them, feeding them, and mounting them with riding equipment for the horse trainers.*
    - *Horse trainers: Help train the horses to obey and do as they are told. Also help break wild horses. If a horse is really wild and the trainers can't break it, they call on the help of the head horse keeper (description to follow).*
    - *Horse riders: Ride the horses. The horses need to be taken out every day in order to keep their speed and strength. Older riders also have the opportunity to help out the school with students who need to learn how to ride.*
    - *Head horse keeper: This is a position for the person who shows exceptionalism when it comes to their knowledge and abilities in dealing with horses in general. This is the highest position possible for this area of study. Chosen by the Elders. Not available to new graduates.*
- **Weapon Makers:**
  - ○ *Job description: the development of weapons. Including, but not limited to, swords, spears, axes, bows and arrows, darts, daggers, clubs, whips, ropes, etc.*
  - ○ *This position may include travel to the North, to the Willow tribe, to learn weapon-making, as they are much more advanced in weapon-making than any other tribe.*
- **Warriors:**
  - ○ *Job description: Peacekeepers. However, if war is to ever break out, their main goal is to protect the people and fight off the enemy.*
    - *Different warrior positions include: guarding outside the tribal boundaries, protecting people from whatever may be out in the wild. Also, making sure no one goes out of the tribe unless they have reason to do so, such as hunters or those traveling to and from different tribes.*

  - ○ *Head warriors: train the warriors. This position is open to seasoned warriors who have shown exceptionality in both strength and wisdom when protecting the people.*
    - *Head warriors are also the judges/punishment dealers if necessary (in extreme situations).*
    - *This position is not available to new graduates.*
- **Healers:**
  - ○ *Different job positions and descriptions follow:*
  - ○ *Head healers: Work with very ill patients. This is the highest position of healer offered, and is only available to seasoned healers who show exceptional healing skills. These healers pass down their knowledge on to up-and-coming healers. This position is not available to new graduates.*
  - ○ *Regular healers: Work with the head healers, but deal with more of the everyday patients. These patients include hunters who get hurt out in the wild. They deal with the basic cuts, infections, colds, etc. This position is available to new graduates.*
  - ○ *Beginner healers: Follow the regular healers around and assist them in their work. This position is available to undergraduate students who are considering becoming healers themselves.*
- **Medicine Makers:**
  - ○ *Job description: Collect different herbs, florae, and parts of trees to make medicine.*
  - ○ *Those that take this position will work closely with the head healers, as they decide what needs to be collected and what medicine needs to be produced.*
  - ○ *Medicine makers will also work closely with hunters, as they will always have hunters with them when they go outside the tribe to look for different plants.*
  - ○ *This position does have a higher risk level, as it can be dangerous to wander in the woods, which are filled with poisonous plants and dangerous animals. This position is available to new graduates.*
- **Gardeners:**
  - ○ *Job description: Keep the fruit and vegetable gardens thriving.*
  - ○ *Like medicine making, this position is for those who have an affinity for plants.*

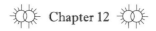

- Gardeners take care of the plants, water them, and pick the fruits and vegetables when they are ready. They also make use of plants that one might not think to eat, such as tree bark, flowers, and different herbs.
- Just like the hunters, there are limits to what the gardeners can plant and where.
- This position is available to new graduates.

- **Teachers:**
  - Job description: this position is open to those who excel at what they do, whether it be weapon-making, horseback riding, healing, etc.
  - There are positions for those who are most knowledgeable of the sciences and history of the world as well. These teachers are former students of the Elders.
  - This position may require travel to different tribes in seek of knowledge
  - Students who show a great interest in learning about history, mathematics, or the sciences, are taken under a teacher's wing and taught extensively about the subject they are most interested in before they can be given to the Elders and study under their guidance.
  - This position is not available to new graduates. Further study of specific subjects in order to become a teacher is available for new graduates.

- **The Elders of the Tribe:**
  - This position is not open to new graduates. Most will not be able to fill this position.
  - There are nine Elders in each tribe at all times. The Elders are the most important and most respected people of the tribe. They pass on the knowledge that they have acquired from their previous Elders. Only the most selfless and most respectable people are chosen by the members of the tribe to become Elders.
  - The Elders bestow their wisdom on the people of the tribe, as it is important for the people to never forget where they came from and how lucky they were to survive. The Great Wave was not a random event. Mankind allowed a lot of things to happen. Things that almost lead to the extinction of the human race. The job of the Elder is to remind everyone about the consequences they might pay they are not careful.
  - Elders take on students who they teach for years, who end up becoming the teachers at the tribe's school.

- The tribal rules are made by the Elders, and they are not random. There are limitations on hunting for a reason. There are limitations on cutting down trees and harvesting different plants as produce for a reason. The world is still at a tipping point. Cut down one extra tree or kill one more bison and the whole system could tip over the edge, like the last time. Being an Elder is not an easy job to have; it is a big burden. However, it is also an honor. For this reason, the Elders are the most looked up to and respected people of the tribe.
  - As the tribal Elders are chosen by the people of the tribe, previous Elders cannot suggest candidates for new members. This eliminates favoritism by the Elders to their sons and family members.
  - For the most part, it is easy to know who the next member of the tribal Elders will be. Students are observed from a young age to see whether they have the greatness and responsibility it takes to have such an important position in the society.

"I would hate to be an Elder," whispers Ivory to herself.

"Yeah, me too," whispers Sparrow over to Ivory. "That's such a big responsibility; it would stress me out to death."

Ivory nods in agreement with Sparrow.

"So do any of you know what you are going to choose?" asks Professor Ganlion at the front of the class.

The students hesitate for a minute, but a few hands go up.

"Yes, Trixie, do you know what position you will choose after graduation?" asks the professor.

"Well," starts the shy girl, "I have been shadowing a healer named Ina and I really love it. So I think I choose to become a healer," she finishes with a small smile.

"That is a wonderful choice, Trixie! Let's all give Trixie a round of applause as a future healer!" booms Professor Ganlion.

The class claps for Trixie, whose cheeks flush pink in embarrassment. Ivory turns to look at Trixie sitting right behind her.

"You are going to make an amazing healer, my friend. I know it." She winks and gives the girl's shoulder a squeeze.

"Thank you, Ivory. I am so excited to do it; I will do my best to make you proud," replies Trixie, with a confidence in her eyes that Ivory wishes she had.

"Okay, Flora! You had your hand up, along with your sister. What have the both of you chosen?" asks the professor.

"I want to be a Medicine Maker," says Flora.

"And I want to be a Hunter," says Fauna.

"Well, would you look at that!" exclaims the professor with a laugh. "Each of you has found the perfect position, and you will end up working together! How wonderful!" he exclaims, giving the two a round of applause. The class follows, clapping for the twins.

A few more students share their chosen position before the professor wraps up the class.

"Remember, no matter what you end up choosing, you are an equal member of this society. No one position is greater than another. In the end, we all strive for the same goal – to make this tribe, this world, a better place. And if you still cannot make up your mind, do not fret. As they used to say in the past, Rome was not built in a day – it took time. It might take you time to figure out your purpose. And if you truly believe that you have no purpose, just look around you, at the people that love you. That is your purpose. This is the last time I will be teaching you as my students. The next time we meet, we will be colleagues. So I want to thank all of you for giving me the pleasure to be your teacher and for trusting me to guide you through your childhood into your adulthood. It has been quite the honor," finishes Professor Ganlion, giving his students a small bow of the head.

The students all clap for their teacher, some cheering aloud for him. They form a line, giving the professor a hug, thanking him for passing down his knowledge before heading out the classroom.

"I can't believe that was the last time we're having class with Professor Ganlion," thinks Sparrow aloud, feeling bittersweet about the whole situation.

Ivory puts her arm around Sparrow as they make their way to the Tribal Center for the mandatory assembly.

"I'm so happy that you guys decided the positions you want after graduation," she says to the twins next to her.

"Thanks, Ive, we're really excited too!" replies Flora.

"Hey guys, we need to move to the side of the path, the warriors are coming through," says Sevastyan to the girls, guiding them out of the way.

Head Warrior Zlato rides by on his horse, followed by about ten more warriors. Ivory looks at the people who had been walking behind them. Oaks;

she can tell by their clothes and sunburned skin. But then she spots something that makes her heart speed up all of a sudden. It's small, but she knows that it cannot be anything else. She could have spotted it from a mile away as it glimmers in the sunlight. Two intersecting suns, hanging on a gold chain.

The Oak wearing the necklace catches Ivory staring at it. He quickly takes the pendant and stuffs it into his shirt, making Ivory's gaze move from the necklace to his face. He gives her a quick smirk before turning back to his fellow Oaks and continuing their talk in hushed voices.

Ivory's face is stark white as she continues to make her way to the Tribal Center with her friends. Her heart doesn't slow down as she looks around at every Oak walking past her. With everyone, she catches a little gold peeking underneath the collar of their shirts. But she also notices that none wear their necklace out in the open. Actually, the only person she sees wearing the necklace obviously is Nazar. Ivory spots him next to the stage, looking like he is in deep conversation with Warrior Zlato. He wears many golden chains, but the longest one is that with the intersecting suns. Nazar's pendant is much bigger than the one she had seen on the other Oak. It is also much bigger than the one in her dream. But she knows for sure that it is the same pendant. And just like he had heard her speaking his name in her head, Nazar turns his gaze from Warrior Zlato straight to Ivory, making direct eye contact. Ivory is taken by surprise at the sudden eye contact, and is further embarrassed when he gives her a knowing smile and wink.

"Hey, you okay?" asks Sparrow, nudging Ivory on the shoulder. "Your face looks hot, are you alright?"

"Huh? Oh, yes, I'm fine. It's ummm…" Ivory rakes her brain for a good excuse. "It's just really crowded here," she says finally.

"Ugh, I know. I'm not a fan of these assemblies, to be honest," says Sparrow before she goes off on a rant about how dangerous these kinds of gatherings really are.

Ivory nods every few seconds to show that she is paying attention to what her friend says, but she can feel Nazar's eyes on her without even looking at him. A part of her wants to look over at him to see if he really is looking, but another part of her is terrified that she is right. What would she do if they make eye contact again? Would she smile? Would she nod her head in acknowledgement of their eye contact?

Thankfully, she doesn't have enough time to make a decision, as Warrior Zlato takes the stage.

"Everyone, quiet down," he orders, looking more stressed than in any of the previous assemblies.

"We've received some news today from the Northern Assimilian tribe; news that changes everything. It would seem that several people have gone missing up in the north. All of the signs that were found after the kidnappings match the kidnapping of our own, Yuri."

The sounds of gasps fill the air.

"The letter we've received from the North also says that similar events took place in the Eastern Tribe about a month earlier. This situation has now become very serious. There is something out there that is moving through the tribes, taking people. We have no idea what it is. We have no idea why it is taking people. And we have no idea if those people still live. As of right now, this tribe is under official lockdown. No one goes in or out of this tribe without going through me first. Keep your eyes open and your doors and windows closed, my friends. We are under attack," he finishes, before walking off the stage.

The tribe goes into immediate hysteria.

Another head warrior walks up to the stage to try and calm the crowd down, but the damage is already done. Warrior Zlato gets back up on his horse and makes his way out, followed by his warriors.

Sevastyan tries to keep the girls together and slowly starts leading them out of the crowd. Ivory gives the stage one last look before she leaves, catching a pair of eyes in the process. The eyes stare back at her, trying to read her expression. She quickly breaks eye contact, turning her back to what's in front of her. But as she walks away, she can feel his eyes burning through her back. And at this moment she can't decide what she's scared of most, that they are under attack, or him.

Chapter 13

Ivory sits at the head of a long dinner table, decorated with plate after plate of the most delicious foods; stuffed roasted birds, an entire lamb, ten different kinds of bread, and vegetables of all shapes and colors. Ivory does not know where to start. And even more, on one end of the room sits a silver cart over-flowing with every dessert pastry Ivory has ever seen, and more. Ivory reaches for the napkin to her right hand, placing it gently on her lap over the scarlet silk dress she wears. Her bracelets chime together as she moves her hands around, serving herself. The first bite of food takes her breath away. The meat melts in her mouth like butter. Cutting another piece with her knife and fork, she puts another piece in her mouth.

"You should try the lemon-glazed sautéed carrots next," his voice dances in her ears.

Ivory reaches for a carrot, closing her eyes at the explosion of flavors that hit her taste buds.

"Try a piece of the pumpernickel bread with some garlic-infused butter next, try that," he whispers.

Ivory does as she is told, eating an entire slice of bread. She continues to eat, fully aware that her stomach is yelling at her to stop, but she can't. It is as if she is under a trance, eating blindly, doing what he tells her to do without question.

"Stop. Ivory, stop eating. Now!"

This new order makes Ivory jump. It's a new voice. Well, a new voice that she is very familiar with.

Ivory looks around the room as if this is the first time she is looking around her. Half of the food on the long cherry wood table is gone. Her stomach feels like it's about to explode. And sitting right across from her on the other end of the table is Nazar. He stares at Ivory, wide-eyed with amusement.

"I think it's time for dessert," he says with a wicked smile.

Ivory feels the haze start to fall over her again. She knows that she cannot eat one more thing, but she can feel her body shifting to one side as she prepares to stand up again.

"Sit down, Ivory," orders the woman. "Do not put one more thing in your mouth."

Ivory sits back down on the chair, back straight. She looks directly at Nazar, whose face is now stone cold.

"What are you doing here?" he asks, looking straight at Ivory. But Ivory knows that he isn't talking to her.

"It's time for you to go away now," replies the woman.

Nazar's face completely transforms into pure fury.

"HOW DARE YOU?! THIS IS MY DREAM, WITCH! IT BELONGS TO ME!"

"Not anymore," replies the woman, with what Ivory thinks is amusement.

Nazar bangs his fists down on the table, making it vibrate. He completely loses his composure and starts yelling profanities at the woman. He then grabs the two corners of the table, and with incredible strength, tosses it to one side of the room. The table and everything on it crashes into a wall, breaking in half. Ivory sits across from Nazar with nothing in between them now, stunned. And just as she had feared, Nazar stands up and starts stomping towards her. Ivory braces herself, holding on to the sides of her chair. But the woman speaks out before Nazar reaches the halfway point between himself and Ivory.

She chants in a language Ivory is familiar with; Arabic.

"Ith'hab ya man'oul. An'alouka kama na'alaka rab ul'alamin. Ith'hab. Ith-'hab. Ith'hab!"

Nazar freezes dead in his tracks. He screams as his body starts to disappear.

"This is not over yet, witch! Mark my words, I WILL FIND YOU!" he yells before disappearing completely.

Ivory doesn't move from her spot. Her knuckles, white from holding on to the chair so tight, start to feel numb.

"It's over. You're safe, for now," says the woman.

Ivory's grip on the chair softens. But as soon as she lets the chair go, she feels sick. She quickly leans forward on her chair, holding her stomach. She gags and coughs a few times before vomiting what looks like black tar. It chokes her, not allowing her to take a breath until it's all out. Ivory pulls her feet up off the ground and wipes her mouth with the sleeve of her dress. The black stain left on her sleeve makes her look down at the ground again. The black tar completely surrounds her chair, and slowly, it starts moving outward. Ivory brings her knees to her chest, trying to get as far away from the tar as possible.

"It is time for you to wake up, child," says the woman softly. "And remember, some of the most rotten things in this world are painted with beautiful strokes of color. Do not let beauty distract you from what is right and what is less than that."

Ivory looks down at her once-beautiful dress, now a simple gray one with little stains and holes on one side. The room starts to fade away, slowly getting replaced by the usual darkness. Soon enough, the walls are gone, the broken table is gone, and the chair and tar are gone.

"I am sorry," whispers Ivory.

"You need not be sorry, child. Not for human nature. We were created to want more – the best. But soon, you will begin to learn that having it all is the biggest burden there is."

"Who are you?" Ivory asks suddenly. "He called you 'witch.' Do you have a name? Something I can call you by?"

The woman does not reply.

"Please! I just need something, anything, to know that all of this is not in my imagination, that I am not going insane," pleads Ivory.

Seconds go by without a reply from the woman. Ivory loses almost all hope before the woman replies.

"My name is Zohra."

Ivory's eyes fly open.

"No, no, no…go back to sleep!" she yells at herself. But she can't. The woman had jolted her out, like she usually does.

The woman…Zohra.

Ivory has never heard that name before; Zohra. But it's a name she will never forget.

Breakfast at the Skye household is a quiet affair this morning after the events that took place last night. Ivory watches her mother in deep thought as she prepares lunches for the girls before she heads off to the healing clinic. Ivory's father, Nadi, had left before the younger girls had gotten up, but Ivory caught a glimpse of him before he headed out. He had shared a long, private embrace with his wife at the door before telling her to take care of herself. Nadi is an optimistic man, always happy, as he is kind. But the situation has changed – Ivory could see the worry on his face, no matter how hard he tried to make the girls feel like everything was ok.

"Ivory. Ivory."

Ivory snaps out of her thoughts as her mother tries to get her attention again.

"Yes, Mama, I'm sorry. I didn't hear you. What is it?" she asks, shaking her head.

"That's fine, Ivory; I just need you to do a favor for me. I was going to leave the girls home today, as they're done with school, but I'm not very comfortable with that anymore. Do you think you can take them with you to the tribal center today? I've packed a blanket for them to sit on the grass, and lunch. They can bring whatever else they need with them."

"Yes, Mother, of course I understand. I would feel weird leaving them home alone, too," replies Ivory with a nod.

"Don't worry, Ive, I'll be with them at the tribal center, you won't even know we're there," says Hayden, joining in the conversation as she walks into the kitchen.

"That's good to hear, Hayden, I need you to really help me out with your sisters now, ok," says Constantina. "If we don't stick together as a family and help each other out at times like these, then there's no point in having each other. I am trusting the both of you with the responsibility of Anya and Diana, ok?"

"Yes, Mother," reply Ivory and Hayden in unison.

- - -

Sparrow walks up to Ivory as Ivory finishes helping her sisters set up on a grassy area underneath the shade of an Alder tree.

"Hello, stranger," says Sparrow softly, placing her hand on Ivory's shoulder.

Ivory turns around at the touch and sound of her friend's voice.

"Hello, friend," replies Ivory in a tired voice, also placing a hand on Sparrow's shoulder.

"Yeah, me too…" says Sparrow in response to Ivory. They share a long silent moment before embracing each other tightly.

"I couldn't sleep last night. For the first time ever, I had nightmares all night long," whispers Sparrow, still embracing Ivory.

Ivory sighs. If only Sparrow knew the last time she had had a good night's sleep. Ivory couldn't remember herself.

"Me, too," is all Ivory replies to her friend.

- - -

"So the pattern you want is three white, one pink, and repeat. Once we're done, we'll wrap some green vine around the base and add in a few leaves to fill in the empty spaces," says Flora to the three girls.

Ivory, Sparrow, and Fauna all watch as Flora demonstrates how she weaves the beautiful flowers together to make a flower crown. Flora had volunteered to make the crowns for the graduation ceremony, and she'd volunteered her friends to help her. The girls didn't mind, but Sevastyan had to go help set up the stage with some other boys.

Ivory looks over at her sisters every once in a while, just to make sure they're all present and alright. She looks down at the flower crown she is currently working on in her lap.

"Ouch!" jumps Sparrow.

"Oh, watch out for the needle, Sparrow, I've jabbed myself a few times already," says Flora.

"Yeah, this is definitely not going to be the last time I poke myself," replies Sparrow with a sigh, shaking her head.

The girls sit in silence for a few minutes, each engrossed in the work in front of them.

"So, guys, are we going to talk about it or not?" asks Fauna, breaking the silence.

"Honestly, I don't really know what to say," replies Ivory. "I mean, Yuri is still missing, there's something out there picking us off one by one, and we're sitting here making flower crowns. The irony of this moment is just way beyond comprehension."

Sparrow chuckles.

"I mean, I do agree with you, Ive, but I also think it's good that we're still preparing for the graduation and festival. It'll help get people's minds off of the issue," says Flora.

"But that is an issue of its own, Flora. Don't you see? The same thing is happening in the other tribes, too, but they're so busy preparing for other things that it has taken so long for us to get the news. If they had sent us the warning earlier, we might have been prepared, and I don't know…Yuri might still be here," replies Ivory, shaking her head.

"Have you guys heard anything new from Acyl and Kai?" asks Sparrow.

The three girls shake their heads "No."

A few hours go by…

"Alright, this is the last one," says Flora as she sets the final flower crown in the basket with the others.

"That actually wasn't so bad; it was almost a little fun," smiles Sparrow.

"Speak for yourself," laughs Fauna. "I poked myself so many times with that needle, I hope you don't end up getting one of my bloody flower crowns!"

The girls all laugh at the thought.

"Hey, do you guys think you can carry the flower crown baskets to the festival planners on your own? I need to drop the girls back off at home before coming to dinner."

"Yeah, we should be fine; you go ahead, Ive," replies Fauna.

"We will be just fine, Ive. Just try to hurry a little bit, though, I don't want you to eat the food cold," says Flora.

"That, and I'm really hungry, and I'm not waiting for you!" smirks Sparrow.

Ivory laughs. "Don't worry, I'll take a horse back. I might even get to your place before you!" she winks at the girls.

The girls all go their separate ways, Ivory making her way back home with her sisters.

"Did you girls have a nice day?" asks Constantina as the sisters put their shoes away.

"Yes, Mother, it was really fun. I'm so happy that school is over. Look, I even made you a painting of the Tribal Center," replies Hayden.

Constantina takes the painting, holding it up to get a better look. "It's beautiful, love! I'm definitely putting this one up. Hmm…it might look really nice in the hallway, on the wall opposite the window. The light will hit it perfectly at sunrise," she thinks aloud.

As the younger girls sit in the kitchen with their mother, discussing their day, Ivory quickly changes her worn-out, dirty pants and now blood-stained top into something a little more appropriate for dinner; a clean pair of black Jodhpurs and her favorite top – scarlet-colored, short-sleeved, with shoulder cutouts. She quickly brushes her wild hair up into a high ponytail before putting on her boots and heading out.

"Not too late, ok, you know the curfew," says Ivory's mother as Ivory heads out the front door.

"Oh, don't worry, Mother, I'll meet you at the tribal assembly tonight, so I'll come home with all of you," she replies.

Ivory gets her saddle up on Snow, a beautiful silver-eyed, snow-white horse, and makes her way to the Ilios household.

"Welcome, Ivory, it's so nice seeing you again, dear!" says Fleur Ilios, kissing Ivory's cheeks as she brings her into her home. "How have you been? Your forehead is healing marvelously; I must say, I am a bit surprised! Although, your mother did patch you up herself," laughs the twins' mother as she lightly touches Ivory's forehead and face.

"Thank you so much for the dinner invitation, Healer Ilios; I hope we didn't add any extra work to your plate," replies Ivory.

"Oh no, love, the girls were so disappointed when they had to cancel the lunch, and you know you are all like my own," replies Fleur.

Ivory chuckles as Fauna comes to the door, taking Ivory by the arm.

"Come on, food is ready and everyone is here!" says Fauna excitedly.

"You have a good time!" says Fleur as the girls make their way into the dining room.

As Ivory makes her way in, her breath is taken away by the delicious scent of food and flowers.

"Flora, I know you did the decorating," says Ivory, making her way to her seat.

The dining table, although small, is filled with food. Pink and yellow roses spill off the sides of the table, along with jasmine vines.

Flora laughs. "If you're talking about the flowers, then yes, of course!" she winks back.

Sevastyan gets up and embraces Ivory in a tight bear hug. "Hey you, I've missed you. How are you feeling?"

"I'm feeling a lot better," replies Ivory into Sevastyan's shoulder. "I've missed you, too. How was the set up today?"

"It was good; we actually got most of it done. The assembly location has been changed so that no one messes up the work we did," replies Sevastyan, heading back to his seat.

"That's good; I was thinking about that today! We don't usually have all of these assemblies during the graduation and moon festival period. This is definitely a first," says Sparrow.

"Yes, thankfully we've found a way to work around it, though," says Sevastyan. "Oh, and speaking of which, I worked with Acyl and Kai today. They send their regards. They don't have any new news about Yuri. We talked about that for a while today. But we did hear that the warriors are giving us something tonight. Not sure what it is yet, though," says Sevastyan.

"Well, thankfully we don't have to wait for too long to find out. We're all heading out as soon as we finish dinner. That being said, please help yourselves, guys; you're not strangers in our home," says Flora, inviting everyone to start eating.

"Everything looks delicious, I'm so hungry!" exclaims Sparrow.

"It really is amazing, guys, thank you!" says Ivory through her first bite of food.

The room falls silent for a few minutes as the gang enjoys their dinner. The sounds of forks and plates clanking and mouths chewing is almost peaceful. As Ivory eats, she looks around the table at her beautiful friends. Flora and Fauna in matching flowing pastel summer dresses – hair braided into two braids, hanging down on either side of their chests. Sparrow in a striking plum-colored top that shows off her perfectly toned arms – short hair and bangs slicked back, off of her face. And then Sevastyan – sweet, brave Sevastyan, looking exceptionally well in a plaid button-down short-sleeved number. As her friends chat away over their dinner, Ivory doesn't say much. Instead, she takes the moment in. She takes in the happy atmosphere, and for a moment, forgets about everything happening outside that room.

I am so lucky, so blessed, to have such amazing people in my life. I don't know what I ever did to deserve such an amazing life, but I will treasure this moment for eternity.

Ivory is lightly shaken out of her thoughts when Fleur walks in with a tray of desserts for the gang.

126

"I hope you guys left some space for some peach cobbler! It's hot out of the oven, so just be a little careful, ok!" exclaims Fleur as she sets the tray down on the table.

The gang cheers and claps for Healer, and now special cook, Ilios. She takes a bow and blows kisses to her big fans before heading out. Flora quickly brings the tea over to the table to go with the cobbler.

"I must say, girls, this is the best dinner I've had in a while. I don't think I'll be able to ride a horse for the next two days, I'm so full!" laughs Sevastyan.

The girls all laugh at the thought. Ivory and Sparrow thank their hosts as well as they begin getting up.

"Hey, Ive, are you taking Snow with you to the assembly?" asks Fauna as they get ready to head out.

"No, if it's ok with you, I was planning on leaving her here and passing by to take her home with me on the way back," replies Ivory.

"Alright, that sounds perfect. Hold on, let me get her a few apples before we leave," says Fauna before she disappears.

The girls wait for Fauna outside as she treats Snow to a few handfuls of sweet yellow apples. And as soon as she makes her way to her friends, they head out to the assembly.

- - -

"Thank you all for making your way here today," starts Head Warrior Zlato. "I would like to start off by thanking you for your cooperation with us, as the tribal center is currently under preparation for both the annual moon festival as well as the student graduation. I would also like to thank you all for your cooperation with the warriors and for abiding by the currently active curfew. We truly appreciate you for all of your help," says the warrior, getting a round of applause.

"As of now, we unfortunately do not have any news on the case of the missing boy, Yuri. However, as agreed upon by the Elders of this tribe, we will be releasing both the names and pictures of all that have disappeared from both this tribe and the others. As you may or may not have noticed, the pictures were posted up about an hour ago on the trees of the main tribal pathways. And although it is unlikely that you will know anything about these people, the Elders have invited anyone with any kind of information to please come forward with it. We can use all of the help we can get, so please do not be afraid to come forward with anything that you might know. I will end this short assembly meeting here, as this is all we have for you today. Once again, thank you all for your time, and please make your way safely back to your homes," ends Warrior Zlato.

"Hmm…that's not really much to go off of, is it?" says Sevastyan to his friends as they turn to make their way back to the Ilios house.

"Yeah, I definitely thought they would have something else to give us. I doubt anyone will know anything about the people that disappeared. How could they? They're not even from here…" replies Fauna.

As they walk, Ivory spots a tree with a few pages stuck on it. "Hold on, guys, I want to take a quick look at it, ok," she says to her friends, making her way to the tree.

Ivory's heart sinks at she looks at the pictures, names, and ages of the people who had disappeared. Most of them were so young, some as young as her sister Diana. She spots Yuri in one of the images. And although she doesn't know any of the others taken, some of them look eerily familiar to her. She can't put her finger on it; she had definitely never met any of them before, they were from different tribes…yet, there was something there.

"Come on, Ive, It's going to get dark soon. We need to head back," says Sparrow, taking Ivory by the arm. Ivory takes one last glance back at the tree as she walks away, arm in arm with her friend. When the friends arrive at the Ilios household, they all say their goodbyes and each head in their own direction.

Ivory rides her horse back to the main trail, soon catching up to her family as they make their way home.

"How was your dinner at the Ilios's? Did you guys have fun?" asks Ivory's father.

"Yes, it was actually really nice…a nice change in scenery from everything that's happening around here," replies Ivory, thinking back to that peaceful moment that seems so far away now.

"That's nice; I'm glad you had fun," says Ivory's mom. "So…tell me what they made for dinner! I need new cooking ideas; I feel like I've been feeding you all the same thing for the past month. I'm stuck in a cooking rut," laughs Constantina.

"Hey, I don't mind eating the same thing every day; I like consistency. And plus, anything you make is always amazing," replies Nadi, holding his wife closer to his side.

The girls all laugh. Ivory looks down at her two younger sisters walking hand in hand.

"Hey guys, do you want to ride Snow the rest of the way home?" she asks Anya and Diana.

The two girls look at each other and back at Ivory. "Yeah, sure, if you don't mind walking," answers Anya.

Ivory jumps off her horse and stops her for a minute while she puts her two sisters up on the saddle. Anya puts her arms around her younger sister in front of her, keeping one hand on the reins. Diana holds on to the saddle while Ivory takes full control of the horse reins, leading Snow forward. Hayden slows down a bit, waiting for her sister to catch up so they can walk together.

"So did you guys have a good dinner too?" asks Ivory.

"Yes, we did, contrary to what Mother says," laughs Hayden.

As the girls make their way home behind their parents, Ivory notices the sun beginning to set in the horizon. *Beautiful*, she whispers to herself as she looks on at the burning embers licking across the purple-pink sky.

Chapter 14

"Ivory…" whispers a young girl's voice. "Ivory, please, wake up. We need you…we need you to wake up and save us. Please…" the voice cracks as the young girl cries quietly.

Ivory's eyes open, and she sees her. A young blonde-haired, blue-eyed girl. She couldn't be any older than Ivory's sister Diana. Ivory walks forward and kneels down as she gets to the girl.

"What's your name?" Ivory asks the crying girl.

"My…my name is Marina," replies the girl through her tears.

"Why are you crying, Marina? What's wrong?" asks Ivory, wiping away the girl's tears. As she does so, Ivory notices something small on the left side of the girl's neck. With her thumb, she traces over what looks to be some kind of…birthmark. Why did it look familiar, though?

This is so weird; where have I seen this before?

Marina suddenly grabs hold of Ivory's shoulders, startling her.

"Listen to me!" starts the girl, eyes wide with fear. "It's not going to stop… more people are going to get taken! You need to find us, Ivory! You know where to find us; all you have to do is wake up!" she screams.

All of a sudden, Ivory is surrounded. She stands back up, looking at the faces around her, yelling for her help. Ivory puts her hands over her ears as the sound starts to overwhelm her. As she tries looking for a way out of the circle she notices something – someone.

"Trixie! What are you doing here?" yells Ivory over the loud screams.

Trixie, huddled in a corner, holding her own ears shut, looks up, face tear-streaked. But before she can reply to Ivory, the kids start getting sucked into the earth. Ivory tries running over to help them, but her feet start sinking in as well. Turning back to look at Trixie, she catches a last glimpse of her hand, as it's the last to sink into the earth.

"NOOO!" screams Ivory as she wakes up in her bed.

Ivory lays in her bed for a while, unable to fall back to sleep. *There's no point in going back to sleep anyway*, she thinks to herself, watching the first rays of sun start to peek through her window. Instead of just lying in bed for the next hour or so, Ivory reaches under her bed and pulls out her memory book. She had been writing in it every other night or so, just recording everything that was happening. As she begins writing down her most recent dream, she realizes something. The name, Marina, and the girl herself...Ivory had in fact seen her before – on one of the posters of the missing children.

I guess it makes sense that I would dream of her; I can't get those poor children out of my mind, thinks Ivory. But then, the more she thinks about it, Ivory realizes that seeing that girl on the posters was not the first time she'd seen her. Ivory looks back down at her book, flipping to a few entries prior to this one. The day she was put in the hospital, the day she had gotten hurt, she'd had another dream. In fact, that dream was very similar to this recent one. As Ivory looks for the specific memory, her hands start to lightly shake.

There's no way; I know that I'm just imagining it...it's not actually possible... she thinks to herself, trying to calm down.

"A beautiful blonde-haired, blue-eyed young girl. Too young. With a little spot on the left side of her neck, although I didn't get close enough to see it..."

Ivory shoots up in her bed, arm hair standing on edge.

"No, no, no...no way. There's no way..." she talks to herself, flipping to the next page.

"The other boy, he looked young, but he was definitely not as young as the other girl. He was probably more around my age. He was dark-skinned and dark-haired, but had the most striking eyes. One brown, and the other...crystal blue."

Ivory looks up from her book. "Tersk..." she whispers his name. She remembers his name from the posters. She quickly closes her memory book. She knows that if she reads another description, she will lose her mind.

Dear God, please, what is happening to me? This is not possible, it's not...people will think I'm crazy. Maybe I am, maybe I'm going crazy.

Ivory holds herself and rocks back and forth, lost in her head. She stays like that for a few minutes, after which she takes a deep breath and decides to just finish off her current entry and hide her memory book out of sight.

As Ivory signs her name at the bottom of the page, she closes her eyes and thinks about Marina and what she'd said. The look in her eyes, the intensity of it, when she'd said those final words…

One of Ivory's feet starts going numb, as she'd been crossing her legs for a while. She stands up, still deep in thought, before walking over to her dresser. As she prepares to close her book and stash it safely between her clothes, she looks down, and immediately drops it to the floor. She brings her shaking hands to her chest to contain her wildly beating heart. She feels the heat rise up from her legs, up through her neck, to her face, before she blacks out.

- - -

"He…Hello? Hey! Is anyone there?" he yells groggily, confused.

"Ah!" he winces, touching the side of his throbbing head.

"Oh my God…there's so much blood. Someone please! I'm bleeding, please! HELP ME!" yells Yuri.

- - -

"Hey, sorry I couldn't get here sooner; what happened?" asks Sevastyan, walking into Ivory's room.

"Her mom said she found her passed out on the floor a little after sunrise," replies Sparrow from the end of Ivory's bed.

"What happened to her? Is she hurt?!" Sevastyan asks as he walks up to Ivory, examining her face and head.

"No, her mother said it's to be expected after the head injury. Don't you remember her telling us the same thing at the hospital?" replies Sparrow in a tired voice.

Sevastyan sighs, shaking his head.

"I remember what she said, Sparrow. It's just so weird; she's been doing so well these past few days…and she looked amazing at dinner yesterday too," chimes in Flora from the other end of Ivory's room.

"Honestly, I think the stress from current events has been taking a toll on her. I was talking to her yesterday when we were making the flower crowns and she told me she'd been having a hard time sleeping at night," says Fauna next to her sister on the floor.

"Post-traumatic stress," says Sevastyan.

"Mmhmm," agrees Sparrow.

Ivory slowly starts moving her head, and then hands. Her eyes start to open, and she turns her head to her right to look at Sevastyan.

"Hey! Look who's finally awake!" he says with a sigh of relief.

Ivory smiles back at her friend.

"Hey, you! We need to stop meeting like this, do you understand?!" laughs Sparrow from the end of Ivory's bed.

"Hey, it's not my fault!" exclaims Ivory. "I blame it on the post-traumatic stress…" she winks at Sevastyan.

Everyone laughs.

"Well, looks like she's fine to me," says Fauna, getting up off the floor.

"Hey, should we tell her mom she's ok?" asks Sevastyan, looking around.

"Her mom's at the Healing Clinic. I need to go and get my stitches checked out, so Healer Skye told me to bring her with me when I go. You can drop us off at the clinic, can't you, Sevastyan? Just in case she passes out again on the way or something," laughs Flora nervously.

"Yes, of course, it's not far from where I need to be, anyway," replies Sevastyan with a wink. "And what about you two?" he asks, turning to Fauna and Sparrow. "Are you coming along?"

"No, we're actually going to stay here with the girls; they can't be alone," replies Sparrow.

"Well…I personally think I can handle my sisters; I'm pretty responsible…" chimes in Hayden from the doorway, popping her head into the room.

Everyone laughs at the unexpected Hayden.

"Hey, bro, you okay?" Hayden asks Ivory.

"Yeah, I'm fine, bro," laughs Ivory.

"Ok, good," replies Hayden. "Just so you know, you're literally the most dramatic sick person ever! Like, you actually passed out. Like, you fainted… who faints?! If you're doing this to get out of chores though, I give you props, because that's super smart…"

"Oh my God, Hayden, I am not fainting on purpose," laughs Ivory, shaking her head.

"Okay, if you say so. Anyway, Mama's waiting for you at the clinic, worried, so you should go soon. I'll be with the girls. Later!" says Hayden as she walks away.

"Well, you heard her. Time to get up," laughs Sevastyan incredulously.

"What do you guys think; do you think I'm a good actress?" teases Ivory as she slowly gets out of her bed with the help of Sevastyan.

"Hmmm…no, I don't think so. I mean, maybe to other people. But I feel like we would know if you were up to something," replies Sparrow.

"Oh, is that so?" laughs Ivory. "I guess we'll see, won't we…" she says in a mysterious tone.

"Oh please, along with my sister, you're the last person that would be up to something," snorts Fauna.

"Hey!" exclaims Flora, punching her sister on the arm.

"What?! We all know it's true!" exclaims Fauna, rubbing her arm where Flora punched her.

"You two are kind of like…teacher's pets? Is that the term? But like, not with just teachers, with everyone. You always do the 'right thing,'" she says, using her fingers to make quotations around the words.

"Hmmm… have you ever thought about doing the right thing, even though it's technically the wrong thing…" Ivory shakes her head and smiles. "You know what, never mind. I need to change really quick, so if you don't mind, I need a few minutes of alone time, please," she says.

"You sure you'll be ok alone, Ive?" Asks Flora.

"Yes, I'll be right out, love. You guys go ahead," replies Ivory.

Everyone leaves the room; Sevastyan closes the door on his way out. Ivory swiftly throws on the first pair of clothes she can see and takes a small bookbag out. She looks around the room, quickly locating her memory book half-sticking out from underneath her dresser. It must have been there from when she'd dropped it a few hours earlier. She stuffs the book in her bag and tosses an empty bottle of medicine in there as well, in case anyone asks questions. She takes a moment to sit on her bed to take a few deep breaths when an idea crosses her mind. She takes out her memory book and quickly writes:

There's someone, something, out there taking people. I have a hunch, but it's a dangerous one. I need to look further into the matter before I can say anything for sure. But if I'm right, everything will change. Something big is happening here; something bigger than all of us…I'm not going to stand around, though. I will not fall under the spell. It feels like…like I've been sleeping this whole time. And It feels like I'm finally starting to wake up.

Ivory gasps at her choice of words.

"Wake up, Ivory…"

She quickly signs her name at the bottom of the page, but instead of putting her full name, she only uses her initials. After all, if anyone found this page…she didn't want to think that far ahead just yet.

"Okay guys, let's head out; I feel really bad making my mom wait and worry," says Ivory as she puts her shoes on.

"Alright, we'll be here. We'll see you when you get back," replies Sparrow, giving Ivory a quick hug before she heads out.

As Flora walks into the clinic, Ivory looks around for a staircase that could lead to the basement.

"Hey, Flora, why don't you go ahead and do what you have to do, and I'll go find my mom," says Ivory, still looking around.

"I actually don't mind waiting for you; I'm not in any rush, really," replies Flora.

"Oh no, please…I umm…I have a few things I need to do around here. I need to get a refill on my medication, I need to use the restroom…trust me, I'm going to be a while. How about we each do what we need to do, and then meet up on the benches outside next to the flower garden when we're done," says Ivory, hoping Flora will take the bait.

"Alright, that sounds fair. It is more time-effective to split up," laughs Flora. "Okay, I will see you in a bit, then." She waves as she makes her way to her mother's office.

Ivory waits until Flora disappears, then heads the other way. She could swear that she had seen a staircase in the eastern side of the building. As she looks around, she spots a door with an exit sign.

"Yes!"

She opens the door, finding the staircase behind it. She quickly starts making her way down to the basement, where the Records Room is located. She hesitates a moment outside the door, listening, making sure that no one is actually in the room, before slowly opening the door and making her way in.

She leaves the door slightly ajar as to not make too much noise on her way out. Turning now to look at the room, she is shocked at the sheer size of just this one room. She could swear that this room is bigger than the library; it definitely has more file shelves and cabinets than any other library. Ivory's breath quickens as her heart starts to race a bit faster. She is both overwhelmed and on a very tight schedule. She has no more than ten minutes at the most to find the files before she'll be noticed missing.

"Oh my God...think...where would they be?" she asks herself as she starts running around, trying to figure out the organization of the files.

The records room holds the file of everyone who was born in the tribe, lived in the tribe, or even died in the tribe. Everyone has a record...Ivory also had a hunch that there would be records of the people taken, as their files would have been sent along with the letter explaining the kidnappings. It would only make sense in case the people were to be found. The warriors would need those files to identify the people. The only question now is, under what category do these files fall? Are they filed by last name, like the rest? Surely not; that would be too much of a hassle for the warriors. Ivory briskly makes her way around the aisles of shelves, taking note of the filing pattern. She stops for a minute to think.

Alright, I'm only on the letter D right now, and if I keep going, I'm just going to work my way through the alphabet. There was nothing before the letter A...but if there is a special or different type of filing system, it will probably be after the letter Z...

Ivory sprints for it. She only has about three minutes left, and the room is just too big. She makes her way to the other side of the room, stopping as she reaches the last shelf.

"Okay, okay, okay...Zx, Zy, Zz...well hello, what's this?" she asks herself as she gets to a box of files on the lowest panel of the shelf. The box is un-marked, but this is Ivory's last chance. She opens up the first file and is met with the picture of a boy she'd never seen before. Right under the boy's name, in bold letters, is written "Missing."

She puts the first file down and opens another. This one makes Ivory pause for a moment, because she knows the boy's name before she even looks at it on the paper...Tersk. As she is almost out of time, Ivory closes Tersk's file and sets it down with the rest. She quickly takes off her book bag, opens it up, and puts all of the files inside.

Oh no, I hope Flora doesn't notice how much bigger my bag just got.

She puts her memory book and the empty medicine bottle on top of the files, just in case anyone asks questions. Ivory quickly makes her way out of the room, closes the door, and runs up the stairs. She opens the Exit door as slightly as she can, making sure that no one is around first. Once she sees that she's in the clear, she makes her way out. She tries to make her way out of the corridor as fast as she can, almost crashing into her mother as she turns the corner.

"Mama!" she exclaims, trying to hide how startled she actually is.

"Ivory, what are you doing here? When did you come?" asks Constantina, taking her daughter's face in her hands and examining her eyes.

"I, umm…I came here with Flora; I was looking for you. I'm feeling much better, honestly. I think I just jumped out of bed too quickly, causing the blood to rush to my head and whatnot…" rambles Ivory.

"Honey, I told you to take it easy. You need to start listening to me…" sighs Ivory's mother.

"I'm listening. I promise," replies Ivory with a nervous smile.

Her mother looks her over suspiciously. Ivory knows that if anyone would notice something weird about her, it would be Constantina. Sparrow once said that she has a sixth sense and that her mother does too. They always seem to know what's going on, no matter how hard you try to hide it.

"Anyway…do you know where I can find Flora? I don't know…oh wait. Haha, never mind. I completely forgot I told her to meet me outside on the benches. Wow," Ivory shakes her head in disbelief at the momentary memory loss.

"Alright, you go straight home, understand?" replies Constantina, still looking Ivory over suspiciously. "I made lunch for you, your sisters, and your friends. So please make sure everyone eats, including yourself."

"Healer Skye! We need you at the delivery room; she's crowning!" yells another healer across the hallway.

"Alright, I'm coming!" Constantina yells back. She gives Ivory a quick kiss on the forehead before she turns around and quickly makes her way into the delivery room.

Ivory stands in her spot for a while, taking deep breaths, trying to lower her heart rate back to normal speed. Once she feels a little more relaxed, she makes her way out to Flora, who's already waiting where she was told.

"Hey, how did it go?" asks Ivory, walking up to Flora and taking a seat next to her.

"Well, they said I'm almost fully healed, but they want to wait one more day before they take out the stitches. So I'm going to need to come back tomorrow for that," replies Flora with a shrug.

"I'll come with you, then," offers Ivory quickly.

"Really? Are you sure? It's kind of a long walk; I don't want to make you come back here for nothing," says Flora.

"Oh no, I actually need to come back too. They, umm…they didn't have my medication ready for me, so I need to come back and get it," says Ivory, trying to think of something on the spot. In fact, she needed to come back to return the files. They might not be missed for one night, but more than that, and someone might notice the box of files missing.

"Alright then, that's perfect! Do you think you're up to ride to my place and both make our way here by horse? It would definitely be quicker…but only if you feel better! We can totally walk too; I have no problem with that…"

Ivory laughs at the always-thoughtful Flora. She takes her hand and the two start making their way home.

"You know that I love you, right?" asks Ivory, laughing. "I'm so lucky that I get to call you my best friend."

"Of course! If I had another twin, or I guess in that case it would technically be called a triplet…you know what I mean. It would totally be you!" laughs Flora, holding onto Ivory's arm tightly.

The girls giggle and laugh all the way home – except for one moment. As they pass through the tribal center, right off of the main road Ivory notices two people huddled next to a tree. The first person she didn't know. But judging by his clothes, and just the way he held himself, he was definitely an Oak. The other person, however, she could spot from a kilometer away. If his perfectly coifed blond hair and fancy clothes weren't enough, his demeanor, even from far away, was a dead giveaway – Cassius.

As Flora chatters on, Ivory slows down her pace a little bit to try and catch as much of the exchange as she can. Unfortunately, she's not close enough to hear anything. As she's about to give up, the Oak man reaches into his pocket and takes something out. Ivory can't see what it is, but he gives it to Cassius, who puts it in his pocket. The Oak then gets really close to Cassius, almost in an intimidating manner. But Cassius holds his ground and replies to the Oak with a demeanor that Ivory thinks is just as fierce. The two keep eye contact for a few seconds before the Oak backs down, turns around, and walks away.

Cassius stands in his spot for a few moments, fixing his hair, making sure that his shirt is tucked into his white pants properly. He reaches into his pocket, the one that had whatever the Oak had given him. But he doesn't take anything out. He keeps his hand in his pocket as he walks away, not noticing that Ivory had seen the entire exchange.

Ivory looks at the time – midnight. *Everyone should be fast asleep,* she thinks to herself before getting out of bed. She had been waiting for this moment all day long. It wasn't safe to take the files out with people around. Even after dinner, anyone could have walked into her room at any time, especially her mother. So she had decided to wait until everyone slept before doing anything.

Ivory quietly sneaks into the kitchen and grabs the lantern. She could turn on her brighter bedroom light, but she doesn't want to take any chances. Once in her room, she turns on the lamp and starts laying the files out on the floor, making half a circle around her. There are about twenty files, all of which are just from the Northern Assimilian Tribe. Well, all but one, as she discovers. Someone had put Yuri's file in the box with the other missing people's.

Ivory starts getting nervous as she opens the first file – Marina's file. The file is only a few pages long. It starts off with the girl's name and age.

She's only ten years old…right in between Diana and Anya.

Ivory's heart breaks the more she reads about the girl, but she reminds herself that she doesn't have time to dwell on the details…at least, not these specific details. She moves on to the second and finally the third page. At the bottom of the third page is a section for unique traits. Under this section is one trait, along with a picture of it; this is what Ivory had been looking for. She takes out her memory book and opens it to the last dream entry she had written. She looks at the drawing she'd made at the bottom of the paper subconsciously and holds it up next to the picture.

"Perfect match."

Ivory takes a deep breath as she starts going through every single file. She can feel her face getting warmer by the moment as her stomach drops deeper into her gut. It takes her about twenty more minutes go through the majority of the files before she is fully convinced that her theory is a reality. As the truth starts to really sink in, she sets the files down and stands up to pace around her room.

She feels sick to her stomach, like she might vomit or even pass out again. But most of all, she is terrified. What will she do with this new knowledge?

Warrior Zlato had pleaded with the tribe to come forward with information, so maybe I can go to him with it? But then, I have to really think this through...what if they don't believe me? What if they think I'm crazy...I mean, I really don't have proof; it still is a theory, isn't it? And this theory – I'm pretty sure it falls under the category of treason. So I could end up dead, along with everyone else who's been taken. Even if I tell them what I think and they believe me, how will they make it in time to save everyone? It would be too conspicuous. No...I can't; I won't. No one can know about this. No one but me.

Ivory quickly puts all of the files back in the order she had taken them and stuffs them into her book bag. She sits on her bed with her memory book and a pencil and starts to write:

In my previous entry (I've stopped counting entries), I confessed to having a dangerous hunch as to who is taking the missing people. I will now leave a full confession of my theory and how I can prove it...

I believe, with reasonable purpose, that Nazar Yilan II is responsible for these kidnappings. I have stolen, borrowed, the files of the missing people. And I have found one thing in common with all of them – a birthmark. With the exception of two, everyone is documented to have an interesting birthmark somewhere on their body, all of the exact same design – two intersecting suns. This is the same design that I have personally seen on a pendant around Nazar's neck, as well as one of his people. I do believe that everyone that works for Nazar wears the same golden pendant as some kind of sign, as his followers. However, they hide it. Nazar wears his pendant out in the open. But along with his other chains and pendants, it only gets lost.

I don't think that Nazar is personally grabbing people out of their homes, but I definitely think that he has some help. It only makes sense, that every time he has been at a tribe in the past year, people have gone missing. And how does one coincidentally forget to inform a whole tribe that the one before it was attacked?

I cannot say these words to anyone, for an accusation like this against a tribal Elder...it could get me killed. And when I'm dead, who will help those poor people; the children? My heart breaks as I write this entry, but I know what has to be done. There is no other way. The whole tribe might be fast asleep right now, but I am finally wide awake.

Signed, I.S.

Chapter 15

Ivory lies in her bed, eyes wide open. She should have been asleep hours ago. But as dawn slowly starts creeping up, she can't seem to get comfortable enough to sleep. It's so hot and humid; she feels like she's suffocating. Her racing mind isn't helping, either. Cracking open a window would not help this time; it would only make it worse, as the mosquitoes would find their way into her room and attack.

Ugh, I should have stolen a sedative or something, from the clinic. Maybe then I could fall asleep...

LOUD BANG. GIRL SCREAMS IN THE DISTANCE

Ivory shoots up from her bed.

No, no, no...this can't be happening, not now...

She runs out of her bedroom toward the front door, but she's not alone this time. Her parents and sisters are all awake, her mother holding up a lantern and her father putting on his riding boots.

"You all heard it too?!" she asks, breathing hard.

"Yes, we did. Your father is going to see what's going on. Something is very wrong here."

"Father, let me go with you. Please!" pleads Ivory.

"No! It's too dangerous, Ivory! You have to stay here with your sisters!" refuses her mother.

"But Mother, Father, please!! I must go! I can't just stay here, you know that!"

"Fine. But hurry up, we need to go quick. Before the warriors make their way here and lock us in," says Nadi.

"Are you serious?! It's dangerous!" replies Constantina.

"I know…but it's good for Ivory. The world, this tribe, it's not the safe little bubble we thought we lived in anymore. As the eldest sister, she needs to know how to protect you all if anything happens to me."

Ivory's mother huffs. She knows her husband is right, but that doesn't make the situation any less stressful.

In the meantime, Ivory finishes putting her boots on over her pajama pants. It's so hot out, she doesn't bother putting on anything over her tank top.

As she starts making her way out after her father, Constantina catches her arm.

"Be careful, do you understand?! Don't let your father out of your sight; make sure you're on his flank at all times," says Constantina to her daughter.

"Yes, Mother, I promise I'll be careful," replies Ivory.

As Ivory starts making her way to the little arena on the side of the house, her father comes around the corner on his horse, with another for her.

"Hurry and get on. No time for saddles tonight; we're riding bareback," he says.

Ivory grabs onto the horse's mane and throws her right leg over his back, pulling herself up. In seconds, Ivory and Nadi are riding toward the sound. This time, Ivory has a premonition of whose house they were headed too. As her father prepares to turn toward the direction of the tribal center, Ivory yells over to him to follow her.

As Nadi prepares to question their new course, he stops. Out in the distance lies a scene from what seems to be a horror film. A little house, one side completely broken open. Windows, glass, shattered on the ground. Blood, bright red, splattered all across the road. Parents holding each other and weeping beside their home. Warriors scattered, trying to piece the scene together.

Ivory's heart sinks into the lowest depths of her stomach. She'd known where to go because she had known who was taken. She'd hoped that for once, she would be completely proven wrong, but she wasn't. As she and her father reach the scene of the crime, she can't bear to look at the parents crying on the ground. She looks away, but their screams fill the air as reality sets in more and more by the second. Their only child was just taken. And they don't know if she's alive or dead.

And to think Trixie had introduced Ivory to her parents just a few days ago.

"Trixie..." whispers Ivory, her voice unable to surface.

Nadi goes straight to the source for his questions.

"Silver, what's happening?"

"The girl that lives here, she was taken. Whoever took her didn't want to use the front door. Her bedroom windows and that whole wall of the house is destroyed."

"Did they use explosives to break down the side of the house? I feel like that would be a lot of work to just end up killing someone."

"No, there are no signs of gunpowder or explosives at all. Not even a hint. It's more like if a boulder knocked it out. But from the inside of the house..."

"What do you mean? How is that even possible?" asks Nadi.

"Inside the bedroom is most of the shattered glass. And outside where the wall used to stand is the rubble. And it all happened really quick, in less than a minute. The parents ran to the girl's bedroom as soon as they heard the window shatter, followed by the wall being knocked down. She'd already been outside screaming when they got to her door. She was long gone after that."

"So they broke the window to get in, and broke the entire wall to get out."

"It, not they."

"What do you mean??"

"I mean, there's only one pair of footprints, Nadi. One. They're big, but they look human."

"What are you saying, Silver? There's a person out there knocking down walls with their bare hands?"

"I don't know, Nadi. I don't even know if this thing is even human. The footprints are similar, but like I said, they're too big. If you use them to estimate the dimensions of this thing, assuming it's human, it would be as big as the side of the house," replies Silver, looking incredulously at the rubble.

Nadi shakes his head, sighing at the horrid predicament in front of him. He speaks with Silver for a few more minutes, then eventually makes his way back to his daughter.

Ivory sits in silence, staring out into the darkness.

"Hey, did you know her?" asks Nadi solemnly.

"She, umm... she was my friend," whispers Ivory, a tear betraying her. She quickly wipes it away.

Nadi rides up to his daughter, putting a hand on her shoulder.

"Let's go home," he whispers back.

They ride home in silence, moonlight guiding their way back.

"Thank you all for making your way here so early this morning for this emergency assembly," starts Head Warrior Zlato, sounding very tired. "I am going to assume that most of you have already heard the news. Early this morning, about three hours past midnight, a home was targeted and another member of this tribe was taken. Trixie Stone was fast asleep when someone, or something, broke in through her window and took her. As news travels around here pretty quickly, I am sure that a lot of you have already heard about the large quantity of blood found at the scene of the kidnapping. However, we have been testing samples of the blood, so we can now conclude that the majority of it did not belong to the girl. We have also compared the blood samples from this incident to that of the other kidnapping, and the samples are identical. As of this moment, my warriors are out in the forest with our trained wolves, tracking this thing. I would like to believe that all of you are smart enough to know not to set foot out of this tribe without directly coming through me first. However, I have put out extra warriors to guard the gates at all times. We appreciate your cooperation. Thank you," finishes Warrior Zlato before turning around and leaving.

The grumbling crowd starts to sound like a swarm of bees as people start to panic. The annual moon festival, and graduation, happen in two days. But how can they even happen with current events looming over everyone's heads?

"May I have your attention, please?" shouts one of the tribal Elders, standing up and approaching the people. The crowd falls silent immediately, pointing all of their attention to the Elder speaking.

"There once lived a beautiful writer," starts the old man. "She inspired people, changed lives, with her words. To this day, some of her words live, passed down from generation to generation. One of my favorite quotes of hers goes something like this; even on the stormiest of nights, a small spark can turn into a lightning that illuminates the entire night sky."

Elder Elias smiles to himself, then looks up to the sky. He watches the birds fly, only closing his eyes when a cool breeze makes its way through the silent crowd. Elder Elias takes his time, choosing his next words wisely as his people wait intently.

"I am old," he starts again, looking back at his people. "I have seen much in my days; things that might lead one to lose all hope to despair. But her words, they got me through it.

Sadness, darkness, hatred...we have the power to overcome them all, if only we chose to do so. Love will always trump hate. So I ask you, my people, to choose love above all. Do not let fear or hatred taint your pure hearts. Love your people and love yourselves. Only together can we truly defeat the evil out there. I would not be standing here if I did not truly believe so myself. So I stand as your witness, as well as your example. After a rainy day, the sun always shines. After night, we have day. The sun will shine again, and tomorrow will be a new day. Do not let evil smother the flames in your hearts; breathe, live on. The annual moon festival, the celebration of life, is closing in on us all. We shall celebrate this one with more passion and fervor than any that have passed. I thank you all for your courage, and may you all blessed be," finishes the Elder.

Instead of making his way back to the other Elders, Elder Elias walks forward and places his right hand on the shoulder of the first person standing in front of him. The man mirrors the move by placing his right hand on the left shoulder of Elder Elias. Silently, every person in the crowd reaches their right hand forward, holding onto the shoulder of the person in front of them, making a weave of arms, connecting everyone together. And although the moment is an especially sad one for Ivory, the connection brings with it a spark; a spark of hope. The spark moves through the silent crowd, and everyone feels it. They will be alright as a people, and they will live on protecting each other, just as they have in the past. Elder Elias slowly lets go of the man's shoulder, thanking him in the process; the rest of the crowd follows. And just like that, the people start making their way out, heading back to where they need to be.

"Are you going to be alright, love?" whispers Sparrow.

"I will be," whispers back Ivory, giving her best friend's hand a squeeze.

Ivory, Sparrow, Flora, Fauna, and Sevastyan all make their way back onto the main road, walking in silence. Since the assembly could not be held at the tribal center due to preparations, it was held in front of the school. As the gang reaches a fork in the road, Ivory finally speaks up.

"Well, Flora and I need to head back to the Healing Clinic. So we'll be heading this way," says Ivory, pointing to one of the paths.

Sevastyan walks up to Ivory, embracing her in his arms. Flora hugs Sparrow goodbye, as she will not see her for the rest of the day.

"I'll pass by your place later; we need to talk," whispers Sevastyan in Ivory's ear.

"Alright," whispers Ivory back.

Sparrow and Fauna both give Ivory a hug before they start down the other path with Sevastyan, making their way home.

Flora and Ivory's walk to the Healing Clinic is a silent ordeal. The two hold hands, but no words come to either of them. When they finally reach the clinic, Ivory agrees with Flora to meet up when they are both done.

"If I get my medication quickly, I'll come look for you," says Ivory.

"Okay, sounds great. I'll see you in a bit," replies Flora, turning to leave.

An exhausted Ivory starts walking in the other direction, only quickly checking to see if anyone sees her going through the exit door and down the stairs. She pauses for a brief moment before entering the Records Room and closes the door halfway behind her. Once she reaches the end of the room with the empty box, she sets down her book bag and takes out all of the files. She puts them back in the box in the same order she had taken them out. She can't help but sigh in the process.

What can I actually do, though? I wouldn't even know where to begin. I think I'm way in over my head with all of this. I can't keep this a secret to myself anymore; I need to tell someone. Sevastyan...I'll tell Sevastyan. I trust him more than anyone, and maybe he can help me out, tell me what I can do. Alright then, that's what I'll do; I'll tell Sevastyan when I see him later.

Ivory puts the box of files back in its place and makes her way out of the room. It doesn't take long for Ivory to find Flora, but she is surprised to find her friend still waiting to get her stitches out.

"You've been waiting here for a while; when will it be your turn?" asks Ivory.

"Flora Ilios," calls out a healer.

"Oh, well, there you go, it's my turn now," replies Flora, stunned at the perfect timing.

Ivory goes into the room with Flora for moral support. She also doesn't have anything better to do. The healer takes a few minutes explaining to Flora how to take care of her wound once the stitches are removed before asking her to pull her shirt up so he can take a look at it. Flora, sitting on a bed, pulls her shirt up, revealing her abdomen. A large piece of gauze covers the entire wound and some of the skin around it. Now, although Ivory does not personally want to become a healer, she has always been fascinated with surgeries and pretty much anything that involves putting people back together. So she leans in closer to see the healer as he carefully takes the large bandage off of Flora.

Ivory freezes…

Her mouth drops open as her eyes look on in utter disbelief. Her heart, beating violently, feels like it might burst through her chest. It takes her a moment to shake the humming sound in her ears, as it drowns out any other sound trying to go in.

"Ive, Ive…Ivory…" says Flora, waving her hand at her friend to get her attention.

Ivory looks up and sees Flora's mouth moving, but she can't hear the words. She shakes her head quickly, trying to get her ears to work. She looks back at Flora, some sound starting to get through again.

"Ivory, is it bad?!" asks Flora, too afraid to look down.

"No, no…no, it's not. It's not bad. It's, umm…" Ivory struggles to find her words. "Flora, I didn't know you had a birthmark," says Ivory, looking at the two intersecting suns on Flora's ribcage.

"Oh, yes," replies Flora with a wave of the hand, dismissing the birthmark comment. "But the cut, it's not that bad, is it? I mean, your face, it looks like you've seen a ghost, it's kind of freaking me out…"

"No, Flora, look down, it's gotten a lot better…how long have you had this birthmark? I mean, like, I'm guessing you were born with it, but maybe you weren't, so I don't know…"

"Oh yes, I was born with it," replies Flora, a little engrossed in the stitches getting pulled out of her abdomen.

"It's, umm…it's a really interesting birthmark," says Ivory, clearing her throat. "I have a question; have you ever told anyone about it? Like, do you discuss it with people? Because you've never personally mentioned it to me," says Ivory.

"Oh no, it's definitely not something that comes up in most conversations. Although it's really cool because Fauna and I have it on the exact same spot but on the opposite halves of our body. It's kind of like a mirror image," laughs Flora.

Ivory chokes on her saliva.

"Hey, are you alright? There's water right next to you over there," jumps in the healer, pointing to the water on the table behind Ivory.

Ivory turns around and pours herself some water. She tries steadying herself, but her shaking hand spills some of the water onto the table. Ivory takes a sip, but her throat feels like it has a ball of wool blocking anything from going in or out. She takes a quick deep breath before turning around to look at Flora again.

"You and Fauna both have the birthmark?" she asks.

"Yup, we sure do. Why?" replies Flora, oblivious to the entire situation.

"Oh, no reason. Umm…I just remembered something, Flora, I need to go see my mother. Yes, I have to go see her. I will just meet you outside, okay?"

"Alright," replies Flora before Ivory dashes out of the room.

Ivory runs down the hallway, knowing that she probably shouldn't draw too much attention to herself, but she can't wait. There is no time. Flora and Fauna might not have told people about their birthmarks. They also have their birthmarks placed strategically, where no one will ever really see them. But their records…Ivory is sure that it's on their records.

Ivory had been doing a lot of thinking. People like Marina, and even Yuri, who has his birthmark on his wrist…they were easy to find. But for a lot of the other people taken, their birthmarks were very hard to identify. The only way they would have been discovered is through their files.

As Ivory reaches the exit door, she stops to take a deep breath before heading down.

The Oaks have been down here. That's the only way they could have known about Trixie. I still don't know where her birthmark is, or if she has one. But if she does have one, which is more probable, this is where they would have found it…

Ivory listens intently, making sure no one is in the Records Room before she heads in, leaving the door slightly ajar. She makes her way down the right side of the big room until she gets to the letter A. From there, she runs back the way she came until she finds the letter I.

Ii, Ij, Ik, Il…ok, it should be here somewhere. Ilios, Ilios, Ilios…where are you…

"AHA! Found it!" whispers Ivory to herself.

She quickly pulls out the two files, one for Flora and the other for Fauna. She opens Flora's file to the last page, and there she finds it, under the "unique traits" category. Instead of taking the whole file, Ivory takes the last page, along with the picture provided. She quickly does the same thing for Fauna, stuffing the pages in her bag. As she puts the files back, a thought crosses Ivory's mind.

Oh my God, what about my other friends? OH. MY. LORD. WHAT ABOUT MY SISTERS AND PARENTS? What if they have birthmarks that I just don't know about?!

Ivory starts making her way back to the letter A when she hears voices.

"Hey! What did I tell you?! You have to be more careful; you know what he'll do to you if you even flinch at the wrong time," says a man's voice.

"I know, I warned the kid; he shouldn't be a problem...hey, why is this door open? Hello!" screams the second man as he walks into the Records Room.

Ivory gets on the ground, holding her mouth shut as to not make any noises.

"Hey! Is anyone here?!" yells the second man again.

"Hey, dumbass, do you want them to find us here?!" says the first man in a quieter voice.

"Someone has been in here within the last thirty minutes, a girl. I can smell her perfume," spits the second man.

"It doesn't matter; she's gone. It was probably one of the stupid healer women. We need to be quick, just grab the files and go," says the first man. "We'll come back later to finish looking through the files. You heard what master said. Destroy the pictures."

The two men continue talking as they make their way to the opposite side of the large room.

They're going to destroy the pictures of the birthmarks from the files in the box...

"What about the two from this tribe?" asks the second man.

"I gave them to master; he's probably already destroyed them," replies the first man as he ruffles through the files in the box.

Shoot, even if I go tell someone now, they won't believe me. The main part of the evidence is the pictures. The description doesn't do much in describing the birthmarks. Ugh, great...

"Ok, good," replies the second man. "How many more letters do we have to go through? This is literally the worst job ever. I can't wait till we leave this dump of a tribe."

"You started with the letter A, and you just ended with the letter H. And I started working my way from the letter Z, and I just finished the letter L. So if I'm right, we just have the letters I, J, and K left," replies the first man.

Ivory gasps, but no sound comes out through the hands covering her mouth.

151

"Ugh, I can't believe we've only found two so far," huffs the second man. "Do you remember how many we found up in the North?"

"Yeah, well, not every tribe can be special," laughs the first man, making the other man laugh. "I'm done; let's get out of here before we get caught. We can come back after dark."

Sparrow Avere, Sevastyan Lanza, and my family, the Skyes…All of these letters have been checked, and they didn't find anything.

Ivory's tense body relaxes a little bit. There is a bit of hope after all.

The only letters they still have to check…I, J, and K…if I had caught Flora's birthmark any later, the two might have ended up being in a lot of trouble. I need to get out of here. I need to hide these pictures and descriptions where they will never be found. And I definitely can't talk about this to Sevastyan anymore. It's too messy. I'm going to have to find my way in; I just need a good opportunity…

Ivory waits around for another five minutes before quietly making her way to the door. She turns to look back at the rows of files on the shelves. If she actually had time, she would have loved to go through the remaining files and make sure no one else would get hurt.

One thing that the students had learned in school is that no one is to ever get left behind or forgotten. The only exception to this rule is if the greater population is in danger. If Ivory gets caught in the Records Room, it's over, both for her and the people that need her.

As Ivory makes her way out of the clinic, she knows that she's ultimately made the right decision. But she knows that if someone else goes missing, it will be her fault.

Chapter 16

As Ivory shuffles around the kitchen, putting away clean dishes, someone knocks on the front door. Ivory sets down her dish towel to open the door for Sevastyan.

"Hey, come in," she says, letting him in the house.

"Hey, thanks," he replies, taking his shoes off before walking in. "What are you up to? I hope I'm not interrupting anything important," he starts, taking a seat at the table in the kitchen.

"No, you're fine. I'm just cleaning up a bit around here," says Ivory as she finishes putting the rest of the dishes away.

"Are you here alone, or are the girls here?" asks Sevastyan, looking around.

"Oh, they're here, but they're busy in their rooms. I don't think they'll be coming in here, if that's what you mean."

"Ok, good."

Having finished putting everything away, Ivory takes a seat across her friend.

"Well, you said that you needed to tell me something earlier. What is it?" she asks curiously.

Sevastyan takes a deep breath, pausing for a few brief moments before starting.

"I ran into Warrior Emile earlier this morning, before the assembly..." he finally says.

"Oh wow, I totally forgot about him. How is he doing? The last time I saw him was when he took us to the hidden beach…" replies Ivory, thinking back to that beautiful, peaceful moment. It seems like it was so long ago.

"Well, he's as good as one can imagine, given the circumstances…" says Sevastyan, bringing Ivory back to the present day. "He was one of the first warriors on the scene at Trixie's house."

"NO WAY!" gasps Ivory, shocked.

"Yes. Honestly, he said he was alright, but I could see that he was shaken a bit from the whole thing."

Ivory sighs, remembering the scene from earlier in the day.

"I forgot to tell you guys this morning…I was there too, with my father. I didn't even notice Emile, the whole thing was just…too much," she says, laying her head on her crossed arms on the table.

"I knew you were there; Emile said he'd seen you. I didn't want to probe, though, because I know it must have been really hard to see. Trixie was our friend – all of us. But I know she meant the most to you. And I know she felt the same way about you. That's why…I need to tell you what I know – what Emile told me."

"I mean, I think I know how the story went; I overheard Silver talking to my father" says Ivory, looking up from the table. "Someone – something – broke in through Trixie's window, grabbed her, then broke through the wall, taking her along."

"Did Silver mention anything to your father about the blood…?" asks Sevastyan.

"No, we got there only a few minutes after the warriors. But Warrior Zlato talked about it at the assembly today."

"See, that's the thing, though," Sevastyan says, leaning in closer to Ivory. "He mentioned the blood, but not the weapon or what actually happened."

Ivory sits back upright in her chair, suddenly much more interested in the conversation. "Go on…"

"Emile said that they found a knife outside the house. A big kitchen knife, all bloody. And apparently, when they checked with the Stones to see if they'd ever seen it, Trixie's mother said that she had been missing that knife for the past few days," says Sevastyan.

"Okay, so the knife belonged to them, it was from the kitchen. So did the bad guy use it? I mean, if it was all bloody…"

"No, no…" starts Sevastyan, cutting Ivory off. "The blood on the knife wasn't Trixie's! Just like Zlato said this morning, most of the blood wasn't hers…Don't you see? She was defending herself!"

Ivory gasps as this new revelation. She had never thought of Trixie as one to defend herself; she was just too sweet. In fact, there were many occasions where other people had to defend Trixie…but not this time. Ivory feels something new, but she's not sure what it is. Pride?

"Trixie used the knife to defend herself! Oh my God…that's actually good to hear! I mean, it doesn't change the situation, but I don't know…I feel a little better knowing that she didn't just sit there doing nothing, you know?"

"Yes! But here's the thing…did you notice how I said that Trixie's mother had been missing the knife for a few days?" asks Sevastyan.

"Yes."

"And there is no way that Trixie would have had time to grab the knife from the kitchen…"

"Okay, go on."

"Well, Emile, along with a lot of other warriors, thinks that she had taken the knife days earlier to protect herself. Like, she knew that something was going to happen," finishes Sevastyan, eyes wide with disbelief.

Ivory's face mirrors Sevastyan's as the wheels in her head start to turn. She doesn't say anything as she waits for Sevastyan to finish saying everything he knows.

"So pretty much, Emile was asking me if I had recently spoken to Trixie and if she was ever acting weird. He thinks that she knew that something was going to happen to her. Or that she at least had an idea…I told him that I hadn't spoken to her as of recent, because that's the truth. So he told me to ask you because you're close. And because he saw you there," finishes Sevastyan.

"Umm…wow. I'm actually speechless right now. I don't really know what to say…" replies Ivory in disbelief. "I mean, yes, I have seen her around the past few days, and we do speak when we see each other. But none of our conversations have lasted more than ten minutes, and she'd seemed fine to me."

"That's what I told Emile. I told him that if you'd seen anything wrong with her, you would have spoken up and told us; you always do…" says Sevastyan as a matter of fact.

Ivory looks away, knowing that she doesn't actually live up to her friend's expectations. In fact, the first night that Ivory had met Trixie, Trixie hadn't been doing so well.

Actually, now that I think about it, it makes sense. If Trixie had a feeling that something bad was going to happen, it was probably the dreams that tipped her off. Maybe she had a feeling just like I did when she got taken...

"Anyway, I knew I had to tell you; you have a right to know. And I thought I should ask anyway, about if you ever saw Trixie acting weird, or just out of the ordinary in general," says Sevastyan, leaning back in his chair.

"Mhmm...no, I've never seen anything that would make me think, 'Wow, she's in trouble,'" replies Ivory, a little uncomfortable stretching the truth from her friend.

Sevastyan nods, then leans his head back and closes his eyes.

"I'm tired Ivory – mentally. Physically, I feel like I could demolish an army. But mentally...I wouldn't mind taking a hundred-year nap."

"Me too, Sev, me too..." agrees Ivory, lost in her own mind.

"Ivory," whispers a small voice from the kitchen door.

Ivory and Sevastyan lean over at the same time to look at the doorway.

"Hey Diana, come in. What do you want, love?" asks Ivory, taking her sister in her arms.

"I'm thirsty," whispers the girl in her sister's ear.

Ivory smiles, then gets up to fill up a glass a water for her sister. She pats Diana's hair as Diana drinks her water.

"Thank you," says Diana as she places her glass down on the counter.

"Hey, can I get a hug?" asks Ivory, arms open.

Diana embraces her sister, nuzzling her face into her sister's stomach. Ivory stands with her sister for a long minute, trying to live in the moment as long as possible. But soon enough, the moment ends.

"Go have fun with your sisters; I'll call you guys out for lunch in a little bit," says Ivory as she lets go of her sister.

"Okay, thanks Ive," replies Diana as she makes her way out of the kitchen.

"Do you want to stay for a bit longer and have some lunch, Sev?" asks Ivory, still standing.

"Oh, I would love to...but alas, he has much to get done before he graduates in two days," laughs Sevastyan as gets up to leave.

Ivory laughs at Sevastyan's impression.

"Unfortunately, she understands, as she procrastinates getting her chores done," she replies.

Shoes on, Sevastyan motions to Ivory to come in for a hug.

"Thank you for telling me; about Trixie, I mean," whispers Ivory into Sevastyan's shoulder.

"Of course, love, you know I would never keep something like that from you," he whispers back.

Ivory waves goodbye to her friend as he walks off, closing the door behind him. She can feel her eyes starting to water, as she feels extremely guilty for not telling him everything she knows.

It's for his own safety, she tries to convince herself. Still, one tear manages to escape the rim of her watery eyes.

As soon as Ivory's mother arrives back home, Ivory heads out towards the stables. She hasn't seen Thunder in a while, which is out of the ordinary. The walk is a long one, but Ivory appreciates the alone time to think. Once at the stables, she takes her horse out for a quick half-hour ride, cleans him up, then feeds him back at his stall.

"That's my good boy...I've missed you so much," coos Ivory as she brushes through Thunder's mane with her fingers.

"Sometimes I wish we could just ride right out of those gates...and never come back..." she whispers to her horse.

Thunder looks up from his hay, making eye contact with Ivory, and nudges her on the shoulder with his muzzle.

"I knew you would love the idea," smiles Ivory, planting a kiss on Thunder.

"Hey, fancy seeing you here," says a familiar voice from the other side of the stables.

Ivory turns around, spotting Cassius walking in with his horse Stallion. She remembers when she'd first heard what he named his horse. It was extremely ironic, as his horse was actually an Appaloosa. But she eventually grew to really love his name. It also helped that Stallion actually ended up running like an actual stallion.

"Hey, Cassius, it's been a while," replies Ivory.

The two make eye contact and smile at each other before Cassius turns to put his horse back in his stall. Ivory turns her attention back to Thunder as Cassius puts away his riding equipment and brings over a bale of hay for Stallion.

"They're great, aren't they?" he says, not looking away from his horse.

"They are," agrees Ivory with a smile.

"What made you fall in love with horses in the first place? I've always wanted to ask you, but I never really got the chance," says Cassius, glancing at Ivory from Stallion's stall.

Ivory is a little taken aback by the question. In reality, no one had ever asked her that question before.

"Well, I've never really thought about it, honestly; why I love them so much. I guess…I don't know; they're just so…peaceful. Like, sometimes I feel really bad that we bring them in, break them, and pretty much force them to be our slaves, in a way. Horses are meant to be wild and free. Actually, maybe that's why I love them so much…I envy them, their freedom."

"Hmm…I respect that. I think we all want some form of freedom – some of us more than others…" replies Cassius as he caresses his own horse.

Ivory continues caressing Thunder as she thinks about her answer. Maybe this is why she really wants to solve this problem on her own – a chance to leave, to go somewhere else. Maybe a chance at having the freedom she'd always dreamed of…

Ivory quickly finishes up with Thunder, takes a deep breath, and starts making her way to Cassius.

She stands right in front of Stallion's stall, looks Cassius in the eye, and says, "I want to go with you."

Cassius is both a bit startled and very confused. So Ivory says it again.

"I want to go with you."

"Come with me where?"

"Everywhere. Away from here."

Cassius is shocked.

"Take me with you and the Oaks and Nazar. I want to be one of you."

Cassius gets out of Stallion's stall so he can stand face to face with Ivory.

"I don't know what you're talking about Ivory; you're starting to sound a little cr…"

"I saw you," she interrupts him. "I saw you with the Oak in the trees. I saw the both of you talking and then he gave you something."

"Ivory, I think you're imagining things. That was probably someone else…"

"Oh yeah? What's this, then?" asks Ivory, reaching into Cassius's shirt, pulling out the gold necklace with the pendant hanging on the end.

"Hey!" exclaims Cassius, quickly hiding the pendant with his hand. "How do you…"

"Cassius! You don't need to lie to me. I know everything. Just like I know your father wouldn't let you go if you actually asked him," says Ivory in a matter of fact.

Cassius sighs, shaking his head.

"This girl…Ivory, do you know what you're asking? Do you actually want to leave your family, everything you know, behind?"

"Well, you're leaving everything behind, aren't you?"

"Ive, I don't have anything left for me here. I'm not leaving anything behind."

"You sure about that? What about Caius?"

This hits Cassius like a slap in the face. He turns his back to Ivory, takes a deep breath, then turns back.

"It's best for Caius if I leave now."

"Cassius, how could you say that? You are all he has. You are his everything, his life. How could it be better for you to leave him?"

"If you can't already tell, Ivory, I'm not the best role model for Caius," he says, eyes hard but heart burning for his younger brother.

"I think he might actually have a normal life, with friends and people who love him, if I leave."

"But he already has friends. And everyone loves him. After Seraphina…" Ivory's voice trails off. "…everyone took care of Caius like he was theirs. This tribe raised him and loves him."

"But he will always be the younger brother of Cassius Zlato, Ivory. Just like I will always be the first son of Magnus Zlato. That is, unless I leave. I'm not the selfless person you think or wish I was, Ive. I'm leaving for my own gains as much as I am for Caius. I think I was meant for greatness too. But I can't have that here. So at midnight the day after tomorrow, after the graduation and full moon festival, I will take off with the last group of Oaks."

"And you're really not going to say anything to your father?" asks Ivory, shaking her head.

"Come on, Ivory, you know the man almost as well as I do. Do you really think he would let me go if he knew? He doesn't think I have what it takes to survive out in the wild by myself. According to him, the 'greatness and bravery' gene skipped a generation. He doesn't see in me or Caius what he saw in himself growing up. And don't worry about Caius, because once he is of age, I will come back and take him with me. He deserves a real chance too."

"Wow, I'm so sorry…I had no idea you felt that way about your father or that he felt that way about you," replies Ivory, both shocked and hurt for Cassius.

"Yes, well, the Zlatos are masters of disguise when it comes to making people like us. It's a family trait, you know," he says, rolling his eyes.

"Is that why you try to make people hate you? Rebelling against your destiny?"

"You're very smart, Ivory. You have a good eye. You see things that other people don't."

Ivory laughs sarcastically. "You have no idea."

The two stand in silence for a moment.

"I don't think I can explore my full potential here either, Cassius," starts Ivory again. "Just like you, I don't want to follow in the footsteps of my parents. I don't want to be that perfect child with the perfect, boring job. I want to leave; I want to explore. I want to live my life day by day out in the wilderness. I want to challenge nature and win. Please, I know that we haven't been the greatest of friends, but think what they will say when they find out. I know you love to make a good scene. Think of what they will say when they find out that the unpredictable first son of Magnus Zlato and the perfectly prim first daughter of Nadi Skye ran off to join Nazar's group of wild explorers. We will be the talk of not only our tribe, but all four of them – the Collection. You know how fast word travels around here when it comes to gossip." Ivory pleads with Cassius.

Cassius looks at Ivory, eyes narrowed. He can't decide if she's playing some kind of joke on him or if she's being genuine.

"Cassius, please, I'm begging you. My future hangs in the air, between your hands," she pleads some more.

"Your safety is not guaranteed," he says in a warning. "When you leave the tribal borders, you're on your own. The Oaks, they move fast. You either keep up, or you don't."

"I understand. I will do my best to keep up, and if I don't, the wilderness can have me."

Cassius thinks some more, letting out a loud sigh.

"Like I said, we leave the day after tomorrow at midnight. The caravan waits for no one," he finally says.

"Oh my God, Cassius, thank you! Thank you!" Ivory jumps up and down, hugging Cassius in the process, who stands there, surprised by her reaction. She quickly realizes who she's hugging and pulls away.

"Thank you, Cassius. You have no idea what this means to me. I just… wow…for a second there, I thought there was no way you would agree."

"Yes, well, do you remember what I said to you on the cliff, when we went on the trip to the coast? I told you that you have my respect because you deserve it. And I still believe it. If I could have chosen one person to share this journey with, it would be you, I guess."

"Thank you," replies Ivory solemnly. "So, umm…do you think Nazar will be okay with this? Do we have to ask him personally if I can come along?" asks Ivory. This is the only part of her plan where things get a little muddy.

"No, don't worry about that. I talked to Nazar when he came. He was excited to have me in his group and asked me to bring one or two people along with me if I believed that they were worthy enough. At the time, I didn't have anyone in mind, so I said no. The only problem is that they need to know that you are one of us…hmmm…" Cassius thinks for a moment, and then remembers what he has in his book bag. "Hold on," he says as he looks around the stables for it, finally spotting it next to his equipment. He reaches into it, pulling out the extra clothes he'd brought with him. Reaching into the pocket of a pair of white slacks, he pulls out something small and shiny.

"You see this?" he asks, pointing to the gold double-sun medallion necklace he wears around his neck. "This medallion – only people who follow Nazar and work for him wear it."

Ivory obviously knows the medallion very well. It is the whole reason she is about to put her entire life on the line – risk it all.

"Do you know what that medallion stands for? What it means?" she asks Cassius, interested to see what his response will be.

"I don't think it actually means anything, other than being a sign of fellowship," he answers.

He doesn't know, thinks Ivory to herself. *That's for the better, anyway.*

Cassius opens up his right hand, revealing a smaller version of his necklace.

"Give me your wrist," he orders Ivory.

Ivory gives him her right hand. He opens up the small chain and wraps it around Ivory's wrist. Hanging from the chain is Nazar's medallion.

"It's slightly loose on your hand, but it doesn't look like it will fall off. Make sure you wear this before you meet me at midnight after the moon festival. If they don't see you wearing it, they might mistake you for someone trying to smuggle out with them."

"What will happen if they think that?"

"Well, I'm not sure, but I wouldn't risk being returned to the tribe. You might get in deeper trouble than if you actually leave."

"Yes, that's probably true. Alright, I will make sure to keep it on."

"Also, make sure that no one else sees it. I keep mine hidden in my shirt. I don't want anyone to know that I'm leaving, and I'm sure you don't, either. So be mindful of that."

"Is that what that Oak told you? To keep it hidden so no one knows you're leaving with them?"

"Yes," answers Cassius, completely oblivious to the actual reason he had to keep it covered.

"Okay, got it. Anything else I need to do before we leave?"

"Well, you might want to write your family a letter. Maybe explain to them that you will be alright."

"Have you written a letter to your father?"

"No. I have not written him anything. I wrote one to Caius. He deserves to know why…why I'm leaving him," Cassius has a hard time saying that last part. It breaks his heart to abandon his brother; especially after his mother had been taken so suddenly. But he knows deep down that he is doing the right thing.

"Okay, I will do that. Thanks, Cassius. And don't worry about Caius; I'm sure he will be alright. I know my mother would never let anything happen to him."

"Yes, I know, and I am grateful. Well," he says with a sigh, "It has been decided, then. I will give you more details tomorrow about where to meet me exactly; I still don't know if we will take the front or back gate. Until then, get yourself ready. Pack light, but don't forget to bring the essentials to survive."

"Alright, sounds good. Thank you."

"You can stop thanking me, Skye. I'm not doing anything special; I'm just letting you tag along."

"I know, but I still appreciate your trust," replies Ivory sincerely.

Cassius looks down to hide his smile.

"I have to get going. I don't have much time before…there's just places that I need to be. And you should be getting back as well. This is not the time you want people questioning your actions and behavior. Try to act as normally as you usually would. And do not, under any circumstance, draw attention to yourself."

"Got it. I'll see you tomorrow," Ivory nods to Cassius as he begins to walk away.

"See you then," he replies with a final nod.

Ivory watches as Cassius makes his way out of the stables. She stands in her spot for a minute afterward, then walks back into Thunder's stall. She buries her face in Thunder's shoulder and cries. She has never cried this hard before; she has no idea where all of the tears are coming from. But she doesn't stop. She cries for herself, for her family and friends, for Cassius, for the missing people…by the end, she doesn't know who she's crying for, but that doesn't stop her, either. Everything is just so overwhelming. She cries for a good ten minutes before she decides that it's time to get up and head back home. The next two days will be long, and she has a lot to take care of before she leaves.

Chapter 17

The soothing sound of small, calm waves dances in the air. Bubbling water rushes at a sandy shore, then slowly makes its way back, leaving behind it wet, rolling sand. The sound of the water, along with its comfortable warmth, lulls Ivory quietly to sleep. She lays in the soft water, so relaxed, so serene…

What seems like hours later, another layer of warmth is added into the mix. As a light salty breeze blows around Ivory, soft rays of sun make their way onto her face. She squints her closed eyes before slowly opening one and then the other. She lifts her hand out of the water, shielding her eyes from the rays of sunlight. Small droplets of water fall on her cheek and lips. Eyes shielded, through the cracks of her fingers, she sees blue – sky blue. It takes a moment for Ivory to realize where she is as she slowly looks at her surroundings. Once she realizes her location, she closes her eyes again and smiles.

I thought I would never see this place again, she thinks to herself as she wades her arms back and forth in the water. She lies for a few moments longer before she opens her eyes again and stands up. The water doesn't come up very high as she stands, but this, too, makes her smile.

The Hidden Cave…

Slowly, Ivory starts making her way out of the cave through the glimmering turquoise water, only to be met by the vast, sweeping blue ocean. She looks out into the distance, trying to make out where the water ends and the sky begins. But the two blend so beautifully, she soon quits trying. Making her way back into the cave, Ivory wonders where her friends are, as they were all here the last time she came. But she soon realizes that the reason she's here alone is because it's all a dream…

"Hello, Ivory."

Ivory gasps.

"Hello…Zohra. It's you again. I haven't heard from you in a while," replies Ivory, a bit startled to hear the old woman's voice in this particular setting. "Why are you here? Why am I here? The dreams are usually bad…"

"The dreams, my child, were not meant to be bad. They were meant as a message, a warning. But, as you have decoded the message, I have no more dreams for you," answers the woman.

"Wait, so this isn't your dream? You're not doing this?" asks Ivory, looking around for the woman.

"No, child. How could this be me? This is your memory, along with your imagination. It's the place you were the happiest…all I did was help you re- member."

"But why? Why would you want me to remember my happiest memory?"

"Why not?" replies the old woman. "We all deserve to be happy, Ivory. We all deserve our own little piece of paradise. And you've worked so hard…"

Ivory smiles. She walks over to the sand and takes a seat, leaving her feet in the water.

"So I was right, huh? About it all? Am I doing the right thing, leaving?"

"I cannot answer that question for you, Ivory. My purpose was to give you the message and protect you from the outside sources that were trying to in- fluence you in other ways…" replies Zohra.

"What outside sources? Are you talking about the dreams that I had about Nazar?" asks Ivory, trying to forget those horrid dreams.

"There is much for you to learn, child. All in good time; do not fret. As for now, enjoy this moment, bask in it. Take in these last rays of summer sun, as the gray clouds of autumn are slowly rolling in. This winter will be a long and cold one. You're going to need every last drop of sunlight you have to keep warm."

Ivory sighs, closing her eyes in the process. She doesn't say anything in reply to the old woman's prophecy.

"This will be the last time I speak with you, Ivory, as my mission is com- plete. Before I leave, I just want to remind you of something – you are a lot stronger than you believe, child…"

"Wait, wait…what do you mean this is the last time?! I'm going to need you; I can't do this by myself," says Ivory, standing back up.

The water dances around Ivory as she impatiently waits for Zohra to speak.

"You have powers, Ivory; powers that you will soon come to realize…the world is not as black and white as you have been taught. Everything you know is about to change. Remember, just keep your mind open and let your heart follow."

"Zohra, what are you talking about?! Can you please stop speaking in riddles and just tell me what you mean, just this once?" shouts Ivory, hands in the air.

"Good luck, and may the light guide you home…" says the old woman, voice vanishing out into the ocean.

Ivory runs through the pool of shallow water to the opening of the cave, but she already knows that she's gone.

"Goodbye, Zohra…" she whispers to herself as she watches the sun begin to set.

Ivory stands at the edge of the cave for a while, taking in the last of the sun's rays. Who knows, maybe this is the last time she gets this chance. The sounds of the waves, consistently making their way to the shore and back, start to lull Ivory back to sleep. She yawns as the last of the sun makes it way down into the ocean. The now dark blue ocean meets up with the purple-orange sky. Ivory is blown away by the colors, but her eyes can't hold on much longer over the sleepy haze washing over her. As the sun finally sets into the horizon, and before Ivory's eyes close, she sees a flash of green light. She'd read about the green flash in books before, but it really is so much more beautiful in person. Sailors used to believe that seeing the green flash was a sign of good luck – smooth travels. Ivory is thankful for the moment. And as her eyes slowly open up again to her bedroom ceiling, she can't help but realize that the old woman was right. She has to take advantage of these last few moments she has, for she has no idea when she will be presented with them again.

- - -

"Good morning!" says Ivory cheerfully as her parents walk into the kitchen.

"Good morning, Ivory," says Constantina, giving her daughter a kiss on the cheek. "I'm surprised you're up so early today. And what's this…are you cooking?" she asks, laughing.

Ivory laughs with her mother. "Yes, I'm making a proper breakfast, a feast, for everyone!" she replies, pointing the pan in her hand to the covered plates on the table.

Ivory sets down her pan to give her father a hug.

"Someone's in a great mood this morning; I like it," says Nadi as he embraces his daughter. Ivory laughs again.

"What can I say; I had a great dream…" she teases.

"Oh, I thought so," laughs Constantina. "Well, I don't know what to do. Should we just sit? Or do you need any help?"

"I'm actually almost done, just call the girls to come and eat while the food is warm," instructs Ivory as she turns back to the stove.

Constantina and Nadi glance at each other with a smile before heading out of the kitchen to wake the girls up.

"Don't come back into the kitchen until I tell you to!" yells Ivory after them as she rushes to finish setting everything up.

About ten minutes pass before Constantina yells out for Ivory, letting her know that everyone is about to come into the kitchen.

"Okay, come on in, it's all ready," replies Ivory, excited for her family to see the feast she's made for them. Her family's reaction is just as good as she had imagined it would be.

"Wow, this looks amazing!" squeal Anya and Diana together, running up to Ivory on either side, embracing her.

"Did you make all of this, Ive?! It looks so yummy!" says Hayden, joining her sisters.

Constantina and Nadi look back and forth from each other to the table before sitting down.

"Ivory, this really is something special, darling. What's gotten into you?" asks Constantina as she gets comfortable in her seat.

The girls all make their way to their seats to join their parents.

"I don't know; I felt like it was a special occasion, with tomorrow being my graduation," laughs Ivory. "I want it to be special for all of us," she says with a shrug.

"Well, darling, it is," replies Nadi, squeezing Ivory's round cheek. "I don't even know where to start…Ivory, you can have the honors," he laughs, looking around the table.

Ivory had woken up refreshed from her dream around sunrise, so she'd been cooking since. And since neither one of Ivory's parents worked early today, she had a lot of extra time to make the breakfast look perfect. She'd made a vegetable omelet filled with melted cheese, honey garlic baked potatoes, garbanzo bean and avocado salad, garlic bread, baked honey-glazed beans, merguez beef sausages, boysenberry muffins, strawberry/cherry frozen lemonade, and one of her favorites for dessert – the classic apple pie. It really was a feast.

Ivory and Constantina serve Nadi and the girls before digging in themselves. The Skye family eats as they discuss the exciting upcoming plans and events. Ivory lets her parents know that she will be sleeping over at the twins' place with Sparrow as the girls prepare for their graduation together. When everyone is finished eating, Ivory and her mother start cleaning up as the rest of the family head off to get dressed for the day. As Constantina starts washing the dishes, Ivory leans down and wraps her arms around her mother's waist, embracing her tightly. A little surprised, Constantina washes the soap off of her hands and turns around to hug her daughter back. The two stand in the same position for a while. Constantina caresses her daughter's hair as she rocks back and forth with her in her arms. Ivory, eyes closed, tries to take in as much of her mother's scent as she can – so she can remember it when she's alone. She's always loved her mother's scent – jasmines and little pink flowers she doesn't know the names of.

"I love you so much, Ivory, and I am so proud of you," whispers Constantina, finally breaking the silence.

"I love you too, Mama," whispers Ivory into her mother's chest.

The two stay in the same position for a while longer as Ivory takes one last deep breath before she lets her mother go and stands back upright. The two smile at each other. Constantina gives Ivory one last kiss on the cheek before turning back to her work.

- - -

"Hey, Ivory, are we going to see you again today before you go and stay with your friends, or will we see you tomorrow morning?" asks Diana, peeking into Ivory's room.

"Umm…I'm not sure, actually. You guys are going to stay with your friends at their house, right? I'll probably come back a little later, but you might not be here."

"Hmm…okay," replies the little girl, hard at thought.

"See, I told you, we'll have time later. And we can give it to her tomorrow," Ivory hears her sister Anya whispering outside her room. Diana's head disappears and she whispers back at her sister. Ivory giggles to herself at how adorable her sisters are.

Waving goodbye to her mother and the girls, Ivory makes her way out of the house toward the market.

Wow, it's such a beautiful day, thinks Ivory to herself as she makes her way down a quiet path. A light, cool breeze blows through the trees on either side of the path. Ivory's hair floats with the falling leaves and flower petals. Ivory closes her eyes and lifts her chin up to the sky, also exposing her palms in the process. She takes in the few rays of sunlight that can find their way through the branches as she walks. She only keeps her eyes closed for a few moments, though, in fear that she might trip and fall again. As she continues to walk, Ivory soon notices a tall figure walking far out in front of her, seemingly heading in the same direction. She speeds up her pace as curiosity takes ahold of her and as she tries to make out who it might be. It takes her a minute, but she soon figures it out as she sees the sun bouncing off of his sandy locks. Ivory picks up her pace into more of a jog as she tries to catch up with Cassius.

"Hey there!" she says, slowing back down as she reaches her classmate.

"Oh, hello. Didn't think I'd see you so soon," replies Cassius with a dazzling smile, a little surprised to see Ivory.

Ivory looks down and smiles to herself, as it's been a while since she's caught Cassius in a genuinely good mood. *He really does have a beautiful smile,* she admits to herself as she tries to ignore the momentary inconsistent beating of her heart.

"So where are you heading?" asks Cassius, still looking at Ivory, smiling.

"Oh, umm…" Ivory laughs off her awkward moment. "I'm heading to the market. I just need to pick up a few materials; I'm meeting up with the girls later to prepare for graduation," she says, looking back up at Cassius.

"That sounds fun," replies Cassius with a nod, looking back at the path in front of him.

"And you? Where are you headed?" asks Ivory, turning her gaze back in front of her as well.

"I'm headed to the market too. I actually need to grab a few things for tomorrow as well, just not for the graduation exactly…" replies Cassius, with a nervous laugh.

"Oh, wow…" Ivory laughs nervously too as she remembers what's to happen after the graduation and festival. "Yes, I might actually need to grab a few extra things then too. Thanks for the reminder."

Cassius chuckles while shaking his head.

"You really are a piece of work, aren't you, Ivory?" he says playfully in a deeper voice, almost as if he's speaking to himself.

Ivory smiles and shrugs, keeping her eyes forward.

"Oh, I just remembered," starts Cassius, turning his full gaze back to Ivory. Ivory looks up at him as she listens intently. "We will meet up tomorrow two hours past midnight, at the stables. With the extra guards at the Tribal Center, there will not be anyone at the stables. At least, not for a while. From there, once we get our horses, we'll ride out through an unguarded path that I found on the eastern border of the tribe. The Oaks will be waiting for us there, out in the wild," he finishes.

Ivory takes a deep breath, nodding in understanding.

"This is going to be a close call. We have to be super careful not to run into anyone between our houses and the stables…" she says, already trying to plan out her path in her mind.

"Yes, it will be. I think we can do it, just make sure that no one knows or even thinks that you might be up to something. The smallest unexpected thing can throw the whole thing off. And remember, I can't wait for you for too long because the Oaks will not wait for me. Make sure you're there on time."

"Yes, of course," nods Ivory.

The two walk in silence for the rest of the way to the tribal market. Once there, the two stop at the edge of the market before they go their separate ways.

"We can't let anyone see us together; can't have them talking," smiles Ivory as she stands face to face with Cassius, hands in her pockets.

"No, we can't. Don't worry, I'll be sure to cause a scene at some point to-morrow, just to put the last nail in the coffin, you know?" laughs Cassius, running his hand through is sandy blonde hair.

Ivory laughs with Cassius. The two stand for a moment, and as Ivory pre-pares to start moving, Cassius grabs her right wrist. Surprised, Ivory looks down as Cassius takes her hand out of her pocket and brings it closer to his face. He delicately holds her wrist with one hand as he moves her flowing sleeve slightly up with the other.

"You need to be careful with this, ok?" he speaks with a low, deep voice, looking up at Ivory through the tousled pieces of hair fallen over his eyes.

"Yes," manages Ivory, a little taken aback at the abrupt motion. It takes her a moment before she realizes that he's talking about the bracelet he gave her.

Cassius looks back down at Ivory's wrist, fixing her sleeve so that it fully covers the bracelet before setting it back down to her side. As he quickly brushes his hair back and out of his eyes, Ivory can't help but notice the cologne he has on; she really likes it. She'd never been so close to him before... she'd never noticed how built his arms were, either...

"Umm..." starts Ivory, shaking the thought completely from her brain. "Well, it was great seeing you; good luck with preparations, and I will see you tomorrow," she says with an awkward wave as she slowly starts backing away, turning to leave.

"It was great seeing you as well, Ive. I'll see you tomorrow," replies Cassius, one hand in his pocket, watching as Ivory walks away. He waits in his spot for a few moments before making his way into the market himself, in order to not draw attention, of course.

Cheeks burning red hot from that unexpected encounter, Ivory makes her way to the fabrics stand.

- - -

"So we have the lavender blush, light rose, or more of a dusty rose chiffon."

"Oh perfect, I just need a little bit more of the dusty rose chiffon; I ended up making the dress a lot longer than I expected."

"That sounds beautiful. I also saved the beads you asked me for. We got the shipment with Nazar's arrival, and you know how in demand they are..."

"Thank you so much, Emilia; you have no idea how much I appreciate it," says Ivory to the woman selling her the fabrics and beads for the dress that she is working on for graduation. "I'm cutting it real close this time; I had no time to finish it. It ended up being a much bigger project than I had anticipated," sighs Ivory, a little stressed out.

"And how will you proceed?" asks the woman.

"Thankfully, I have amazing friends that are going to be helping me out with the beading. That's going to take the longest time," laughs Ivory.

"Yes, she really does have amazing friends, doesn't she? You should tell her to take better care of them!" jumps in a voice behind Ivory.

Surprised, Ivory turns around to find Sparrow standing right behind her, shaking her head at her. Ivory laughs and hugs her friend.

"You startled me a bit; when did you get here?"

"Oh, I've been here for a while, actually," replies Sparrow, narrowing her eyes at her friend. "I have seen something that we need to discuss for sure, but for now, have you gotten everything you need?"

Ivory's face starts to flush as she realizes that her friend might have caught some of her conversation with Cassius.

"Umm…yes, I got the chiffon and the beads. That's all I really need. I'm still not sure if I want to put a thin belt on it though…" Ivory thinks out loud.

"Hmm…it depends on how it turns out in the end," replies Sparrow. "Look, just get it and we'll decide once it's all done. If you don't end up using it, you can use it for something else. But if we finish and it's past sunset, we won't even be able to go back out because of the curfew."

"Your friend is right," jumps in Emilia. "Better to be safe than sorry."

"Oh, alright," Ivory finally gives in after some thought. "I'll take a very thin piece of that pink leather over there," she says, pointing to the color she wants.

"Perfect choice; this will go nicely with the chiffon," replies Emilia, putting the leather along with a buckle in Ivory's bag.

"Thanks again, Emilia, that should be it for me. How about you, love? Are you getting anything?"

"I actually do have a list of things that I'm picking up for the twins," replies Sparrow, reaching into her pocket and taking out the list.

Emilia opens the list and starts reading it, a little taken aback and confused at what the list contains. She looks up at Sparrow questioningly.

"Hey, don't ask me. They just said to give you the list and that you'd have everything," says Sparrow, putting her hands up in surrender. Ivory laughs at her friend.

"I though the girls were done with their dresses…" whispers Ivory to Sparrow, a little confused herself.

"I know; they are done. They said that it was a surprise," whispers back Sparrow.

"Okay, everything is in here. Is there anything else you girls need?" says Emilia, handing Sparrow a large cloth bag with all of the materials inside.

"No, that's all Emilia, thanks!" replies Sparrow, paying the woman in the process.

"Did all of you end up making long dresses?" asks Emilia as she gives Sparrow her change.

Ivory nods in response to the woman.

"I was going to make a short one, but the girls convinced me otherwise," says Sparrow, rolling her eyes. Emilia laughs.

"I can't wait to see you girls tomorrow; I know for a fact that all of you will look stunning!" says Emilia excitedly.

"Thank you, Emilia! Seriously, for all of your help…We'll see you tomorrow!" says Ivory, waving goodbye to the woman and heading off with Sparrow.

Sparrow and Ivory get to the edge of the market before Ivory remembers that she needs to buy a few more things for when she leaves.

A new travel bag, rope, dried fruit…I already have a water flask, and I have my sword that I'll bring with me. Maybe I should get a few more bandages in case…

"Hey, Earth to Ivory!" Says Sparrow, walking out in front of Ivory, waving her hand in her face.

Ivory quickly snaps out of her thoughts.

"Oh sorry, did you say something?" asks Ivory, a little dazed.

"Umm…would you like to explain to me what I saw exactly earlier?" asks Sparrow, as she stops walking and stands in front of Ivory.

"Well, that depends," starts Ivory. "What exactly did you see?" replies Ivory in a confused tone. Even though, deep down, Ivory knows exactly what Sparrow is talking about. She just doesn't know to what extent Sparrow had seen.

"Really?" replies Sparrow, unimpressed. "I saw you standing with Cassius, talking. And then Cassius holding your hand…" says Sparrow, waiting for Ivory to take over at any time.

"Oh, yes, of course" starts Ivory, playing down the situation. "I saw Cassius yesterday at the stables, and his horse wasn't doing so well. He was just catching me up on the whole situation because I'd asked him to, that's all," Ivory finishes. She isn't completely lying to her friend. She had seen Cassius at the stables; it's just the conversation that was different.

"Mhmm…and the hand-holding?" asks Sparrow suspiciously.

"There was this disgusting bug crawling up my pants and into my sleeve. He saw it, so he kind of just shook it off and checked if I'd gotten bit. That's all," replies Ivory, stone faced.

Sparrow looks Ivory over, but Ivory's expression doesn't falter.

"That's it? Really?" asks Sparrow one last time, almost looking a little disappointed.

Ivory laughs at the disappointed Sparrow. "If I had known better, I'd think that you wanted there to be something more…" mocks Ivory.

"You bet your big booty I wanted there to be something more!" replies Sparrow, shaking her head. "He's handsome, and you're getting old," she says as she starts to make her way to the path home. Ivory hesitates in her spot. She needs to buy the last few things she needs, and this is her only chance.

"Why are you standing there? Aren't you coming?" asks Sparrow, stopping again.

"I actually just remembered, I need to get a few more things for my parents. It's really annoying; you go ahead and I'll meet you at the twins," replies Ivory, praying her friend agrees to leave without her, just this once.

"If I didn't need to meet with my mother I would totally stay with you, you know that, right Ive?" says Sparrow, feeling bad that she's leaving her friend behind.

"Oh, of course, love! Please go, we all have those last-minute errands to run. I'll see you in a bit!" replies Ivory, thankful to Sparrow's mother for the save.

The two girls wave goodbye to each other as each make their way to where they need to be. Ivory already has a list in her head of what she needs to buy, so it doesn't take her long to get everything together and head home. Once there, she makes her way quietly into the house, hoping to get to her room before anyone notices she's there. She quickly hides her traveling stuff under the bed. Once the coast is clear, she calls out to anyone that might be in the house, but she gets no answer – she's alone.

With a sigh of relief, Ivory takes her time packing her traveling clothes and materials in her new travel bag. After that's done, she gets another separate bag for the night ready. Once she has all of her ducks in a row, Ivory takes a break and lies down on her bed and closes her eyes. With so much happening all at once, she had forgotten the excitement and fear that she had about graduating. It all seems so irrelevant to her now, though.

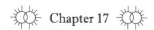

Ivory lays in her bed for about fifteen minutes before deciding to finally get up and get ready to leave. As she hides her travel bag under her bed once again, she remembers something that she had forgotten to do. She quickly pulls out her memory book and rips out a clean page from the end. On the page, she begins to write her goodbye to her family.

Chapter 18

Dearest Mother and Father,

I have gone to chase after my destiny.

I wish I could have stayed and explained this in person, but I am not so sure that I would be able to convince myself to begin with. I thought it might be easier this way…

I just want you to know that I love you very much. And I hope you know that you have raised an intelligent, independent young woman who will work hard to play her role in society. All that I have ever wanted to do in my lifetime was make you proud. But I have come to realize that I cannot do that if I stay here.

Please, put your trust in me, as you have all of my years growing up.

And I promise you that when I return, you will be proud to call me your first-born daughter. I promise…

With all of my love,

Ivory.

- - -

"Good afternoon, darling! Please come in, the girls have been waiting for you. They're in the room; you know how to make your way there," smiles the twins' mother.

"Thank you, Healer Ilios," replies Ivory politely as she makes her way to Flora and Fauna's bedroom.

"Time to get this party started!" shouts Ivory excitedly, quickly shutting the bedroom door behind her as to not disturb the twins' mother with the noise.

"Ivory!" the twins shout in unison, both jumping up excitedly to hug their friend. Sparrow joins the three girls in their hugfest with Ivory. The girls stand around for a bit, all talking at the same time, too excited about the upcoming events. It takes a few minutes before Ivory can set her things down in a corner.

"Alright, Ive, let's see what we're working with!" exclaims Fauna, excited to see Ivory's dress.

"Okay, but remember, it's not done yet. I still have to add the last few layers of chiffon inside the dress and I need to add the beads," replies Ivory as she takes her long, blush rose-colored dress out of its special covering.

The three girls all gasp and start squealing together at the same time, gushing over the beautiful dress.

"Ivory, I can't even begin to imagine how beautiful this will look tomorrow, especially when we add the accessory we're making for you!" screams Fauna, too excited to hold it in anymore.

"Fauna! You weren't supposed to tell!" yells Flora at her sister. "But on a serious note, Ive, it's going to blow minds, just wait and see!" laughs Flora, jumping up and down with excitement.

Sparrow and Ivory laugh along with their friends.

The four girls all take a seat in the middle of the large room on the soft, tan-colored fur rug. They lay Ivory's dress out on their legs, each taking a corner of it. Ivory explains to Flora and Fauna the beading pattern on the top portion of the dress.

"Each of the flowers gets a pearl bead in the center, and then the little empty spaces in between the flowers get filled with the different beads. There's really no pattern there; just mix the beads around, like up here," instructs Ivory, pointing to a part on the dress that she's already finished.

The twins nod along with Ivory and start working right away. In the meantime, Ivory and Sparrow start working on the skirt of the dress.

"Ive, are you sure you want to add more? It looks nice as is…" says Sparrow, turning the skirt layers over in her hands.

"Yes, I want a little more volume. I feel like it looks very…I don't know if the word flimsy works in this situation. But do you know what I mean? Trust me, it will look a lot more complete," replies Ivory, taking the chiffon out of her bag.

Ivory and Sparrow finish the skirt of the dress in about two hours. Once done, they move on to help the twins with the beading on the top part of the dress.

"You guys have seriously done so much; I can't thank you enough!" sighs Ivory, unable to put into words how grateful she is to her friends.

Fauna and Flora look up at Ivory and wink at her at the same time, then look back down at their fast-working fingers. Ivory laughs at their twin moment – she lives for these moments. As Sparrow and Ivory join the twins with the beading, it only takes them about one more hour before they are completely done with the dress.

"Oh my God, I cannot believe we finished it this fast!" gasps Ivory, running her fingers along the top of her beautiful dress.

"You know what they say, eight hands are better than two," laughs Fauna, stretching her arms. The three other girls burst out laughing at the same time.

"I've actually never heard that one before," replies Sparrow as she makes her way up off the floor. The girls all stand up, and Flora and Ivory put the dress up on a hanger.

"Alright guys, before we head out to dinner, I need one last opinion," says Ivory, reaching into her bag. "Belt, or no belt?" she asks, wrapping the thin piece of leather around the waist of the dress so the girls can picture what the final result would be.

"You know what, I actually really like it with the belt," starts Flora. "It's so pretty and glossy; I feel like it adds a little playfulness to it, honestly."

"I agree; it gives the eye a little break from the intricate beading. It balances it out very nicely," adds Fauna.

"And the belt is so thin it's not going to take away anything from the dress, you know? I say yes too," finishes Sparrow.

"Well, the crowd has spoken, then. Belt it is!" laughs Ivory, setting the leather down on her bag. "I'll quickly put the buckle on it after dinner; I need a break now."

"Yes, food first, and then accessories after. We've already started working on all of the accessories we're making for you two; we'll let you know what we need help with later," says Flora with a mysterious look in her eye.

Fauna mirrors her look. "You guys are going to love it, trust us," she winks. "But first, food!" she exclaims as the girls start making their way out of the bedroom and into the dining room.

As usual, the twins' mother doesn't disappoint with the food. Ivory admires the beautiful tablescape as she makes her way to her seat. Tonight, Flora has set the table up with a lavender theme. Ivory lightly brushes her index finger over the small bouquet of lavender flowers on her serviette.

"Is this lavender from our trip?" she asks, looking back up at Flora.

"Yes and no," smiles Flora as she helps her sister set the food down on the table. "I took some of the lavender that I brought back with me and grew more in my window garden. So it's technically from here."

"It's beautiful," replies Ivory, looking back down at the pretty flowers, remembering the miles of stretching lavender hills.

"Alright girls, dig in," says Fauna, bringing Ivory back to the table. "Mother kept it on the lighter side today so we can all fit into our dresses tomorrow."

"It looks delicious, as usual!" exclaims Sparrow as she starts serving herself some quinoa salad and lemon grilled fish.

The girls all eat until they are full. And just as they think they can't fit any more food into their bodies, Fleur Ilios brings out a large bowl of red and white cherries. The girls eat a few cherries before they really can't fit anything else into their stomachs.

"Thank you for the dinner, Healer Ilios; it was amazing," says Sparrow as she and the girls help bring the dishes into the kitchen.

"I'm glad to hear you girls enjoyed it; you're always welcome here," replies Fleur with a genuine smile.

Once the table is clean, the four girls make their way back into the bedroom, each finding a comfortable spot to work on their separate projects. Flora and Fauna sit sprawled out on the floor with their materials around them, working on the hair accessories for Sparrow and Ivory. Sparrow sits on the bed, putting together white rose corsages for the four girls for the full moon festival. It is a tradition for everyone to wear white on the full moon festival and to decorate themselves with flowers. The girls had already helped make a lot of the flower crowns that would be distributed to the people in the tribe on the day. The corsages were Sparrow's gift to her friends for the special day and occasion.

As for Ivory, although she hasn't told her friends yet, she had made bracelets for her friends from the seashells she had collected at the beach inside the hidden cave. She had collected a lot of small shells and braided them into her bracelets, which she will be giving to her friends after graduation. For the moment, however, she sits working on the belt for her dress, attaching the latch and buckle onto the leather.

The girls share some small chat as each works, engrossed in what they have in front of them.

"Sooo…" starts Sparrow, elongating the word. "Guess who I saw today speaking to our little friend Ivory?" she asks with a smug smile on her face.

"Really?" asks Ivory, rolling her eyes and shaking her head. "You're going to do this now?"

"Who?" asks Flora, not looking up.

"Cassius…" replies Sparrow, waiting for the twins' reaction, which she gets right away as the two of them look up at the same time. Sparrow laughs, happy with the reaction.

"Where did you meet Cassius, Ive?" asks Fauna.

Ivory sighs and throws a dirty look at Sparrow, who returns the gesture by sticking her tongue out at Ivory.

"I saw Cassius yesterday at the stables, and then I ran into him again this morning at the market," replies Ivory, finally.

"Did you guys talk?" asks Fauna as she continues her work.

"Yes, we talked," answers Ivory, looking back down at her belt.

"Oh, they talked all right…" says Sparrow with a knowing voice. Flora and Fauna catch it.

"Did something else happen?" asks Flora, a little confused, looking back and forth between Ivory and Sparrow.

"No, nothing happened. Sparrow just caught a random moment that she interpreted wrong because she didn't know the context of the situation," explains Ivory.

Sparrow laughs out loud. "Yes, Ivory. Please explain to them the context of Cassius holding your hand."

"Woah, there! Holding hands? Girl, speak!" commands Fauna.

"Oh, I'm sure there is a perfectly good explanation if you just give Ivory time to explain," chimes in Flora, giving Ivory a quick wink that only she sees.

Ivory laughs at her ridiculous friends.

"You girls are insane, I hope you know that," she starts. "Like I already explained to Sparrow over here, we were just talking. He was having some trouble with his horse; I gave him some advice and he was just getting back to me on it…"

"So why was he holding your hand?" asks Fauna, narrowing her eyes at Ivory.

"Give her time to finish!" Flora yells at her sister.

The two exchange a silent conversation through their eyes. Ivory sighs out loud.

"There was a bug on my shirt, well…in my shirt…it crawled up my sleeve, and he saw it. So he took my hand, pulled up my sleeve, brushed it off, and put my hand back down. That's the whole story," finishes Ivory, taking a deep breath.

"Eww…was it a spider?" asks Flora, cringing.

"Spiders are cute; I don't know why you're all scared of them," says Fauna, rolling her eyes.

"I'm not scared of spiders at all," chimes in Sparrow.

"No, it wasn't a spider; I wouldn't be that still if it was. I HATE spiders," replies Ivory, feeling the hairs on her arms stand up. "It was one of those twig-looking bugs. Still nasty, but not as bad as spiders."

"Hmmm… I still think the whole situation is questionable," says Sparrow.

"I think it's sweet…" says Flora, smiling to herself.

"I mean, I'm not that surprised, to be honest. We've all known that he likes Ivory," says Fauna in a matter of fact.

"WHAT?! What are you going on about now?" asks Ivory, a little annoyed. "We almost never talk, and when we do it's different each time. Some days he's normal, and other days he's your typical, chauvinistic idiot."

"Well, you know what they say. Guys who are mean to you are the ones that like you," replies Fauna.

"Agreed. And you're the only one he's ever genuine with, even if it is just once or twice a year," agrees Sparrow.

"Honestly, I don't think he's as bad as you guys all think he is. I feel like he's just a little bit more complicated than your everyday tribal male," thinks Flora out loud.

"I don't think he's bad, and I completely agree with you, Flora. That's exactly why I try with him. Because as much of a terrible person he's shown himself to be, I know there's more. I grew up with him; I've seen the good parts, along with the terrible ones. That's all," finishes Ivory, looking back down at the belt in her lap.

The girls all silently agree with Ivory's assessment of Cassius.

"Well, at the end of the day, we are coming of age now. Winter might be coming, but as soon as the spring flowers begin to flourish, the hunt begins…" says Fauna with an evil grin.

The girls all look at her, confused.

"What are you talking about?" asks Sparrow, for herself as well as the other girls.

"BOYS!" replies Fauna with an uncharacteristic squeal as she pretends to swoon.

The girls all laugh at her impersonation.

"Oh my, you girls have no idea what I have to deal with when I'm alone with this one…" starts Flora, giving her sister a funny look.

"Oh please, have you seen Sparrow in the spring time?" asks Ivory, unable to hold back a fit of laughter. "I have to hold her back by her hair, I swear!"

"This one right here has had her eye on a specific warrior ever since last winter, and especially after our trip to the coast…" says Flora. Fauna holds her face in her hands to cover her flushing cheeks, but doesn't deny the allegation.

The girls all pretend to swoon with Fauna as she lays flat on her stomach on the floor, covering her head with her arms.

"I can't help it; he's too handsome and strong…" she mumbles from underneath her arms.

"Fauna, who is it?!" asks Sparrow, bouncing up and down on the bed now.

"I think I have a feeling I know who it is…" says Ivory, looking over at Flora for the nod of approval. "Emile?" she asks with a questioning smile.

Flora nods, holding her hand over her mouth as to not laugh out loud.

"OH MY GOD, EMILE!" yells Sparrow, jumping off the bed and onto the floor next to Fauna.

"SHHH!" say Flora and Ivory at the same time, trying to keep Sparrow quiet.

"You guys are so mean!" mumbles Fauna from underneath her arms, still on the floor, laughing.

Sparrow pulls at the resisting Fauna, finally breaking through her arms and getting her to sit upright. Fauna sighs out loud before looking up at her friends.

"That's not fair," she says with a pained laugh.

"Hey, you started first!" laughs Ivory along with her friends.

"Why didn't you say anything before?" asks Sparrow, still holding Fauna up.

"I don't know! I haven't really tried talking to him too much. Just on the occasional school trip…" she replies.

"Fauna! You should have said something; I'm pretty close with Emile! And just for the record, I think you two would make the perfect match. He's not that much older, only about five to six years. You know what…I'm going to get you two together, it's official!" says Ivory with a wink.

Fauna holds her face again in her hands, laughing.

"You guys are ridiculous, I swear," she says.

"So you don't want Ivory to get you a proper introduction, then?" asks Flora, giving her sister a knowing look.

Fauna gives her sister the *I'm going to kill you later when we're alone* look. Flora brushes the look off, still very happy with her decision to speak up. Ivory puts down her finished belt before crawling over to her three friends.

"Give me some more work to do, please, I'm all done," she says to Flora, who is surrounded by some of the most beautiful crystals that Ivory has ever seen.

"Yes, alright. Girls, back to work, come on! We have all day tomorrow to freak out over boys," laughs Flora.

Sparrow and Fauna share a few more giggles between themselves before each heading back to their spot to complete their work. Ivory stays next to Flora, watching her glue the large crystals to the headband intertwined with pieces of metal and leather.

"I really don't mean to bring down the mood, but I have a question that's been eating at me all day today…" says Fauna suddenly.

Flora makes eye contact with her sister; she already knows what her sister is about to ask.

Ivory and Sparrow look over at Fauna expectantly, waiting for her question.

"Do you think they're going to mention Trixie and Yuri tomorrow at the graduation?" she asks after some hesitation.

Sparrow and Ivory look at each other; Ivory's heart sinks a bit. She had almost forgotten about them – almost. The truth is, she had told herself to try and make the most of her last two days. She's tried pushing the thought of her lost friends out of her mind and heart, but it seems to be an impossible feat at this point.

"I would hope that they mention their names," sighs Ivory. "They are a part of the graduating class, after all. It will be very bittersweet though…"

"It's not going to be easy for their parents and families, especially. They were so close…it really is a shame," adds Sparrow solemnly.

"I just, I wish I could do something, you know?" says Fauna with a fire in her eyes that Ivory recognizes. It's the same fire that she had felt in her heart when she had made her decision. "If I just knew what happened to them, I would go and bring them back myself. That is, if they are still alive..."

"All we can do at this point is pray, sis. Pray that they are alive and un-harmed," says Flora, touching her sister's shoulder. "I can't begin to imagine, sweet Trixie – someone hurting her." Flora shakes the thought out of her head. "We must stay positive and believe that they will be okay in the end."

"Do you think they can find them before our next trip to the coast?" asks Sparrow. "Trixie had such a great time with us the last time," smiles Sparrow, remembering her time with the girl.

"I think it's possible," speaks up Ivory. "That will be the goal, to find them before the next trip. That way, we can all ride out together and explore to-gether again..." Ivory closes her eyes as she tries to picture a possible future where everyone is safe again and together.

"We can take Trixie back to the hidden cave; she really loved it," smiles Fauna at the thought. "We can take Yuri, Acyl, and Kai with us too. I'm sure they'd all love that."

The girls all reminisce about their previous trip and make plans for their next trip to the coast, making sure to include their missing friends. They finish all of their work as they talk and prepare the bedroom for sleep once they are all done. It doesn't take long for Sparrow, Fauna, and Flora to fall asleep. But Ivory can't seem to find the same peace as her friends to sleep, as her mind wanders in a million different directions. She lies around for a bit before finally deciding to take out her memory book and have a seat next to the window. Al-though the moon is not completely full tonight, as it will be tomorrow night, it is still bright enough for Ivory to use its light to write in her book.

- - -

Greetings again,

It's me, Ivory. To anyone reading these entries, I apologize for the lack of organ-ization in my last few entries. A lot has happened in the past few days – a lot of rev-elations have come into the light for me...but you already know.

At this moment in time, I sit at the window of my friends, Flora and Fauna. My special friends that I now have to make sure I protect. And then there's Sparrow...she is not the most peaceful sleeper, I must admit, as I watch her toss and turn in her sleep. Nonetheless, I love her as if she was my sister. And although he's not here with us to-night, there's also Sevastyan – the brother that I've always wanted. One of the few men that I will trust unconditionally for as long as I live.

Tomorrow is the big day – for too many reasons.

It seems that everything is falling into place for everyone. Except for me; it's all falling into the wrong places. Nonetheless, I am grateful for having such an amazing day today, bonding with my family and friends. I will take this day with me on my travels, and I will look back on this entry whenever I feel lost or hopeless.

In other news, I have found a surprising ally in Cassius. I can't lie and say that I didn't have the intention to use him and drop him as soon as I got what I needed from him. But he's starting to really surprise me – I'm starting to see that old Cassius again, the Cassius that I knew before his mother died. Actually, I'm even starting to question myself on possibly telling Cassius my real intention for leaving at some point... If I'm right about him, he could become a very important ally when I need all of the help that I can get. It would be very foolish to think that I can do this all by myself with no help whatsoever.

I guess, I'm just hoping – praying – that I will be surprised with help when I lose all hope at some point...

Maybe I should be a little more positive about the situation, I don't know. In any case, I am ready. Ready to graduate, ready to celebrate, and ready to go on an adventure.

Also, on a side note, I can't believe I'll be turning twenty-three very soon...I'm really a grown-up now. But I still feel like a child sometimes. I wish I was still a child, honestly...

Anyway, I have no idea what point I'm trying to make at this point. This is probably the worst memory book that ever existed.

I will go ahead and end this entry here and leave you with a final quote as I prepare to embark on this new journey:

"When a man has done what he considers to be his duty to his people and his country, he can rest in peace. I believe I have made that effort and that is, therefore, why I will sleep for the eternity." – Nelson Mandela, 1918-2013.

This is one of my favorite quotes by one of the most influential people of the twenty-first century. That was a long time ago, but we must not forget people who've made such a big mark on the world. I wish to be like him some day. It would truly be an honor...

I will do my best to do my duty as an Alder of the Western Assimilian Tribe and as a human of the human species.

Sincerely,
I.S.

Ivory closes her book, lays back down on her pillow, and closes her eyes. She is soon transported to another dimension as the moon travels across the dark night sky. As she sleeps soundly, the first rays of sunlight make their way through the window onto her body. She doesn't know it, but the light gives her power along with its warmth. It fuels her body and settles her mind as she prepares to embark on her journey through a new world.

Chapter 19

"Oh…"

"My…"

"Goodness…"

Flora, Fauna, and Sparrow all hold their mouths with their hands as they look on in awe at their best friend as she makes her way out of the house.

"So, do I look nice?" asks Ivory, a little embarrassed at her friends' reaction.

"Ivory, you're not just beautiful," starts Flora.

"You're breathtaking," finishes Fauna.

Sparrow crosses her arms and laughs out loud. "See, you're all surprised, but I knew that my best friend was HOT!" she says with a smirk. "You look on point, Ive! And the headband, crown, whatever you want to call it, it seriously pulls the whole look together."

Ivory blushes as she slowly makes her way to her friends. As she walks, she quickly catches a glimpse of herself in a window, and she can't help but feel proud of her work.

Ivory's blush rose dress turned out even better than she had expected. The dress is off-the-shoulder, with see-through lace half-sleeves that reach her elbows. The color of the sleeves and bodice of the dress matches the skirt portion perfectly. The top of the dress, including the sleeves, is completely beaded with small florets and pearls and tapers off to a flowing chiffon skirt. The top of the dress hugs Ivory in all of the right places, while the bottom tapers out in more of a bouffant manner. The little belt Ivory added sits at the smallest part of her waist, showing off her larger hips in the classiest way possible. For accessories, Ivory had decided to just wear the headband that Flora and Fauna had made for her, as it turned out to be more of an extravagant crown. The girls had gotten different sizes of marbled pink quartz crystals and put them together in a way where they almost looked like they were spiking up. Ivory had decided to wear her long hair down in its natural curls, placing the pink quartz crown delicately on top of her hair, keeping her hair out of her face. A little lip stain on the lips that Flora had made out of flowers finishes off the look as Ivory floats towards her friends.

"You guys, I can't begin to explain how amazing YOU ALL look!" Ivory gushes at her beautiful girl friends. The girls all take turns giving Ivory a twirl so she can get a complete look at all of them.

Flora and Fauna had made the exact same dresses, just in different colors. Flora had made her slinky silk dress a pretty sky-blue color. In contrast, Fauna had made her dress in a darker eggplant hue. The girls' dresses flow straight down to the ground, with a long slit coming up to their mid-thigh. Flora's slit is on her left side, while Fauna's in on her right. The dresses both have thin spaghetti straps, a high neckline in the front, and a dip in the back, showing off the girls' backs. The girls wear thin crystal chokers that each have a long strand of crystals falling down their backs, disappearing into their dresses. As for hair, Flora had convinced Fauna to let her braid both of their hair up in an updo. Intertwined in their braids are flowers matching each of their dresses, respectively. The two girls look drop-dead gorgeous in Ivory's eyes.

As for Sparrow, her look is striking, as Ivory had predicted. Of course, Sparrow had chosen to make her dress black – her favorite color. Her dress is the simplest of the four, in terms of it being a long satin black dress. However, Sparrow had decided to add a long cape to the dress that flows down to a train behind her as she walks. The bold shoulders of the cape give the dress a beautiful form, as it sits perfectly on her. A very low dipping neckline gives Sparrow's dress a touch of smoldering sexiness, while the spiked leather statement necklace the twins made for her adds an edge that only Sparrow could pull off. The twins had originally planned on making Sparrow something for her hair too, but turned it into a necklace at the last minute. Short cropped hair slicked back and black kohl lining her light brown eyes, Sparrow looks like she could stop traffic with one look.

The girls all stand outside the Ilios house as they wait for their families and Sevastyan to arrive so they can head to the Tribal Center together.

"HOLY SMOKES!" exclaims a voice suddenly.

The four girls, huddled in a circle, all turn at the sound of their friend Sevastyan, who is clad in a navy suit, white button-down shirt, and matching tie.

"Who are you people, and where are my boring friends?" asks Sevastyan as he walks up to the girls, eyes wide in awe.

"Well, well, look who we got here…" starts Fauna, giving Sevastyan the up and down.

"Sev, you look AMAZING!" says Ivory, holding her hands up to her mouth. Flora nods in agreement.

"Give us a twirl, sexy man!" says Sparrow, motioning to Sevastyan with her hand.

Sevastyan gives the girls a quick twirl, making them clap and cheer.

"Seriously, though, I'm not kidding, you girls look out of this world…" says Sevastyan, getting back to the girls.

"Sparrow, you look insane! Like you look like you can walk down the runway, but also rule a kingdom under an iron fist at the same time; it's crazy!" he says, laughing.

"Fauna and Flora," he starts, lingering a bit longer on Flora, who immediately starts blushing.

"Drop dead gorgeous, the both of you; period," he finally says.

"And Ive," he turns to Ivory, taking her hands. "You are just A PRINCESS. No, A QUEEN. A sight to behold by all…" he finishes, almost getting emotional.

"I honestly feel so lucky to be walking with you girls to graduation," says Sevastyan, squeezing Ivory's hands. "I feel so blessed right now…" he finishes with a sigh.

The girls all surround Sevastyan, hugging him together.

"Sevastyan, I swear, if you make me cry right now…" warns Sparrow, fanning her face. The girls and Sevastyan all laugh at her.

"Ugh, I can't believe it! Today's the day!" squeals Ivory, unable to contain herself.

"We have been waiting for this day for so long; it's a little unbelievable, to be honest," says Fauna incredulously.

"Oh guys, look! Over there, your families are here!" says Flora, pointing toward Ivory and Sparrow's families walking towards them.

Ivory's parents had run into Sparrow's parents, Elliot and Myna, on their way to the Ilios household. Both of Sparrow's parents are weapons masters, which explains why Sparrow is such an amazing shot herself. She could use a bow and arrow before she could run. Her father, Elliot – The Hawk – Avere, is known in the tribe for having a sharp eye for his target at all times.

The four of them stop and chat with Gallus and Fleur Ilios, as well as Sevastyan's parents Felix and Moira Lanza; the biochemist and linguistics professor, respectively. The four sets of parents continue to speak for a few minutes before turning back to their children.

"Ivory, you look beautiful, daughter," says Nadi, holding Ivory's hands delicately in his, afraid of ruining anything.

Constantina, on the other hand, has no such reservations as she pulls Ivory forward. She tightly holds her daughter in her arms as she tries to hold back her tears.

"Ugh, when did you get so big?" she asks as she finally pulls away and wipes at her eyes. "It feels like just yesterday you were running around the house naked with your little butt out in the open."

"Well, mother, my little butt has grown quite a bit, as has the rest of me," teases Ivory, trying not to get emotional herself.

"Excuse me, can we have a turn to get a good look at her?" asks Hayden impatiently from behind her mother.

An emotional Constantina moves to the side, allowing Ivory's sisters to walk up to Ivory.

"Nobody touch her, she's too perfect! This is a rare moment, let's not ruin it…" says Hayden to her sisters while holding her arms out, making them all laugh.

"Sooo…what do you guys think?" asks Ivory, spinning for her sisters.

"I think I'm taking that dress when you're done graduating," replies Hayden in a matter of fact.

"I get to have it next!" calls Anya. "This will be the best hand-me-down EVER!" she cheers.

Ivory laughs at her sisters, then looks to her youngest sister, taking her hand.

"How about you; do you want to wear the dress someday?" she asks Diana.

Diana nods eagerly. "You look like a princess, Ivory," she says, carefully touching the little flowers and beads on Ivory's dress.

"Aw, thank you! Surprisingly, that's not the first time I've heard that word today…" laughs Ivory.

"Don't worry; I'm sure it's not going to be the last time you're going to hear it. You and your friends are going to cause a scene at the graduation today," predicts Hayden confidently.

"Well, we should get on our way, then," says Ivory. "I can't wait to see what happens…"

- - -

Walking into the graduation setup at the tribal center in front of the Elder Building is a bit nerve-racking, to say the least. Ivory is taken aback at the beautiful scene in front of her as she walks with her four friends on either side of her. Next to one side of the large stage built for the graduation ceremony is a large orchestra of violins, harps, flutes, a large drum, and other instruments Ivory doesn't know the names of. The orchestra plays the most beautiful, soft, happy music that she has ever heard. The trees surrounding the tribal center have lines of flowers connecting them all. The white flowers come down, creating a curtain effect all the way around the tribal center.

There has to be about a hundred seats or more set up in a half-moon around the stage. The chairs are all lined with white linen and more flowers in pinks, blues, yellows, and of course, white. Flower petals line the aisle as Ivory and her friends slowly make their way to the stage, where the rest of their classmates stand excitedly, all dressed to the nines.

As Ivory is so engrossed in the transformation of the venue, it takes her a moment to notice her classmates' loud, excited voices changing into quiet, hushed whispers. Ivory stops walking, feeling a little awkward for a moment.

"Umm…why are they all staring at us?" whispers Ivory to Sparrow, who stands to her left.

"Because we look amazing, of course!" whispers Sparrow excitedly back at Ivory.

Turning on the charm to a full one hundred percent, Sparrow takes Fauna and walks towards the stage steps and up on the stage. Ivory looks over to Sevastyan and Flora, who shrug at her and start making their way to the stage as well. Left standing alone, Ivory takes a deep breath before walking forward behind her friends. A little flushed, she watches the people up on the stage as they gawk at her and her friends. Some of the boys whistle at the girls as they make their way up the steps. *This only fuels Sparrow's confidence*, Ivory thinks to herself, smiling. She also notices some of the girls on the sidelines glaring at her friends as they mingle with their classmates, obviously jealous that they're not getting the attention themselves.

Finally having reached the steps, Ivory looks down at her dress, carefully pulling it up as to not step on it and fall on her way up. Now THAT would be a real catastrophe. As she slowly walks up, one step at a time, she takes a peek up to find a hand held out in front of her. Desperate to not fall, she takes the hand before noticing the person holding it out. Once she is standing completely on the stage, and after making sure that her dress is fixed, Ivory looks up at her momentary savior.

"Cassius!"

"Fancy meeting you here…" smirks Cassius, obviously looking Ivory up and down. This makes Ivory's cheeks glow hot pink.

"Well, well, don't you clean up nicely," teases Ivory playfully as she tries to regain her composure. But, in fact, Cassius did clean up VERY well; not that he wasn't always impeccably dressed…

Cassius had decided to dress in all black for the occasion. Black suit, black button-down, black shoes, black belt, black pocket square, but no tie. Instead of a tie, Cassius wears the first few buttons of his shirt undone, making him look like he didn't really try, even though he is the best-dressed boy present.

"I must say, Ivory," he says, one hand in his pocket and the other touching the back of his neck. "You look marvelous," he finishes, finally looking back up into Ivory's eyes.

"You should wear this dress more often," he teases with a wink.

Ivory scoffs, rolling her eyes in the process. "Gee, thanks!" she replies sarcastically. "The next time I get dressed I'll keep your advice in mind."

Cassius chuckles in a low voice, then looks over at Ivory's friends and waves at them with his free hand. He turns back to Ivory and tilts his head, getting one last good look at her before speaking.

"I should get going; don't want people to think anything weird," he says.

"No, we wouldn't want that," Ivory says with a knowing smile.

"Tell your friends they all look really nice," he says before turning to leave. "Cheers."

"Cheers," returns Ivory, before turning and heading toward her friends.

Her friends wait for her eagerly, leaving a space open for her in their circle so she can join them.

"Oh my God, he looks so good!" squeals Sparrow quietly, quickly taking a peek at Cassius as he walks away, then quickly turning back to Ivory. "Did he say you look nice? What did you say?!" she asks excitedly.

"Oh God, here we go. Girl talk…the only downside to having girl friends," sighs Sevastyan with a chuckle.

"Don't worry; we usually keep the majority of the girl talk for when you're not around," giggles Flora with a nudge, still holding on to Sevastyan's arm from when they walked up the steps together. The two start their own quiet conversation as Sparrow and Fauna impatiently wait on Ivory's response.

"He did say I look nice, and I told him that he cleans up well," shrugs Ivory with a small smile.

"Girl, did he say 'You look nice,' or did he use other words? Because the way he was looking you over, he was definitely thinking more than just 'nice!'" giggles Fauna, shaking Ivory's arm.

"You guys are so embarrassing; he's going to know we're talking about him with us all huddled here and Sparrow looking over at him every few seconds!" barks Ivory, smacking Sparrow's arm as she continues to look over at Cassius from across the stage.

Sparrow and Fauna laugh at Ivory as her face continues to glow pink from her encounter as well as all of the eyes staring in her direction.

"Anyway, he wanted me to tell you all that you look very nice," she finally says, bringing Flora and Sevastyan's attention back into the circle.

"That's very nice of him," says Sevastyan with a nod.

The friends stand around for a bit longer before breaking away from their little circle and going off to socialize with their other classmates. Before long, the tribal venue is jam-packed with parents, siblings, and friends. Professor Ganlion soon shows up and starts handing out black dress robes to all of the students, instructing them to take their seats on the stage. In the meantime, warriors make their way around the crowd of people, kindly asking everyone to take their seats so that the procession may begin.

Ivory takes her seat on the third row with Sparrow and Sevastyan to one side and the twins behind her. And of course, as if on cue, Cassius takes the empty seat to Ivory's right hand side. He doesn't speak to her as he sits, but Ivory knows why.

Time to put on a show, she thinks to herself with a small smile that turns much bigger as she spots her sisters in the audience, waving at her. She waves back at her sisters, making the little ones excited that she had noticed them.

The students all sit to the left side of the stage while the nine Elders sit on the right-hand side of the stage. Ivory and Sparrow watch as the Elders make their way slowly out of the building, one by one. Some of the Elders are a lot older than the others, as each Elder serves up until they are too sick to serve anymore or die. Completely white-haired and hunched over their canes, a few of the Elders don't look like they have that much longer to serve, thinks Ivory. Ivory had asked her parents once why the Elders were allowed to serve at such an old age, thinking that a younger person might be a much more efficient candidate. But her parents had explained to her that white hair comes from wisdom. The Elders were the wisest people in the tribe, and they were a necessity for the tribe's survival. This conversation had changed Ivory's perspective on the situation, as she looks on at the Elders in awe.

With the music coming to a soft halt, Professor Ganlion makes his way to the middle of the stage along with applause from both the audience and his students.

"Thank you, thank you very much," he says with one hand on his chest and a small bow.

"I would like to start by welcoming you all to this year's graduation ceremony!" he begins, and waits for the applause to die off before he can continue.

"Once upon a time, our world was struck by a disaster – The Great Wave," he begins again as the audience and students listen on intently.

"We thought it was the end, not only for our kind, but for life as a whole. Most of us were not able to pull through. Those of us that survived the first round of the Great Wave did not live long to survive what came after. Yet, look at us all here right now, celebrating this beautiful occasion. In our greatest time of need, when all hope was lost, we found a way. But the only way we were able to do that was by working together. Throughout the centuries, Post-Great Wave, we have pulled what we were able to remember, all of the knowledge we had, to help get us to this moment right here, right now. Knowledge is the key to life. People have known this fact since the beginning of time, but over time, we became too comfortable with the unknown. At one point, a lot of us believed that what you didn't know couldn't possibly hurt you. Alas, we were proven wrong."

Professor Ganlion paces slowly back and forth on the stage as he continues to deliver his speech.

"Today, we come together to celebrate the movement of another generation of students into full adulthood – into society. We have successfully taken these young bright minds and transformed them into brighter minds that can help keep our species going if we are ever in that dire need again. As the founding fathers and mothers of The Collection once inscribed in stone, no child shall ever be left in the darkness as we make our way into the light. A brighter future cannot be in order when there those of us still left wandering in the dark. Our children here," says the professor, pointing to the students, "We have taught them all they need to continue on and assimilate into society as well-versed, intelligent adults. And looking at some of you here today, the parents, I can see how difficult it may be to hear me calling your children adults, as they will forever be children in your eyes. Regrettably, however, in order to move on, we must learn to let go."

Ivory looks into the audience, seeing some of the parents lightly blotting at their tears. She knows somewhere in the crowd her mother is crying, but she can't bear to think about that, as she may start tearing up herself.

"Before we move one, I would like to have a moment of silence in respect of two of our graduates that are not here with us today; Yuri Lyasin and Trixie Stone. Although they are not here with us right now, these two remarkable students are graduates as much as any of these students here today. To the families and friends of Yuri and Trixie, I hope that you can all feel the same pride that we feel here for them today. And may they return to us safely," says the professor with a bow of the head. The crowd and students all go silent for a bit in respect of the two missing students before the professor moves on.

"Now, with that being said, one by one, I would like to introduce you to our graduates," finishes Professor Ganlion before pulling out a piece of parchment from his jacket.

Professor and Head Flight Instructor Silven "Silver" Drakonas makes his way onto the stage with a small box in his hands and stands to the right side of

Professor Ganlion. The Elders all stand up together, making a line as well. Professor Ganlion starts by calling out the first name on his list.

"Theodore Blackwood," he says out loud. The student stands up and walks toward the professor and Silver as the crowd and students give him a loud applause. Silver takes out a pin from the box, the size of a child's palm, and pins it on the shoulder of the boy's dress robes. One by one, Professor Ganlion, Silver, and each of the nine Elders take a turn congratulating the graduating boy and giving his free shoulder a squeeze. As the boy makes his way down the line of Elders, Professor Ganlion calls out the second name, and so on.

Ivory watches on with pride, and cheers loud as her friends get called up one by one. Her turn comes soon after.

"Ivory Skye," calls out Professor Ganlion, meeting Ivory with a big smile as she makes her way toward him. Out of the corner of her eye, Ivory can see her sisters jumping up, cheering for her loudly. Her classmates all cheer for her as well, her friends cheering the loudest of all.

"Congratulations, Ivory, I expect to see great things from you," says Silver as he pins the beautiful Alder pin on one shoulder and squeezes the other tightly. Ivory returns the shoulder squeeze, a sign of complete respect, to her professor. She slowly makes her way down the line of Elders, making eye contact with each one for the first time in her life. Once she finishes greeting the Elders, she makes her way to the back of the stage next to her excited friends. Sparrow takes Ivory's hand as the two wait for the rest of the students to be called out. Ivory's hand quivers lightly in Sparrow's as the adrenaline pumps through Ivory's body.

"That was so surreal; I feel like I blacked out for the majority of it," whispers Ivory to her friend.

"Oh my God, I thought I was the only one," whispers back Sparrow with a nervous giggle.

The two friends stand hand in hand as they watch the last student on the list, Cassius, make his way through the Elders. Ivory takes a quick look at her pin as she waits, admiring it. The pin is the emblem of her tribe – a golden Alder tree inside a golden circle. Each tribe has their own emblem with respect to their representative tree.

Once Cassius makes his way to his classmates, Professor Ganlion motions for the whole class to walk forward toward the front of the stage. The two professors stand to the side of the stage with the Elders, leaving the center stage for the new graduates. Once the students are in place, Professor Ganlion walks forward for one final announcement.

"Alders, I present to you this year's graduating class! Congratulations to us all, and may we all have a blessed full moon festival tonight!" he finishes with a bow.

Applause and cheers roar through the crowd as everyone stands up for the new graduates. The orchestra starts up again as Ivory and her classmates all take a bow and wave their thanks to the crowd before heading to the back of the stage to return the robes to Professor Ganlion.

Ivory and her friends all hug each other as they simultaneously put their pins on their clothes underneath the robes and return the robes to the professor. Out of the corner of her eye, Ivory can see Cassius getting closer to her. She is a little confused at first, but soon remembers as his back bumps into hers slightly.

"Hey! Watch where you're going, Skye!" he says, loud enough for everyone around them to hear.

*Here we go…*Ivory thinks to herself as she gets into character.

"Excuse you! You bumped into me, Cassius, so maybe you should watch where you're walking!" Ivory spits back at Cassius, turning around to face him at the same time.

"Oh please, we all know you're the clumsy one here. The bruise might have faded from your face, but we all know the extent of your clumsiness, Skye," scoffs Cassius.

"What is your problem?!" asks Ivory, getting up in Cassius's face.

"Right now, you're my problem," he replies, stepping closer to Ivory.

"Hey, Zlato, is that really necessary?" asks Sevastyan, stepping into the conversation, ready to defend his friend.

Ivory holds her hand out, cutting Sevastyan off really quick. She needs to keep the conversation just between herself and Cassius. Cassius glares at Sevastyan for a brief moment, but quickly turns back to Ivory.

"Sev, don't waste your breath, babe. Trust me, he's not worth it," says Ivory, rolling her eyes. "I don't have time for you or your bullshit today, Zlato. Go find someone else who actually cares," spits Ivory with a little wave of the hand.

Cassius takes Ivory's hand in his and grabs her waist with the other, pulling her to him.

"Trust me, princess, that won't take much time," he whispers with a smug smile in her ear, loud enough for some of the people standing around them, gawking, to hear. It takes Ivory a moment to snap out of her shock, as she was not expecting Cassius to play his role this well. She quickly shoves Cassius away, keeping a hand on his chest.

"Just for the record, you're not wearing your suit, your suit is wearing you," she sneers before letting go of Cassius, turning around and whipping him with her hair in the process.

Ivory quickly walks away in the other direction, followed by her friends, who have no words for what just happened.

"What the hell just happened?" Fauna whispers to her sister. Flora shrugs.

"Damn, he really is bipolar. Shame…" whispers Sparrow, shaking her head in disappointment.

"Let's just pretend that this whole thing didn't happen and move on. Please," pleads Ivory as the group starts making their way back to the front of the stage and down the steps to their families.

The friends all nod in agreement as they make their way down one by one. Before making her way down the steps, Ivory takes one last glance behind her, catching Cassius's gaze. He gives her a quick wink as a smile plays over his lips; he's impressed with her acting. She returns a quick smile before turning back around to her eagerly awaiting family and friends.

Chapter 20

The weather begins to warm up as the early-morning sun rises up higher in the sky. The celebrations continue as Ivory mingles with her family and friends after the graduation ceremony. The music picks up to a more upbeat tune, making some unable to stand still. Ivory watches on as her two younger sisters dance to the music. Sparrow nudges her to go on and dance with her sisters, but Ivory tells her that she's saving it for later on, when the real party begins. As the new graduates continue to mingle, a little old lady comes around handing out colorful leis to the graduates.

"Ivory, darling, just a quick heads-up; we've decided to all have breakfast at our house," calls over Constantina from a few feet away.

"Is everyone coming over?" asks Ivory.

"Yes, all of your friends and their parents are coming over, so you can let your friends know," replies Constantina, turning back to her conversation with Fleur and the other mothers.

Ivory turns to Sparrow, who's heard the whole conversation and is basically jumping up and down already.

"Can this day get any better, though?" she asks, ecstatic that she gets to spend the entire day with her friend.

Ivory squeezes Sparrow's hand as she tries to contain her own excitement.

"Hey guys, did you all hear that? You're all coming over to my place for breakfast. Your parents are coming too!" announces Ivory to her other friends.

"No way, that's awesome!" replies Sevastyan, stoked at the idea. "We haven't had a gathering like this in a while!"

"Should we bring our outfit changes to your place then, Ive?" asks Flora.

"True, we can pass by our place on the way so you girls can pick up your bags and we can all eventually change for the festival at your place!" chimes in Fauna.

"Sounds good to me!" agrees Ivory.

"What about you, Sev, when are you going to change?" asks Flora, turning to Sevastyan.

"Hmmm…I'm not really sure. I mean, I could bring a change of clothing and change at Ivory's. It just depends on if my parents are planning on stopping at our place first…" says Sevastyan, looking over at his parents.

"Mama!" Ivory calls to her mother. "Are we all going to our place right away?"

"We're all heading back together, but the ladies want to grab some goodies they made and bring them over. So if any of your friends need to bring anything along from their homes, they'll have the chance," replies Constantina, quickly turning back to her friends.

"Well, you heard that," says Ivory, turning back to Sevastyan.

"Perfect. I'll actually change before coming, that way I won't have to carry anything around with me," he says.

"Yeah…I would change, but then, I want to wear my dress for a bit longer," says Sparrow sheepishly.

"I don't blame you, sister; I'm doing the same thing," laughs Fauna in agreement.

"Alright, it's settled then. The girls will all change together after breakfast. More time to look cute in our clothes," adds Flora, making everyone nod and laugh.

Ivory looks around the venue as she continues talking to her friends. As she's looking around, she accidentally makes eye contact with Professor Drakonas, who stands with his wife. As he makes eye contact with her, Silver waves over to Ivory, motioning for her to come over.

"Hey you guys, can you wait for me for a little bit; I'm going to go and say hello to Professor Drakonas and his wife," says Ivory to her friends as she begins to make her way over.

"You can call him just Silver now, Ive!" Sparrow reminds Ivory as she walks away.

Ivory turns to her friend, giving her a terrified look, jokingly, as if she could never imagine calling the professor by his actual name. Ivory weaves carefully through the crowd of people to get to her professor.

"Hello, Ivory! It's so nice to finally meet you; I've heard so much about you! And congratulations, by the way!" says the professor's wife ecstatically as she brings Ivory in for a hug.

Ivory laughs as she was not expecting the professor's wife to be so different from him. As the quiet, brooding type, Silver Drakonas has the complete opposite personality from his wife. Ivory is also a bit taken aback at the beautiful Mrs. Drakonas. The woman is very basic in terms of looks – average height and build, fair skin, shoulder-length brown hair with side bangs, and brown eyes. But there is something about her face and smile that is so sweet and innocent…

"It's a pleasure meeting you as well! Hopefully, you've heard good things," laughs Ivory, returning the embrace.

"Oh, of course; Silver says that you're one of his best students," says the woman, returning to her husband's side. Ivory smiles in disbelief as she looks between her former teacher and his wife.

"Wow, I'm honored, thank you so much, professor," she says.

"Please, I'm not your professor anymore. You can start calling me Silver," replies the professor with a wink.

Ivory laughs, still a little shocked seeing this side to Professor Drakonas. She watches him intently as he looks over at his wife lovingly – how he smiles at her and holds her close to his side.

There is so much love between these two people, thinks Ivory to herself. The thought makes her smile.

"To be honest," starts Silver, turning back to Ivory, "I've had my eye on you for a while now, Skye. All of us have. It's true, some of the other students may excel more in one specific subject, but you have something that's very hard to teach. You have heart and drive. You don't try to be the best, but you work very hard at everything you do."

"You're also very kind," adds the professor's wife. "I can tell, just by looking at you," she says with a smile and a twinkle in her eye.

"I'm speechless, thank you so much," says Ivory, a little taken aback at the wonderful comments she's getting. "Oh, by the way, I didn't catch your name," she says to Silver's wife.

"Ah, yes, I got a bit ahead of myself there," laughs the woman. "I'm Poppy – Poppy Drakonas," says the woman, looking adoringly back at her husband.

"That's such a pretty name; it's been a pleasure, Poppy!" says Ivory with a warm smile.

"It's been a pleasure as well, Ivory. Hopefully, we meet again soon. And congratulations again!" says Poppy as she brings Ivory in for a goodbye embrace.

Silver gives Ivory a nod and a smile before turning around to leave, keeping his wife close at his side.

Ugh, they are so adorable together, I can't even believe it, thinks Ivory as she watches the duo make their way into the crowd.

Ivory turns to head back to her friends, whom she sees heading toward the edge of the tribal center, closer to the main path that leads home. As she makes her way through the crowd, she is startled when someone grabs her arm suddenly.

A bit alarmed, she turns around only to find Cassius holding her, looking a little bewildered himself.

"Please tell me that you have it with you, by some sort of miracle," he starts, breathing heavily. "You probably don't, but please…"

"Cassius!" exclaims Ivory, trying to take her arm back. "What is going on; you almost scared me half to death!"

"I know, I'm sorry. They want to see you. He wants to see you. I told him I was bringing someone and he wants to know who…"

Ivory's heart skips a beat as her brain slowly registers what Cassius is trying to say.

"He…Nazar?" she asks cautiously.

"YES! We have to go now, but you need to have it, he needs to see it… this is all my fault, I'm so stupid…"

"Cassius!" Ivory yells at him, finally pulling her arm back. She turns herself to face Cassius completely before pulling her dress up, exposing her right ankle. On her ankle is a thin gold chain with the special little insignia hanging off of it.

"Oh my God, Ivory, you are a genius. Thank you, thank you…Ok, let's go," says the boy a bit erratically, pulling Ivory by the arm again.

"Cassius, wait, I'm not ready…" starts Ivory as Cassius pulls her through the crowd. "I didn't prepare anything; I don't know what to say to him!"

"Well, you better think fast then," replies Cassius, a bit disheveled as he looks around for the man.

Ivory sees him first, standing around with a group of professors, laughing along with them. She is a bit bemused, as the last time she'd seen him was in her dream.

Damn, I have a great imagination...thinks Ivory, looking at the man. Nazar looks exactly like he had in her dreams. As usual, he is dressed more like a rich businessman than a traveler. His curly hair slightly moves around as a gust of air rips through some nearby trees. His cape floats up as well, revealing his perfectly tailored three-piece black suit and glossy leather shoes. Unlike Cassius, Nazar wears a white button-down with a red tie embroidered with thin curls of gold. The tie matches perfectly with the red lining of his cape and matching pocket square. And of course, his gold necklaces and rings finish off the look. In comparison, Cassius now looks like the amateur who tried really hard to pull off a similar look, but couldn't.

Cassius finally spots Nazar. He pulls at Ivory's arm again, walking her over to the man. Ivory huffs at Cassius, not sure why he finds it so necessary to drag her around like a ragdoll. She takes a few deep breaths before Cassius comes to an abrupt halt. He clears his throat, making Nazar turn around to see who he's brought for him. Nazar's eyes open wide and his smile grows as he sees Ivory standing in front of him.

"My, my, what do we have here..." he says, taking Ivory's hand in both of his. He bends down as he had done once before and lays a kiss on top of Ivory's hand.

"I asked for a warrior, but I got a princess instead," smiles Nazar as he gawks at Ivory, treating her as if she's a delicate vase that might break at the slightest touch.

"OH MY!" gasps Nazar suddenly, eyes wide. "I see that you heal very well; quick," he says, brushing the side of Ivory's face in awe. "That'll come in handy if you decide to join us on our trip..." he whispers in a lower voice, smirking between Ivory and Cassius.

Ivory looks over at Cassius, who looks almost a bit scared. Cassius motions for Ivory to show her bracelet. Ivory takes her hand out of Nazar's and quickly pulls her dress up, revealing the thin gold bracelet around her ankle, making sure Nazar sees the special insignia. Taken aback by Ivory's quick and abrupt movement, Nazar laughs and grabs Ivory by the shoulders. Ivory tenses up, as now she really is frightened. Nazar is standing so close to her that she can smell the tiny dot of white musk he'd put on the collar of his cape this morning.

"Oh Ivory, my beautiful, special little princess...we are going to have so much fun together..." he says, smiling wide as his kohl-lined, smoldering eyes burn a hole through Ivory's corneas.

If I ever hear that word again, I swear...

"Go now, Ivory. Enjoy this joyous time with your family and friends," says Nazar, finally letting go of Ivory. "We shall have a lot of time to get to know each other in the very near future. Oh, and please forgive the small piece of gold hanging around your ankle. A princess like yourself only deserves the best...I have a special necklace that I think would be perfect for you..." he finishes with a smug smile and a dangerous spark in his eye.

Ivory almost doubles over as she takes in what Nazar just said. But she swallows her fear and proceeds.

"Thank you very much. I really must excuse myself, as my parents are waiting for me. It would be rude to keep them waiting any longer," she finally says with a straight face.

"But of course. May you have a blessed full moon festival, Ivory," says Nazar with a tip of his head.

Ivory nods her thanks and makes brief eye contact with Cassius before she turns around and walks back the way she came. Her walk slowly turns into a jog, as she wants to get as far away from the area as she can. She sees her family and friends waiting for her at the edge of the tribal center, but she stops for a moment next to a tree to take a breath. Her heart is racing so fast; it almost feels like she's having a panic attack.

What he said about the necklace...just like the dream...he's teasing me now. But does he know that I know? Oh my God, Ivory, breathe. Breathe.

Ivory leans at the tree for a few more moments before taking a deep breath and heading in the direction of her friends.

"Hey, you're back! Did you meet Silver's wife? Was she nice?" asks Sparrow, completely unaware of what just happened.

Ivory puts on the fakest smile she can muster as she begins making her way home with her friends. If she'd thought she was afraid before, she was kidding herself. Ivory tries to keep reminding herself that she has to make these last few moments with her loved ones special, as she really does not know what's to come in a matter of less than twenty-four hours.

- - -

Ivory's friends all sit around the small kitchen table, chatting and making jokes as Ivory stands at the sink, mindlessly washing and cutting up a bowl of strawberries. She'd put on a normal face for them the entire way home, but she just needs a few moments to herself to think – to process. She thinks over her entire conversation with Nazar. It was a short but important one. He'd used so many weird nuances, some that she didn't understand.

Why was he so surprised and intrigued that my bruise had gotten better? And the necklace comment…was he talking about the necklace he'd given me the first time I'd dreamt of him? Does this mean that it was actually him? I mean, believing that the woman, Zohra, is real is a stretch. But because I don't actually know her, it's a bit easier for me to believe. But to think that Nazar could actually find a way into my dreams…how is that even possible?! It's not possible; it goes against everything we know, everything we've learned…

"Hey there, baby, are you almost done?" asks Constantina softly, touching Ivory's shoulder. Ivory hadn't seen her walking into the kitchen as she'd been so engrossed in her own mind. She has even more questions now than she did before, and zero answers.

"Yes, Mother, I'm almost done," replies Ivory robotically, taking a look down at the last strawberry she has sitting in the bowl. Constantina doesn't seem to notice her distracted daughter.

"Just put it into the bigger bowl with the other cut fruits, mix everything together, and fill up the cups I've set out over there. Serve your friends and sisters the fruit salad, then bring the rest of the cups over to us in the dining room."

"Okay, Mama," replies Ivory as she subconsciously finishes cutting up the last strawberry and mixes the fruit salad.

Flora gets up from the kitchen table of laughing friends and stands beside Ivory as she fills each cup with the freshly made fruit salad.

"Would you like some help with that, beaut?" asks the girl, too distracted with the others laughing behind her to notice Ivory's somber mood.

"Uh, yes, sure. Can you give each of them a cup and also take one for yourself?" replies Ivory.

"Sure! Do you want me to set one on the table for you as well?" asks Flora, turning to Ivory.

"No, it's ok. I'm not really hungry," replies Ivory, not looking up from the cups.

"Babe, are you sure? You haven't really eaten anything all day. Is everything okay?" asks the girl in a quieter, more serious tone, finally noticing that something is off with her friend.

Ivory looks up at Flora. She studies her friend's face – one that was smiling only seconds ago, now changed into one of worry. Flora's eyebrows furrow closer together as her eyes look back and forth between Ivory's eyes, trying to understand what's happening inside them. Ivory smiles at her sweet, innocent friend. She can't bear to see her beautiful face worried.

"I'm fine," replies Ivory.

"Ive, 'I'm fine' usually means that you're not fine," replies Flora with a suspicious look. "We don't have to talk about it here if you don't want to," she whispers so only Ivory can hear.

Ivory sighs. A small part of her wants to tell Flora. If she could, she would spill her guts, everything that's been eating at her, right here, right now. But her heart hurts her to think of the danger she would be putting her friend into. Instead, Ivory puts on a brave smile and touches her friend's cheek.

"I love you. You know that, right?" asks Ivory, still touching Flora's face.

"I do, and I love you too, Ive," says the girl, still not convinced that something isn't up.

"I promise you that I'm fine and that everything is going to be alright. And I promise you that if I ever need you, I will not hesitate to ask," says Ivory, looking Flora straight in the eye, putting her hand back down.

Flora hesitates as she tries to read into Ivory's expression and words, but Ivory plays her part well. These past few days have turned her into a very convincing actress.

"Alright then. Don't get me wrong, I'm glad to hear that you're fine. I just worry about you sometimes…" replies Flora, her voice still low. This catches Ivory a bit by surprise.

"Why do you worry about me specifically?" asks Ivory.

"I don't know," admits Flora. "I just feel like you're a bit rash sometimes. I can usually expect certain things from everyone else, but not from you. You surprise me sometimes. And…" she trails off, shaking her head lightly.

"And, what?" asks Ivory, intrigued at her friend's accurate sense of her life right now.

"I don't know; it's nothing," replies Flora, trying to play it off.

"No, tell me. Please," insists Ivory, making sure to keep her voice low.

"I just..." starts Flora. "I've been having this feeling; Ever since the day you got hurt. I keep feeling like you're in trouble...or you're going to be. Sometimes I find myself doing something and you randomly pop into my head. But not in a good way. And..." Flora takes a breath as she tries to put her feelings into words.

"I wake up in the morning sometimes, almost in, like, a panic. I don't know why, because I can't remember my dreams. So I don't even know if I'm really having nightmares. But I feel really scared, and you're there too, in my thoughts," finishes Flora.

Ivory's pulse quickens as she watches her friend struggle to explain herself. She wonders about Flora's dreams. She wants to ask her about them, but Flora doesn't remember them, so there's no point in bringing attention to them right now.

"I, I don't know what to say, Flora," whispers Ivory, stunned at her friend's revelation. "Thank you for worrying about me, but I'm good. I don't want you to worry yourself over nothing, my friend. We're all here, happy and healthy on this beautiful day, and nothing can take that away from us."

Ivory smiles reassuringly at her friend, caressing her shoulder in the process.

"Just promise me that you'll come to me if you're ever in trouble, Ivory. I need to hear you say it loud and clear. And we need to shake on it," says Flora, her smile coming back to her face.

Ivory chuckles as she takes Flora's hand in hers, squeezing it hard.

"I, Ivory...that sounds weird," laughs Ivory. "I, Ivory, promise you, Flora, that I will come to you if I am ever in dire need of a friend or accomplice. I promise to come to you if I ever need to bury a dead body or murder anyone else," laughs Ivory along with her friend. The two girls shake on it, making their promise official.

"Alright now, Flora. I need you to help me out with these fruit cups...see, I promised you I would ask for help, and I am!"

"Perfect!" replies Flora, pumping a fist in the air. "I'll deal with the kids in here, and you go take some to the adults..." she says, looking over at her friends.

"Yeah, be careful with those big kids over there, they tend to act crazier than the little ones," teases Ivory as she starts making her way out of the kitchen with a platter of fruit cups and spoons.

Making her way down the hallway, Ivory makes a promise to herself that she won't let herself get so distracted again today. It's too dangerous now that one of her friends is already suspecting foul play.

If there's one thing I know, it's that Flora knows a lot more than she thinks she does. The sooner this day ends and the sooner I leave, the better.

"Come on guys, it's time for the gift exchange!" yells Fauna out to her four friends.

"It's not really an exchange, though, we just made each other a few things for the festival..." says Sparrow.

"Speak for yourself," snorts Sevastyan, pulling a small pouch out of his pocket.

After their late breakfast, the girls had all changed into their festival outfits. This time, all of them wore the same outfit. A comfortable, flowing white cotton dress that comes down just a little bit past the knees. The dress has short flowing sleeves and a low-cut back. Sevastyan had changed when he'd stopped by his place on his way to Ivory's home. He wears white slacks and a flowing white long-sleeved top with a V-neck and two little cords that he had left untied.

Ivory walks into the kitchen with a pouch of her own in her hands, quickly taking a seat on the table next to Sevastyan.

"Okay, all ready," she says with a bit of an excited smile.

"Hold up, did you guys get us presents?" asks Sparrow, looking between Ivory and Sevastyan.

Ivory and Sevastyan look at each other with smug smiles, then turn back to Sparrow.

"Come on, you guys have to start," replies Ivory, avoiding Sparrow's question.

"We'll go first," says Fauna, rolling her eyes at her friends. One by one, she takes out five beautiful flower crowns from her bag, giving one to each of her friends and leaving one for herself. The friends all coo at the intricately made flower crowns as they each try them on.

"These are beautiful; thank you," says Sevastyan, carefully adjusting his crown.

"When did you two make these? They're nothing like the ones we made for everyone at the festival. They're incredible!" says Ivory, turning the crown over in her hands, studying the metal and crystal details added along with the beautiful flowers.

"So, you guys like them?" asks Flora for reassurance.

"Obviously! Well, these are going to put the corsages I made for you all to shame. But whatever, here you go!" says Sparrow, handing out a white corsage for everyone on the table.

"Sparrow, they turned out amazing; what are you talking about?!" comments Flora as she delicately slips the corsage over her hand.

"Why, thank you, thank you very much!" replies Sparrow with a dramatic bow.

"My turn," laughs Sevastyan, reaching into his little pouch. "Here, I made you all little starfish charms. My present is coordinated with Ivory's, so you'll understand what to do with them in a second," he says, looking over at Ivory.

Ivory delicately reaches into her pouch, pulling out what looks like five bracelets.

"I decided to make you all bracelets from the seashells I got when we explored the beach inside the hidden cave. It was one of the happiest moments we've had together, so I wanted us to remember it, along with this day," explains Ivory, handing out a bracelet to everyone at the table.

Flora and Fauna look over at each other, touched at their friend's gesture.

"Ive, that's so sweet," starts Sparrow, getting a bit emotional. "And Sev, the starfish with the shells…it's perfect. Ugh," Sparrow huffs as she looks up at the ceiling in order to stop the water in her eyes from spilling over the rims.

Flora and Fauna help each other get their bracelets and charms on, then hold hands. Fauna extends her hand towards Sparrow on her right, while Flora extends hers to Ivory, who sits to her left. Sparrow and Ivory hold on to their friends' hands, then each extend a hand to Sevastyan, who sits in between them.

"You guys, we have to remember this moment forever. Not a lot of people are as lucky as we are to have such amazing friends that we can call family…" starts Fauna.

"We have been blessed with something far greater than wealth, or power, or even knowledge. We have each other – we have love," finishes Flora.

"We'll have each other's backs through thick and thin, that's for sure. You can always count on me whenever you need me," says Sevastyan, squeezing his friends' hands.

"We are the Reckless Crew. A group of crazy, sometimes hormonally-imbalanced, child-adults, who can take on anything together. Anyone would be crazy to mess with one of us…" adds Sparrow, her tears betraying her.

"That's true," starts Ivory. "Because if they mess with one of us, they mess with all of us. And if anyone EVER tries to hurt one of my friends, my family, they're done," she finishes with a harshness at the end of which only she knows its drive.

The now self-proclaimed "Reckless Crew" all smile and joke about their newly created friendship pact. But as Ivory laughs along, she is stunned at the actual impact this new accord has on her. The power in its words rings in her ears as adrenaline pulses to the beating of her heart. This new promise moves through her body as it prepares itself for what's to come.

If he thinks he can come into my tribe and put my people, my loved ones, in danger…he's messing with the wrong girl. I'm coming for you, Nazar. I'm going to save my people; then it'll be your turn to face the light of day. I will expose you and your sins if it's the last thing I do…

Chapter 21

"Can you guys wait for me outside? My parents need me for just a minute. You better not leave without me!" says Ivory to her friends.

"Don't worry, we'll wait for you. Take your time!" replies Sevastyan, making his way out after the three other girls.

Ivory closes the front door, then turns to head back into the dining room. There, she finds her parents and sisters waiting for her.

"So…what's going on?" she asks, a little confused as to why they all stand looking at her intently.

"Your sisters wanted to give you graduation presents," smiles Constantina, looking back at her husband.

"Really? You guys have presents for me?!" asks Ivory, touched by the thoughtfulness of her sisters.

"Of course we do!" replies Anya, walking forward with Diana. The two hand over their wrapped gift to Ivory, who sits down at the dining table to open it carefully.

"Aww…it's so cute! I love it!" she says, reaching over to bring her sisters in for a hug. The two younger girls had made Ivory a beautiful wooden frame, which they had painted and filled with a picture of the family.

"My turn," says Hayden, eager to give Ivory her present next. Taking the tiny scarlet pouch from her sister, Ivory reaches inside, pulling out a thin gold necklace with a pendant on the end. Taking a closer look at the pendant, Ivory reads the words that Hayden had etched onto it: "Sisters, Always & Forever."

Inside the pendant, Ivory finds one small picture of her sister Hayden and another of her sisters Anya and Diana.

Ivory looks back up at her sister, trying not to get emotional. She puts the necklace safely back into its pouch and stands up to give Hayden a proper hug.

"Does that mean you like it?" asks Hayden into her sister's shoulder.

"That means I love it," whispers back Ivory.

Letting go of her sister, Ivory wipes at her eyes, making sure that no tears escape too far down her face.

"You guys are seriously amazing; I wasn't expecting that at all."

"We still have to give you our present," says Constantina with a mysterious smile.

Ivory laughs.

"More presents?! I should graduate more often!"

Constantina turns around and from behind her picks up a stack of what looks to be clothes and shoes.

"So, this is a shared gift from your father and I," she says, handing Ivory her present.

"Whoa, that is a lot of stuff. What is all of it?" asks Ivory, a little over-whelmed.

"Well, your father and I were not too sure what to get you, and we wanted it to be something practical."

"What you have there is a brand new riding outfit," says Nadi. "It's the latest in riding gear. It will be great when you guys go back out to the coast. The pants and shirt are super sleek, but also breathable. You can also take the sleeves off the shirt if it gets warmer out. The jacket is another layer you can add in the wintertime that will keep you warm without taking up too much space. And the boots; they are pretty amazing as well. They are light and du-rable, perfect for riding while also doubling up as hiking boots – perfect for walking out in the wilderness," he explains.

"Oh my God, this is crazy! I can't believe it...thank you so much!" ex-claims Ivory in shock, embracing each of her parents.

"This is actually perfect; you have no idea..." she says, fully knowing that her parents do not understand how useful this new outfit will be.

"We're glad you like it, baby, we are very proud of you. You have worked very hard to get this far," says Constantina.

"Thank you, again. All of you. I will treasure all of your presents!" says Ivory, bringing everyone in for one last big family hug.

"Alright, well, I need to put all of these presents away and hurry out; everyone's waiting for me outside," she says, picking her presents up.

"We will meet you at the tribal center in a little bit; I'm just going to clean up a bit more around here. Have fun!"

"Thanks!" replies Ivory, quickly making her way to her room and setting her new stuff down on her bed.

This outfit is literally perfect for my travels. And what perfect timing…I'll take the picture frame and necklace with me too, just so I can have a piece of home with me when I need it, thinks Ivory as she quickly puts the necklace and picture frame in her travel bag under her bed. She leaves the outfit out on the bed, as she will be putting it on later on in the night. Finished putting her stuff away, Ivory makes her way outside to her friends.

"Sorry that took a while, guys. Are you ready to head out?"

"Let's do this! I am so ready to party," exclaims Sparrow, speaking for the rest of her friends.

- - -

The sounds of music and laughter fill the air as the gang makes their way into the tribal center. The place has been transformed once again for the full moon festival. The rows of chairs are all gone and replaced with little table stands that people can stand around and chat. A big square in front of the tribal building is left empty as an area where people can dance. Along with the flower decorations that were already up, lanterns have been hung in every tree in sight. Where there are no trees, tall lantern posts are put up instead.

The gang stands around and people-watch for a while before making their way to the tribal market. On a day like today, the market is officially closed. So instead of selling goods, tribal members set up their tables with goodies to give out to the tribe. And although Ivory and her friends have eaten not too long ago, they are excited to see the food waiting for them.

"Okay, I think we should be smart about this. We should start off with the salty foods and then move on to the sweets," starts Sevastyan, getting his game plan ready.

"No, I don't think so, Sev. My stomach likes it when I mix things," interrupts Sparrow.

"Yeah, same. Whatever smells good is going in. End of story," agrees Fauna.

"You guys, I want to go paint a bowl," says Flora, pointing to the activities portion of the market.

"Ohh...me too! I also really want to get a henna tattoo," says Ivory.

The girls all agree with Ivory, as they all have tattoos in mind that they want.

"Well, what do you guys want to start off with? There's a lot to do, so we have to choose how we want to go about this. We're literally just standing around right now..." laughs Sevastyan.

"Let's start off with the activities; I'm not that hungry right now," suggests Flora.

"I agree; I'm not that hungry right now, either," says Ivory, holding her stomach for a more dramatic effect.

"Oh please, you didn't even eat," Fauna rolls her eyes. "But fiiiiine, activities first."

"I will come back for you, food, I promise," says Sparrow dramatically, blowing a kiss to the food stands waiting for her return.

"Good afternoon! Have you all chosen what tattoos you want to get?" asks one of the men working at the Henna Tattoo stand.

"Yes!" replies Flora, going first. "I want a cherry blossom branch going up my arm and onto my chest, with a few petals blowing away," she says confidently.

"I'll get started with you, then," replies the man. "The rest of you can choose from this book of tattoos if you're not sure what you want yet," he says, handing over a small booklet with drawings inside of it.

"Who needs it?" asks Sevastyan passing the book around. "I already know what I want."

"Me too, I don't need it," says Fauna, handing it over to Sparrow.

"I don't need it, either. Ivory?" asks Sparrow, handing the book over to Ivory.

"I actually do need it," laughs Ivory. She looks over the pictures in the book, trying to see if anything catches her eye. And then she sees it.

She is a bit taken aback as it just sits in black and white on the page in front of her. Anyone else looking at it probably wouldn't notice it. But for someone that it means something to, it is a bit shocking. Ivory looks up just in time to see a boy washing off his henna tattoo. The brown color of the henna is almost a perfect match to the birthmarks. And then it hits her...

What if someone gets this tattoo and THEY see it, thinking that it's the real thing? Then again…what if everyone in the tribe got it? Hmmm…

"Ive, have you chosen yet? He's almost done with me and then it's your turn," Fauna interrupts Ivory's thoughts.

Ivory looks up from the book. Each one of her friends is sitting on a chair in front of a different tattoo artist.

"Alright, just let this sit for at least an hour before you wash it off. The longer you let it sit, the darker the stain will be," says Flora's henna tattoo artist. Flora gets up and motions for Ivory to take her spot.

"So what will it be for you, then?" asks the man, waiting intently for Ivory's response. Ivory looks at him for a moment, then quickly makes up her mind.

"I want it on my forearm," she starts, looking down at her left arm and describing what she wants with her fingers.

"I want the stallion this big, and I want the suns above, just like you would have the sun in the sky. I also want hills behind the stallion, and I want him to look like he's galloping," she finishes, looking up at the man.

"Alright, seems simple enough," replies the man, not fazed whatsoever by Ivory's request. He takes a brand new tube of henna, making a small incision at the bottom, and then quickly starts working on Ivory's arm.

Ivory's friends all finish before her. One by one, each shows off their new tattoo.

"What do you think it looks like?" asks Sevastyan, bringing his wrist toward Ivory.

"Umm…it looks like a sword, and it looks like it's inside a rock, I think. Like a boulder," says Ivory, a little unsure.

"You're right! It's the Sword in the Stone! You know that story, right?"

"Oh wow, yes, I do know it! That's great! Is there a reason you got it?" asks Ivory.

"It's just always been my favorite story growing up. It also makes sense, as I am planning on becoming a warrior one day and my sword is my weapon of choice."

"It looks splendid," agrees Flora, taking a closer look at the tattoo.

"What about you, Sparrow? And Fauna?" asks Ivory, turning her attention to the girls.

"I kind of got a whole themed scene on my arm," starts Sparrow. "I got a galaxy tattoo – so a lot of different planets and stars. It looks really cool!"

"It sounds really cool! Fauna?"

"I got a lion on my nape," says Fauna, pointing to the bandage on the posterior part of her neck. "What are you getting, Ive?"

"I want it to be a surprise," teases Ivory. "You guys can see it when I clean it up."

"That's not fair! We just all told you what we got!" laughs Sparrow.

"I know what Ivory got," giggles Flora. "Sorry, I overheard you talking, Ive."

Ivory laughs with Flora. "It's alright, just make sure you don't say anything," she winks.

"My lips are sealed," winks back Flora.

Sparrow and Sevastyan roll their eyes together at Ivory. At the same time, the tattoo artist finishes Ivory's tattoo and puts a bandage on it so it can dry.

"Like I told your friend, give it at least one hour. But leave it on longer if you want a darker stain. And you're good to go. You all have a blessed full moon festival!" He waves goodbye to the gang.

"You know what this means," says Sparrow, looking over at Fauna, who mirrors Sparrows face.

"Time to eat!" they say together, making their friends all laugh out loud.

After hours of hanging out together, eating, dancing, and having a good time, Ivory and her friends head to the Elder Building as the sun begins to set. As today is the full moon festival and a big portion of the festival happens after the sun sets, the curfew is annulled for the day. For this reason, every warrior in the tribe is out and about, making sure nothing gets past them.

The little lanterns in the tribal center start to automatically turn on as the natural light of the sun dims. Glowing fireflies start making their way through the tribal center, illuminating anything they land on. The tribal assemblage starts to grow as more tribal members make their way to the front the Elder Building. Spotting her family, Ivory waves and calls over to her sisters to come over. Everyone stands around for a while, waiting for the Elders to come out of the building for the main ceremony. As the night sky appears to be at twilight and as the full moon shines bright over the Elder building, the first Elder makes his way out onto the stage.

One by one, the Elders make their way out, each taking a seat on the stage in front of the tribe. On the stage, Ivory counts ten chairs instead of the usual nine. She quickly remembers why, as she sees a hooded figure making his way out last onto the stage. Nazar takes the final seat to the right side of the stage.

The tribal center goes silent as Elder Algernon, the oldest Elder, makes his way forward to stand in front of his people.

Elder Algernon holds his arms open, as if to embrace his people. Then, he speaks.

"Welcome, all, to the annual full moon festival," he starts. Ivory watches in awe as the old man stands tall in his white robes, looking out at the sea of white clothed tribal members in front of him.

"The full moon festival marks the end of summer and another successful year, as we move toward the beginning of the autumn months that lay ahead. This particular festival is sure to be a very special one, as the Sun, Earth, and Moon align, and as we witness a Super Blood Moon."

The audience claps for the introduction and then settles down again, listening intently to the Elder.

"We, the collection of tribes, have long believed in the power that comes with the full moon. It is a power that has been used throughout history, specifically by those wishing ill on others. For this reason, we come together on this day to end old feuds, make new bonds, and celebrate the goodness that we have all been blessed with."

The old man takes his time before moving on, as he gathers both his thoughts and his breath.

"Now, for the fear that the full moon might impair some, all hunting activity is to be seized the night of the full moon festival and the day following. No one is to step foot into the forests surrounding the tribe during this time. I must warn you all, the full moon can make you do things against your right mind, with a very dangerous feeling pushing you forward...power. Many before you have wandered into the forests, drunk on the feeling of power, ready to take on the greatest of horrors. Sadly, they have all paid with the ultimate price...their lives."

"But let us not dwell on the negative. This is, after all, a time of celebration, a time of growth. Another year has passed, and we continue to thrive as a species. Remember, my brothers and sisters: if one of us suffers, we all suffer. If one of us thrives, we all thrive. We must continue to work together and make our world a safe, harmonious place for our children to live. We must not forget the horrors that our ancestors faced as a result of arrogance. We cannot sit in our castles while children die of hunger in the streets or drown in the ocean as they seek refuge. Our ancestors did not understand the value of life, but we do. We are not they. We have all made the ultimate promise that selflessness and doing the right thing are the standards we hold ourselves to, above all. We, my friends, are united. We are one. And may we stay that way for eternity."

The crowd claps in unison as Elder Algernon looks ahead, picturing the beautiful future that his people could potentially help create. He knows the potential of his people, especially the new graduates. He only wishes he could be there to witness it all.

"Please enjoy this special time with your loved ones. Eat, dance, and be merry. And may you all have a blessed full moon festival," finishes Elder Algernon.

And as if he had planned it to the minute, the lunar eclipse begins.

Slowly, the large moon glowing bright above the Elder Building starts to change. The bright white orb gradually turns into a bright, blood red color. The tribe watches on, erupting into loud cheers as the full moon reaches its total eclipse. Ivory wishes her family and friends a happy full moon festival as the moon drowns the tribe in its warm red light. And just like that, the moon starts changing again, as the alignment of the Sun, Earth, and Moon comes to an end.

The festivities continue as tribal members scatter around the tribe once again. The orchestra picks up the beat, turning the dance floor that was empty just minutes ago into a full-blown dance party.

Ivory and her friends begin to make their way out of the tribal center, as it is too loud and too crowded for anyone to have a proper conversation.

"Where do you guys want to go?" asks Flora.

"Hmm…can we go to the hill behind the school? You know, where we have classes sometimes," suggests Ivory.

Her friends all nod in approval, changing their course to the proper direction. As they weave through the crowd, they run into a little friend.

"Hey, Ivory!"

"Hey, Caius!" replies Ivory, happy to see the little boy.

Caius, like his brother Cassius, is a blonde-haired beauty. He is sure to grow up into one of the best-looking guys in the tribe. But for now, he takes the award for the most adorable little boy around. Unlike Cassius, Caius is extremely friendly to everyone. They say it takes a whole tribe to raise a child. That was the case for Caius after his mother had passed away. Everyone in the tribe loved him like he was their own. This was the reason that Cassius was alright with leaving his brother behind – he knew he would be well taken care of.

"I haven't seen you in so long, Ivory, I missed you!" says the little boy, tightly embracing Ivory.

"I've missed you too, Caius, how have you been?" replies Ivory with a smile, embracing the boy in a tight hug.

"I'm good! Have you seen Anya and Diana around? I can't find them anywhere…" says the little boy, trying to spot the girls.

Ivory laughs, turning the boy's head in the direction of her sisters.

"Look, over there…" she says, pointing with her finger. "Do you see them next to that lantern?"

"OH! YES! Thanks, Ivory, you're the best!" exclaims the boy, leaving just as quickly as he had come.

Ivory's friends all laugh along as Ivory is left behind in the boy's dust.

"He is so adorable; I could eat him up!" says Fauna, squeezing her sister's arm. Flora nods in agreement.

Turning back to her original direction, Ivory starts making her way out of the tribal center, but then pauses once again as she spots a concerned Cassius making his way through the crowd.

"Ive, why are you stopping?" asks Sevastyan, patiently waiting for Ivory to move in front of him.

"Hey! Cassius!" calls out Ivory, making everyone look in the direction she's looking.

Cassius turns around to the sound of his name.

"He's over there!" Ivory calls out over the crowd, pointing to the area Caius had gone to meet her sisters.

Cassius lets out a sigh of relief, shaking his head in defeat.

"Thanks!" he yells back over with a quick wave of the hand.

Ivory turns back to Sevastyan and smiles.

"If you had younger siblings, you'd understand," she smiles knowingly.

"Oh, trust me, being around yours, I do!" laughs Sevastyan.

And with that, the group finally makes their way out of the bustling tribal center into a much more peaceful and serene part of the tribe.

- - -

"That one, over there. That's my favorite constellation," whispers Ivory as she lies on the grassy hill with her friends on either side of her.

"Orion's Belt...that is a good one," replies Sparrow. "Orion uses a bow and arrow, right?"

"Yes, he does," whispers back Ivory.

"I like that. I can relate to it," smiles Sparrow. "I never asked you...why do you love this constellation?"

"I don't know; I feel like I have a lot of reasons. Stars change. There are so many stars in our galaxy...stars are constantly burning out, with new ones replacing them. But with Orion...I feel like no matter where I am – even when we went out to the coast – I can always look up at the sky and find him. When I see him, I feel grounded, in a way. I feel like I understand the sky and the universe outside of it...it's like home," Ivory smiles.

"Wow, that's beautiful. I've never thought of it that way..." whispers Sparrow, not taking her eyes off of the sky.

"Also," adds Ivory. "I have Orion's Belt on my face."

"What?" asks Sparrow, now looking over at her friend, a little confused.

"Have you never noticed these three freckles on my right cheek? They line up to make Orion's belt..." says Ivory, pointing to her cheek.

Sparrow chuckles incredulously.

"Well, would you look at that. You really do have Orion's Belt on your face. That's magnificent."

Ivory chuckles and turns back to the sky. The full moon is bright tonight, but it only adds to the majesty of the dark blue abyss up above as the hot clouds of gas burn billions of miles away. Sparrow moves closer to cuddle with Ivory, as the nights have officially begun to cool down. Ivory's other friends lay close to each other to stay warm as well, too engrossed in their own quiet little conversation.

The contrast of the loud, bustling Tribal Center to this quiet and peaceful hilltop is striking. The soothing sounds of ruffling leaves and singing grasshoppers soon start lulling the gang into a sleeplike trance. They spend a few more minutes admiring the beauty that is the night sky before getting back up and calling it a night.

As Ivory makes her way inside her house, the clock strikes midnight. Only two hours left...

Her family had made their way home only about ten minutes before her. She goes into each bedroom, wishing her sisters and parents a good night.

This is her final goodbye before she makes her way out. She makes sure to embrace each member of her family as tight as she possibly can, as she does not know if she will ever have this chance again.

Chapter 22

Dear Father,

I have tried to write this letter one too many times, but I can never seem to find the right words.

So, here goes nothing...

Dear Father, everything changed when Mother died. I remember a time when you used to come home happy, and we would sit together as a family over the dinner table, laughing until food came out of our noses. I know losing Mother was really hard on you, as it was equally as hard on me. For the longest time, I wished we could go back to the way we were while she was still alive. And because we didn't, I fell into a dark hole, a place too small to let anyone else in.

I would be lying if I didn't say that I loathed you, because I did, for the longest time. It felt like you abandoned us, Caius and I. So I took it upon myself to help bring him up, the way mother would have wanted.

You see, the thing is, I only ever wanted your approval, your love. That's all I ever wanted, all I needed.

I guess I'm writing this letter now to let you know that I forgive you. I have been doing a lot of thinking and I want to let you know that I understand now what you went through. I understand that every time you looked at me or Caius, all you could see was my mother's face and that tore you apart. I also want to let you know that no matter what we have gone through in the past, or what we may go through in the future, I will always love you. You may be the famous Warrior Zlato to everyone else, but to me, you are Father.

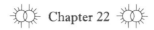

I hope that one day I can make you proud enough to call me son.
Cassius.

- - -

Dear brother,
I love you. Never forget that – no matter what happens. I did it all for you.
Your loving brother,
Cassius.

- - -

Ivory turns off her bedroom light and waits for about an hour before she begins to prepare. She wants to make sure that everyone is fast asleep – she cannot take any chances, not tonight. Very quietly, she turns on a little lantern she had stored under her bed earlier on in the day. She takes out her travel bag, takes everything out, and reorganizes everything back in to make sure that she's not forgetting anything. Once the supply run-through is complete, Ivory finally takes off her festival clothes and puts on her new travel outfit. The pants and top fit her perfectly, almost like a second skin. She takes the sleeves off of the top and stores them in her bag, as it still isn't cold enough to wear them. She does, however, put on the jacket.

Making sure that she is super quiet, Ivory laces up her new boots. She walks around her room, putting everything away, making sure to not leave a mess behind. Once she is happy with the state of her room, Ivory reaches under her pillow, taking out her memory book. She opens up her travel bag to put the book inside. But before closing her bag, she flips through the book's pages and takes something out – a letter. It's the letter she had written to her parents.

Ivory sets the letter down on her pillow so that it can be visible to anyone walking into the room. On top of the folded piece of paper, with beautiful handwriting, Ivory had written her parents' names. Looking at the lonely paper on top of her pillow now, Ivory quickly walks over to her closet and takes out a little pink shell. This was her favorite shell that she had gotten from her trip. She sets the shell down on the right-hand corner of the letter, hoping that Constantina will understand.

It's time…

Ivory blows out the lantern light and opens her bedroom window as quietly as she can. Once the window is fully open, she wiggles the second screen, which is meant to protect against bugs, free. Leaning over the window sill, she sets the large mesh screen down as delicately as she can. A soft thud down the hallway makes her pause for a moment in brief panic, but she hears nothing else in the following moments. Ivory sets her travel bag outside on the grass before she makes her way through the window. Once outside, she takes a fleeting moment to look back into her room. Rays of moonlight find their way into her bedroom, illuminating her wooden bed-frame and closet. From the outside looking in, it all looks so clean and un-lived in – almost cold. Ivory only stands idle for a few more moments before she closes her bedroom window from the outside. As she makes her way onto the main path, she turns around to get one last glance at what she's leaving behind. Her heart aches, as she already longs for her family and friends. But there is no turning back now. Making her way to the stables one last time, Ivory doesn't try to stop her tears, not this time. Because this is the moment where she realizes that all of her dreams of freedom meant nothing – they paled in comparison to the amazing life she already had with her loved ones. It's true what they say – you only truly learn to appreciate something you have, or someone, when they're gone.

Like a black cat in the night, Ivory quietly creeps into the stables, not making a single sound. The boots her parents had given her are perfect for exploring outside the tribe, as she can sneak around quietly without being discovered.

Still walking quietly, Ivory walks up to Cassius, who has his back turned to her.

"Cassius," she whispers.

Cassius jumps high up in the air, dropping the reins he had been holding in his hands. He quickly turns around, startled, only to see Ivory standing be-hind him, a little startled at his reaction.

"Damn you, Ivory! You scared me half to death! Don't you know how to make some sound when you walk!?" exclaims Cassius, trying to keep his voice as low as possible.

"Uhhh…my bad, these shoes are new," replies Ivory, looking down at her boots. "They're really light, that's why they don't make any noise. I mean, I'm trying to make as little noise as possible anyway, so…"

"Oh, never mind!" says Cassius, rolling his eyes as he picks the reins back up off the ground.

"Have you been here long?" asks Ivory, setting her bag down next to Thunder's stall.

"No, only a few minutes. We need to pick up the pace, though; I don't want to take any chances," replies Cassius, hands quickly working on getting his horse set up.

"Okay," says Ivory, turning to do the same.

The two quietly get their horses ready to ride. Cassius had started setting up before Ivory, but Ivory finishes a few minutes before him, as she has spent much more time in the stables with her father.

Ivory stands next to Thunder, one hand on his mane. She watches Cassius as he works. The cold white light of the moon pouring through the stable doors makes Cassius's hair look platinum white. The contrast between his white hair and his black clothing is a stark one. As Cassius turns, he notices Ivory standing and watching him.

"What?" he asks, unbothered, turning back to his horse.

Ivory sighs.

"Nothing," she replies with the same unbothered tone.

"That doesn't look like nothing," says Cassius, only briefly making eye contact with Ivory. "Are you sure you want to do this?"

"Yes," replies Ivory.

"You don't sound very excited."

"Neither do you."

No one says anything else as Cassius finishes up. Once he's done, he walks with his horse up to Ivory.

"Are you scared?" she asks him.

"No, I don't think so. A little stressed, maybe, but not scared. You?"

"I don't know, maybe."

"Your maybe sounds more like a yes than a maybe. I'm going to ask you one more time, because this is the last chance you have to turn back. Are you sure you want to do this? Are you sure you want to leave?"

Ivory looks Cassius directly in the eye. To an outsider, this might seem like Cassius is trying to convince Ivory to stay behind so he can go out on his own. It would be less baggage for him, anyway. But deep down in his hard silver eyes, Ivory can see the fear that Cassius has of her backing out of the trip. Ivory had no intentions of backing out, but seeing this makes her feel a little more reassured, almost at home, if that's believable.

Ivory's lips turn up on one side into a small smile.

"You can't get rid of me that easy, Zlato," she teases.

Cassius looks down to hide his smile. He turns to his horse and lifts himself up with one leg while throwing the other over the horse. He adjusts himself on the saddle before turning back to Ivory.

"Alright Skye, it's time to see what you're really made of," he teases back before turning his horse around and heading towards the entrance.

Ivory smiles to herself as she gets on top of Thunder and starts following Cassius out of the stables. *This sure is going to be an interesting trip. And to just think, how the tables have turned already…*she thinks to herself.

Making their way to the border of the tribe is surprisingly an easy feat for Cassius and Ivory, as there are no warriors to be seen.

"Where are they all?" asks Ivory, looking around, still surprised that they haven't run into anyone yet.

"I'm not sure. They're probably nearby, though. They can't be stationed at every square inch of the tribal border; it's too big."

Cassius carefully looks for the little path underneath the trees that leads out to the wild. He had discovered it with the help of the Oaks.

"Over here," he says to Ivory, pointing toward the direction they need to ride. "Follow me and keep your head low; some of the branches stick out," he instructs.

Ivory follows suit. The trees at one point get so dense that it's hard to make out where the path is. Thankfully, Cassius knows the way out, because alone, Ivory would have gotten confused. Moments later, the trees start giving way again to the moonlight. The number of trees lessen as the small path soon turns into a much bigger one – the main riding path.

"Oh wow, how did we get here?" asks Ivory, surprised.

Cassius turns back to give her a smirk, but the smirk is soon wiped off of his face as he hears voices up ahead.

"Oaks," whispers Ivory, wide-eyed, making Cassius snap his head back forward.

Ivory follows close behind Cassius as he makes his way up to the two men.

"Cassius, you made it…" hisses the first man in a snaky voice.

"Who is that?" asks the second man in a much deeper, ragged voice, eyes narrowed.

"Ghayth, Layth, this is Ivory Skye. She's going to be traveling with us."

"You know that's not how we do things, Cassius," hisses the first man, presumably Ghayth.

"She has one. Show it to them," replies Cassius in a hard voice. He turns to Ivory, giving her a nod to pull out the bracelet. Ivory swiftly pulls her jacket sleeve up, revealing the special insignia to the two men.

"That's not enough; she wasn't accounted for…" growls the second man, Layth. But Cassius quickly cuts him off.

"She was, and she will travel with us. Nazar himself requested it. Now, unless you would like to explain to him how you rejected his special guest, I suggest you get moving," says Cassius with a hard stare, jaw flexing as he holds eye contact with the men. The two men look back and forth at each other and at Ivory. Layth turns his horse around first and rides off. As he turns his horse around, Ghayth looks in Ivory's direction.

"She better be able to keep up," he hisses before riding off.

Cassius quickly turns to Ivory.

"Let's go, it's time to show off your riding skills," he says before taking off.

"Hya!" Ivory gives Thunder a tap with her foot. In the blink of an eye, Ivory finds herself flying through the wild forest on top of Thunder. Within seconds, she's riding next to Cassius again.

"Are we just following straight down the path?" she yells over to Cassius.

"Yes!" He yells back as he gallops through the trees with Ivory. "Hey Ive, why don't you leave these losers in your dust! I'll be right behind you!"

"Thought you'd never ask!" yells back Ivory. "Better keep up, Zlato!"

"Don't worry, Skye, I will!"

"Alright Thunder, it's time to set you free, buddy," Ivory whispers to her horse. She makes a few clicking sounds with her tongue while also giving Thunder a little more room in the reins. And just like that, he takes off. Ivory lifts herself completely off the saddle, positioning herself like horse racers do. Up ahead, she sees Ghayth riding only a few meters behind Layth. Without hesitation, or much effort, really, Ivory smokes past Ghayth, literally leaving him in her dust. Layth looks toward his friend, only to see Ivory racing towards him. Ivory catches a glimpse of his shocked face as she rides right past him, putting herself at the front of the pack. Not taking a moment to slow down,

Ivory keeps riding until she catches a glimpse of moving figures out in the distance. Taking a moment to look underneath her arm to see who's behind her, Ivory notices that she's riding alone. Not one of the three men were able to keep up with her, Cassius included. Having made her point, Ivory slows down to a trot and waits for someone to catch up to her. Cassius reaches her first, slowing down to a trot to match her pace.

"That was insane; I've never seen you ride so fast…ever!" says Cassius, impressed. "You should have seen their faces; it was hysterical!" he chuckles at the thought.

"Well, I'm glad you're amused by my riding skills," chuckles Ivory. "Not going to lie, that felt really good," she says, patting Thunder for the great ride.

The Oaks soon catch up to Cassius and Ivory. The two don't say anything as they ride by; they just narrow their eyes at Ivory and her horse. Ivory smirks at the both of them, happy that she had proven herself worthy to be traveling with the caravan.

"So is that it down there?" Ivory asks Cassius, pointing to the figures out in the distance.

"Yeah, I think so. They were riding slow so the four of us would catch up. Once we reach them, the riding is going to pick up again."

"Alright, sounds good."

The two follow far behind the other two Oaks. The trees soon become really dense, and then open up to a forest clearing. On the other side of the clearing, Ghayth and Layth start making their way back into the dense trees. As Ivory and Cassius make their way through the large, round field, Ivory hears something. At first, she thinks it's in her imagination, but then it starts getting louder.

"Cassius, do you hear that?" asks Ivory, turning to Cassius and stopping in the middle of the forest clearing.

Cassius stops his horse and looks back at Ivory. His eyebrows furrow as he listens.

"Yes, I do. It sounds like…it sounds like your name," he replies, just as confused as Ivory.

The sound gets louder and closer. Someone is yelling out Ivory's name. Ivory's first instinct is to run, to keep going, but something stops her from moving. She doesn't realize what is it until she sees her making her way into the forest clearing, riding Onyx.

"Hayden!" yells Ivory, holding her mouth in shock. She turns back to look at Cassius, who's eyes are just as wide as Ivory's.

"Ivory!" yells Hayden for the hundredth time, riding toward her sister.

"Hayden, what are you doing here!?" yells Ivory, jumping off her horse and walking forward. Hayden mirrors Ivory by jumping down and starts making her way toward Ivory.

"I could ask you the same thing, Ivory, but unfortunately I've already read your letter!" yells back Hayden. "HOW COULD YOU!? How could you do this to us!? To Mother and Father and the girls!? How could you just leave!? And what a pathetic excuse of a letter you left behind; I CAN'T BELIEVE YOU!"

"HAYDEN! WHAT ARE YOU DOING HERE!? ARE YOU TRYING TO GET YOURSELF KILLED!?"

"ARE YOU, IVORY!?"

"Hayden, STOP! You need to leave here now!"

"I can't believe it…How could you do this to Mother and Father, Ive?! Do you know how heartbroken they will be when they read that letter? HOW SELFISH CAN YOU BE, IVORY?!" yells back Hayden.

"Hayden, I'm going to say this one time, and one time only. GO. HOME. NOW. You have no idea what you're talking about. This is so much bigger than you or me or our parents! Leave. NOW!"

Ivory turns around and starts walking away. Hayden goes after Ivory and grabs her by the arm, jerking her back around.

"HEY! LET GO!" screams Ivory at her sister, slapping her hand away.

Hayden stops walking and just stares at her sister in disbelief.

"So this is it then, isn't it," she says, eyes starting to water. "You're just going to leave. No goodbyes, no I love yous…that's how much we mean to you…that's how much I mean to you…"

"Hayden, please," says Ivory, pleading with her sister. "I know you can't understand it now, but you will someday. You'll understand…"

"Understand what, exactly?! Understand that you're a selfish sister who decided that we weren't good enough for her? Is that it? I don't think I can even call you my sister after this…"

"Hayden, don't say that! That's not fair!"

"NO! What's not fair is how sad Anya and Diana will be when they find out."

Hayden wipes away the tears rolling down her cheeks.

"Hayden…please…go home," says Ivory softly, holding herself so she doesn't break down in front of her sister.

Hayden looks at Ivory for a few brief moments before shaking her head in disappointment and turning around.

"Goodbye, Ivory" she says, stone cold, as she walks away.

Ivory holds back the tears because she knows that if one comes down…

She turns around and starts making her way back to Thunder as Cassius watches on with wide eyes.

Then, suddenly, out of the trees in the distance rides out Nazar, a group of his Oaks, and…

Ivory stands next to Thunder, eyes wide in disbelief. She quickly looks back at her sister, who's still making her way to her horse, oblivious to the situation. And if the situation isn't complicated enough, on the other side of the forest clearing, through the trees, ride out Ivory's friends; Sevastyan, Sparrow, Fauna, and Flora. They slow down when they see Ivory, but come to a complete halt when they see it.

It – the monster.

"What is going on here?" asks Nazar from only a few meters away, looking at Ivory.

"It's, it's…it's nothing. There's nothing wrong," Ivory manages to respond.

"I hope not, because if there were a problem, I see a lot of bodies here that would need to be buried…" he says, looking at the monster standing next to him. "If your friends know what's best for them, they will turn around and leave now. They saw nothing," he finishes, directing his words at her shocked friends.

"They're leaving; they didn't see anything…" starts Ivory, holding her hands up and turning to look at her oblivious sister.

Hayden, wiping at the last of her tears, looks up and notices the terrified faces of Ivory's friends. A little confused, she turns around to see what they're all gawking at.

In the middle of the silent forest clearing, Hayden screams – loud. Loud enough for the wolves near the tribal gates to hear her and start howling.

"Hayden, stop! Hayden!" yells Ivory to her sister.

Hayden stops screaming, but the look of horror on her face scares Ivory more than she had already been scared.

"Who is that?" asks Nazar, obviously annoyed.

"That's, that's just my sister. She's going home now; she won't say any-thing," pleads Ivory, looking back and forth between Nazar and her sister.

Hayden stands there, terrified, unable to move from her spot. She doesn't look at Ivory or Nazar, because she can't take her eyes off of it...

"Hmm..." starts Nazar, "I don't know if I really believe that..." he says with a shrug and an evil smile playing over his lips.

"No, I promise! Hayden, just go!" Ivory yells at her sister. But Hayden doesn't move. She can't; she's frozen with fear. Ivory looks back at Nazar, who looks at the monster.

"Detritus, you know what to do," he whispers to it.

"Cassius, say something!" Ivory pleads, now turning to her travel com-panion.

"Oh, there's nothing for him to say, is there, Cassius?" asks Nazar, as Cas-sius looks on, unable to move himself. "Did you think that joining me would really be as easy as wearing a little bracelet or necklace?" smirks Nazar. He laughs out loud at the thought. "My darling, I need proof of sacrifice. And you know what, I think I've just decided what yours is going to be..."

Ivory's heart falls to the ground.

The next few seconds, as Nazar gives the monster the nod of approval, as the monster pulls on the bow, and as the arrow releases...

THUD

Ivory takes in a sharp breath as she hears it. Her whole world comes to a com-plete halt. She knows that she should look, but she can't. The only thing she can see is the smug smile on his face as his name rings through her ears.

It feels to Ivory as if she's been standing in the same position for hours, when in fact...

As she turns around, Ivory sees her sister still standing, arrow protrud-ing through her chest... Ivory's eyes move up to her sister's wide eyes, catching them as they roll back into Hayden's head before she collapses to the ground.

Ivory hears Nazar telling his people to move out. She hears Cassius whisper something, but she can't make it out – he soon follows after Nazar. Thunder neighs as he runs around wildly before making his way out of the forest clearing as well.

As for Ivory's friends…the girls' screams ring through the forest trees as they cry on the ground near their horses, unable to move toward Hayden. Sevastyan stands, frozen in shock.

And Ivory…Ivory is dead.

Physically, she is alive. But on the inside, her soul is gone – taken away with her sister's.

Slowly, she starts making her way to her sister's body. Her feet drag in the dirt as she tries to get there…it's so far away, and she can't feel her legs anymore.

Up to this point, Ivory has yet to react.

It's not real. This is a dream; this is just a dream…

And then she reaches her…

Ivory stands for a while, unable to comprehend the picture in front of her. That's all it is at the moment, just a picture. But reality soon hits Ivory like a meteor as she collapses to the ground.

Ivory tries to talk as her fingers weave through Hayden's hair. Her lips move, but she can't hear herself. In fact, she can't hear anything. All she can hear is a faint beep…like the heart monitor for someone whose heart has stopped beating. It gets louder and louder, to the point where Ivory can't take it anymore. She closes her eyes and clutches her ears with her hands, trying to drown out the ear-shattering sound. But as she tries holding herself together, she comes to the realization that the sound is in fact coming out of her. The sound is her screaming and crying.

As the realization hits her, she slowly lets her hands go and tries to breathe. But as she opens her eyes, she sees her again.

Eyes closed, one tear making its way through her eyelids. Not moving. Not breathing. Her baby sister…dead.

Ivory reaches her arms forward, bringing Hayden close to her chest, holding her and crying into her hair.

As she sobs on the dirt ground with her dead sister in her arms, Ivory's friends watch from afar, sobbing into a pool of their own shared sorrow. Fauna and Flora sit collapsed on the ground, unable to support each other any longer. Sparrow shakes in Sevastyan's arms in shock. Sevastyan tries his best to console his friend but is in too much of a shock himself, crying silently.

"Please, please don't be gone…please come back!" Ivory chokes her words out into her sister's hair.

"I'm so sorry...I was, I was supposed to protect you. I was su...supposed to pro...pro...protect you, and...and I didn't." She stutters. "I'm sorry, I'm so sorry. Please!!"

Ivory gets back up on her knees. She tries shaking her sister awake, caressing her face.

"Hayden...Hayden...please wake up! I'm begging you, please!" She pleads in agony.

Hayden doesn't move, doesn't show any signs of life. Ivory's cries and screams start getting louder again.

"What have I done...WHAT HAVE I DONE?!"

Tilting her head back, Ivory lets out a cry so loud it can be heard back at the tribe. She grabs at her chest with her blood-soaked hands as she screams to the heavens. But nothing can fill the hole that was ripped through her tonight.

She starts losing control...of herself, and her emotions.

"Please Hayden, PLEASE!! You can't be gone...YOU CAN'T BE GONE!" she screams, and bangs her fists in the dirt.

"NOOOO!"

Ivory loses herself in her pain, hitting the ground underneath her hard with her hands. As she cries, her tears mix with the dirt. She hits the same spot, over and over and over again.

The ground beneath her starts to shake slowly. It shakes harder and faster with every fist she throws at it. Her standing friends fall to the ground from the earthquake happening below her fists. A loud exploding sound from inside the earth is followed by a crack, which lengthens in size with every punch. Ivory is too blinded by her tears and broken heart to see what she is doing. Her friends huddle up in a group as they witness the event in complete shock.

But Ivory is so lost in her sorrow that she doesn't feel the ground shaking underneath her knees. She doesn't see the large crack in the earth underneath her hands, getting bigger – heading in one direction toward the tribe and in the other toward the forest.

She doesn't feel the earth shaking, crying, with her. How could she, after all? Her body might be here, but like her sister, she is gone.

Ivory's friends call out to her, desperately, as they try to hold on to each other over the shaky ground.

"Ivory! Ivory, please, you have to stop! Ivory!!" Sparrow yells out.

But Ivory doesn't hear them. She doesn't hear anything, except for the foreign sounds making their way through her quivering lips and the beat of her pulsing heart, exploding in her ears.

Blinded by her own tears, Ivory gathers up every last bit of strength in her to stand up.

The earth stops shaking. She reaches up and wipes at her tears...she wants to get one last good look at her sister so she can remember her face. She kneels back down one more time, this time reaching toward her sister's face, giving her a final kiss goodbye.

I am so sorry, Hayden. I was supposed to protect you under any circumstance, and I failed you. I failed you as a protector, as a sister. But I vow to you that I will avenge you. I will find them and I will kill them – every single last one of them. I will not stop until either my mission is complete or I die myself. I love you so much beautiful, sweet Hayden. I hope that you can forgive me. Farewell, and may you rest in peace.

As Ivory's lips unlock from Hayden's forehead, a large wind makes its way through the forest trees into the clearing. With it, it brings the scent of salty oceans and blood. Ivory knows what she has to do. And she knows that she has to do it alone. She will kill Nazar and every single one of his men, including Cassius, or she will die trying.

Still sobbing, Ivory stands up. She wipes the last of the tears away and looks over to the forest ahead of her. She looks back down on her sister one final time – eyes closed, hair laid out around her like a halo, looking almost alive...almost.

"I will do the right thing. I promise," she whispers to Hayden and herself.

She turns around, unaware of anyone or anything around her except for the mission at hand. Then, she runs. Her friends call out her name, but Ivory had left her old life behind her the moment her lips had touched her dead sister's forehead.

Within seconds, Sevastyan, Sparrow, Flora, and Fauna, all watch as their friend quickly disappears into the trees. The last thing they hear is Ivory's whistle to her horse and the sound of hooves taking off.

"She's gone."

To be continued…

On the next installment of *The Settlement: Earthborn* -

"Earthborn; they were born on earth, but touched by light. All came into this world as the sun rose from the horizon. Some say that anyone born at sunrise is blessed with its powers of life. Others say that only a specific few born at this time of day are blessed with powers. We may never know the truth behind our powers, our abilities, but we are thankful to have been tasked with this honorable purpose; the purpose to save the world." – Zohra